THE
ACADEMY

T.Z. LAYTON

Books for Young Readers

This is a work of fiction. Names, characters, organizations, places, and events are either products of the author's imagination or are used fictitiously.

Published by First Touch Books for Young Readers
Cover design by Robert Ball
Interior by JW Manus

TO COACH JOCKO

DRAGON SQUADS

IGUANAS

Leo	Striker	United States
Robbie	Midfield	United States
Alejandro	Defender	Costa Rica
Dayo	Striker	Nigeria
Kaito	Striker	Japan
Garika	Defender	Zimbabwe
Oliver	Winger	England
Javier	Winger	France
Sven	Winger	Denmark
José	Midfield	Brazil
Brock	Defender	England
Julian	Midfield	England

GILA MONSTERS

Miguel	Striker	Nicaragua
Sebastian	Winger	Poland
Conor	Defender	Ireland
Sergi	Midfield	Spain

MONITORS

Mateo	Defender	Argentina
Hans	Defender	Germany
Mahmoud	Striker	Egypt

KOMODOS

Diego	Striker	Mexico
Fabio	Midfield	Italy
Simon	Defender	Canada

SNAPPING TURTLES

Charlie	Goalie	Australia
Koffi	Goalie	Ivory Coast

Note to Readers

I've never written in a journal before. I've never written much of anything at all, except for those boring assignments they make you write in school, usually about a family vacation or some walk in the woods with your parents. But this is different. I've got a story to tell that feels like it's wriggling beneath my skin, dying to get out, and my friends are all thousands of miles away, in a different country. I want to write down my experiences to make sure I don't forget anything.

In case you're someone who finds this journal, which I plan to turn into a movie one day, maybe I should start with a little bit about myself. My name is Leo K. Doyle, I'm 12 years old, and I just finished the sixth grade. I love soccer and video games, I'm a little bit lazy, and I have a pet lizard named Messi who I talk to like a real person. Oh, I also love graphic novels and banana pancakes and reptiles of any kind—especially dangerous ones. School is lame, my sister's lame, and my mom died two years ago.

Since I drew a big fat ball on the cover, I know you love soccer too, and I feel like whoever you are, no matter what you look like or where you go to school, what country or city or village or barn you call home, you'll agree that what you're about to read is the most incredible story about soccer you'll ever hear.

Now, I'm not talking about regular soccer. I'm talking about the best soccer in the world. You've heard of the English Premier League, right? Arsenal, Chelsea, Man City? Did you know all the clubs have academies where they train and develop the most talented youth players they can find, hoping they'll join the adult teams one day?

Sound like a dream come true?

I'm just a regular kid like you, from a normal town in America, but I was *invited* to one of these academies. I traveled all the way to London, England to train with a group of kids from around the world. If you stick with me for a few pages, I'll tell you all about it. The whole inside story. I even got to meet a few famous people.

I bet you're curious now, but I've got to start from the beginning, because that's how stories work. Not the very beginning—not all that stuff like when I was born and where I go to school, because who wants to read about that? I promise to start right when it all happened.

Here's another thing: I don't know the ending to this story. Yeah, I got invited to the Academy summer camp, but I don't know whether I'll be good enough to make the youth team and be allowed to stay full-time.

I also don't know if I'll be able to use the money that professional youth players make to help stop the bank from taking away our house. I probably shouldn't be talking about that, even in a journal, but there it is.

Anyway, I promise I'll let you know what happens by the end of the story, as soon as I find out myself. But I need to catch you up first.

It all started on one of those perfect spring mornings for soccer, a crisp blue sky and a cool breeze blowing, dew on the grass and the feeling the day will last forever— are you ready?

I'm a Scoring Machine

The game was almost over. My team was down 3-2 to one of the best teams in Ohio, the Columbus Tigers, an elite team that practices four times a week and stays in fancy hotels when they travel to other cities. They wanted me on the team but my dad couldn't afford to pay the dues, or take time off work for all the practices. I never cared, because those kids from Columbus were all rich jerks anyway.

"One minute left! Let's push!"

That was our coach shouting. He's a good guy but he doesn't know very much about soccer. He's a basketball fan who only agreed to coach us because his kid was on the team, and he was always telling us to do things a basketball player would do, like play zone or start a full-court press or something. He's obviously never even played FIFA on his son's PlayStation.

A few minutes ago, I had scored my second goal of the day to cut the Tigers' lead to one. All my life I've played center forward because, well, I'm a scoring machine. No one really kept track in our league, but I probably had double or triple the goals of anyone else, even though I'd just turned 12. I wasn't even supposed to be in this division yet. It wasn't like I was this oversize kid, either, who already has to shave and has chest hairs. I was one of the smallest players in the league, as thin and wiry as the neck of a rooster. But I have a wicked shot, the most creative passes you'll ever see, and moves that could break the internet.

All the parents were cheering on the sidelines like it was the World Cup, and America was in the finals. Well, all the parents except mine. My mom used to cheer like that when she was alive, and it was pretty embarrassing, though it also felt good if I'm being honest. But my dad was standing on the sideline with his arms folded like he always does. Dad is tall and strong and pale, with thick red hair and hands the size of baseball gloves. He was a star football player in high school—American football. Some bald guy I'd never seen before, wearing a long wool coat with buttons, was trying to talk to him on the sideline. Dad didn't seem to notice.

I know he loves to watch me play but he never says very much. That's just him. With Mom gone, he works all the time to pay the bills, and has a ton on his mind.

Oops. Watching my dad made me miss a tackle. Billy Hood—our left fullback—stopped their forward from scoring, but Billy kicked the ball downfield to no one in particular, and the Tigers got the ball back. Billy's fast and strong and a good defender, but I've seen neighborhood dogs with better ball skills.

Soon I got another chance. The ball was knocking around midfield, and I managed to intercept it. I created some space with a pullback move, and took a moment to see what I had to work with.

I was at half field. Too many defenders stood between me and the goal to take it in myself.

I passed to my center midfielder, Dennis, then took off running. "Back to me!" I yelled.

Dennis got the hint and rocketed the ball downfield. I ran it down near the penalty box. When someone tried to tackle me, I cut right and dribbled around him.

Two defenders between me and the goal. I hesitated, trying to decide if I wanted to take them on. Normally I wouldn't have thought twice, but the Tigers were stocked with big, fast, skilled players. We were running out of time and down one goal, so I decided to go for it. I faked a pass left. The first defender bit hard. I cut right again, a quick one-two hook, and moved past him like he was standing still. Now I had to deal with Ronnie Lewis, their center defender and best player. He might be the best center back in the whole state. He was twice my height, growing a moustache, and looked about 18.

Ronnie came right at me. I couldn't just kick the ball around him and run. He was too fast for that. I danced around the ball, faking one way and then the other. He stayed with me. If I didn't get past him quickly, the other defenders would trap me, so I made a split-second decision to try a new move.

I pretended to be scared and turned my back to him, as if I was going to shield the ball and wait for help. He got right on my back, trying to bully me. Exactly what I wanted. As soon as he was close enough, I rolled the ball backwards with the top of my foot, right through his tree trunk legs, and spun around him. I just nutmegged him from behind!

I collected the ball and saw the open goal right in front of me. Just as I pulled my leg back to shoot, Ronnie tripped me from behind. I fell hard and got a face full of grass.

It was a dirty, dirty play. My knees and elbows were bleeding. I ignored the pain and pushed to my feet as the ref blew the whistle. I could have stayed down, but I didn't want anyone to think they could push me around.

The ref ran over and held a hand in the air. He gave Ronnie a red card for taking me down in the box—and my team a penalty kick.

All the parents were screaming again. When I looked over at my dad, his face twitched but he didn't move. For some reason, the bald guy beside him was staring at me curiously, like I was an animal in a zoo.

"Leo, you take it!" our coach shouted. "It's the last play of the game!"

I stepped up and put the ball on the penalty mark, on a level piece of ground with no rocks. If I made the shot, we tied the game and went into overtime. This was just a friendly for the Tigers, because our coaches knew each other, but the game was a big deal to us. I'd have a hat trick, too.

The goalie was dancing back and forth, clapping his hands like the pros do. I took a few steps back. Penalty kicks were easy. Just blast them high in the corner. I made them all the time.

My teammates patted me on the back and walked back to half field. When the parents quieted down, I could hear the birds in the trees and the traffic on the street beside the city park. I took a deep breath and inhaled that juicy smell of cut grass.

The ref blew the whistle. The goalie stopped moving and held his arms out wide. I ran forward, straight on to the ball, then leaned to my left at the last moment and kicked hard to the right, aiming for the top corner.

It felt good. That sweet smack when you realize your foot hits the ball just right. The goalie wasn't anywhere close. I smiled, knowing I was about to score and the game would be tied—right before the ball clanged off the crossbar and bounced over the top of the goal.

The ref blew the whistle long and hard, three times in a row.

Game over.

A Visitor You'll Never Believe

We lived a mile from the soccer field. Dad always let me ride shotgun in our old Ford Ranger pickup truck on the way home from games. He loved his truck but never cleaned it, and it smelled like dirty socks. He kept a photo of Mom on the dashboard, and a stack of classic rock CDs on the console. That's right—my dad's truck is so old it has a CD player.

My little sister Genevieve was in the backseat, singing a Disney tune. On the way home, as I was drinking a Gatorade and munching on a chocolate chip granola bar, I couldn't stop thinking about the missed penalty kick. I kept replaying it in my mind, trying to visualize what went wrong. I did that sometimes, so I wouldn't make the same mistake twice.

"I can't believe I lost the game for us," I said.

Dad turned down a song by Bruce Springsteen, who was about 90 years old and sounded to me like two cats fighting in a box of gravel.

"What are you talking about, Leo?"

"That penalty kick."

"Didn't you score two goals?"

"Yeah, but I missed the one that counted."

"Your team wouldn't have been in a position to tie the game without your goals. And didn't you have a great time playing?"

"Yeah, but—"

"No buts, Son. Don't worry about winning or losing. Just do your best and have fun. That's all that's important."

My dad totally didn't get it. Winning wasn't everything, I knew that—it was just that I hated to lose. I couldn't help it. I was born that way.

Come to think of it, my dad didn't understand much of anything at all, especially when I got in trouble at school. But that was okay, because I knew he loved us, and worked hard to pay our bills and make sure we had food and everything. And even though he didn't know a thing about soccer—he only watched football and baseball on TV and had no idea what offside was even though I'd explained it a hundred times—it never felt right to me if he had to miss one of my games.

Genevieve piped up from the backseat. "Who was that man with the funny accent?"

Ginny was six years old, refused to wear anything that didn't have a unicorn or a princess on it, only ate hamburgers and mac and cheese and spaghetti with meatballs, and liked even worse music than Dad. My mom had been a music teacher at the high school and taught me all about good music. *I* knew good music.

"That was an Englishman in town to see his sister," Dad said. "She lives in Columbus with her family, and her son plays for the Tigers."

"A *what* man?" Ginny said.

"Someone from England. It's a country in Europe, much older than ours. They have a queen, and a long time ago, the Pilgrims came—"

"They have a *queen*?" Ginny squealed.

"It's the home of the Premier League, is what it is," I said, reaching for my packet of Cheez-Its. "The best soccer league in the world."

"Is that right?" my dad said, in that voice he used when he wasn't really listening. He especially used it when I started talking about video games and professional soccer.

"Well, the Spanish league has Barcelona," I said. "PSG and Juventus and Bayern Munich are in other leagues, and are also top teams. But the Premier League is the best."

"What's the queen's name?"

"I don't know, honey," Dad said. "Elizabeth, I think."

Our town was about as big as a movie theater. My dad said 20,000 people live here, but let me tell you, there was never anything to do and it *felt* as big as a movie theater. On a Tuesday afternoon. During a school day.

That was okay. I had my future all planned out. As soon as I was old enough, I was joining a professional soccer team so I could travel around the world and do exactly what I wanted: play soccer all day and video games all night. My friends and I would live in an apartment in a big city and eat whatever we want.

For now, we lived in a neighborhood like all the others in town. Small homes with gray siding, built really close together. But I liked my house. I've lived there all my life, and I was worried we wouldn't get to stay. When Mom was alive, our family had good job benefits. I wasn't sure exactly what that meant, but I knew we had health insurance if we needed to go see the doctor. My dad was a carpenter, but he was self-employed, so he didn't always have enough work. I overheard him talking to Aunt Janice about not having enough money for doctor visits and house bills. I worried that if things didn't change, we might have to move to an apartment or something.

When we got home, I changed clothes and fed Messi, my pet lizard. Have I told you I'm into reptiles, especially anything venomous or poisonous? By the way, they don't mean the same thing. A venomous creature injects its toxin into a victim, usually with a bite or a sting. A poisonous toxin is delivered in what scientists call a passive manner, like something that is inhaled, swallowed, or absorbed. Think of it as offense (venom) versus defense (poison). I really want a poison dart frog but Dad said they were too expensive and dangerous. I told him they're not poisonous in captivity, though the scientists aren't sure why not. They think it depends on the food the frogs eat in their natural habitat. I don't think my dad believes either me or the scientists.

After changing out of my soccer uniform, I played some FIFA on my PlayStation while my sister danced to music in her bedroom, and Dad puttered around in his shed. My friend Carlos swung by. After lunch, we ran down to the park to play some pickup soccer with our friends. When I got home, I practiced a few ball tricks in the backyard before it got dark.

Yeah. I played a lot of soccer.

It wasn't just that I loved the game and was good at it. Somehow, when I had a ball at my feet, I didn't have to think about getting in trouble at school, or worry about Dad and money, or dwell on why my mom died so young.

I just played.

"Leo!" my sister said, poking her head out of the screen door. "You have to come inside."

"Why?"

"There's someone here to see you."

"Who?"

"That England guy."

"What does he want?"

"I don't know. Do you think he knows the Queen?"

"He doesn't know the *Queen*, Ginny. Queens and kings don't talk to regular people." It was almost dark, I was still working on a new move, and I didn't want to go. "I'll be there soon."

"Dad said to come now."

"Shut up, Ginny."

"Dad says don't say *shut up*."

She frowned and disappeared into the house. I ignored the request. Soon after, my dad came out, followed by that bald guy I'd seen at my game. His pants fit too tight at the ankles, and he was wearing the same wool coat. Dark circles under his eyes made him look tired, and he had a leather bag that resembled a purse slung over his shoulder. He was as tall as my dad but much thinner, and even paler. My mom was skinny and short like me, and while everyone said we looked alike, my hair is dark blond, and her skin was much browner than mine. I definitely got my crazy curls from her, though my hair is a total pain to brush, and sometimes I have to cut the knots out.

The English guy's eyes were kind of intense, and he was staring at me again, like at the game. Not in a creepy way, just like he was . . . judging me or something.

"Leo," Dad said, with a funny catch to his voice. "This man would like to meet you."

"Hi Leo," he said, sticking out a hand. "I'm Philip Niles."

I looked him in the eye like my dad had taught me, walked over, and shook his hand. His grip wasn't firm like Dad's, and the inside of his palms felt clammy like Jell-O. "Hey," I said.

"Practicing until dark, eh? You like the game quite a bit, don't you?"

His accent sounded as if he had a toothache that caused him to swallow the ends of his words. "Yeah, sure," I said.

Ginny rolled her eyes. "He *loves* soccer. It's all he ever talks about. Except for lizards and video games."

I returned to juggling the ball, wondering what the guy wanted but not caring too much. Maybe he had just moved into the neighborhood and had a kid my age. I juggled a while with my feet and thighs, kicked it up to my head, and kept going.

Philip and my dad were still watching me.

"Show him a trick," Ginny said.

I brought the ball down to my left foot and caught it with my instep. I held it for a second, never letting it touch the ground, then tossed it up again and swung my leg around the ball. That was called an *around the world*, and it's pretty hard to learn. Or it had been at first—now it was easy. I did five in a row, kicked the ball higher, and this time I balanced it between my shoulder blades.

"Very impressive," Philip said. "Where did you learn all that?"

I shrugged. "YouTube, I guess." After a few more tricks, I looked over and saw him exchange a glance with my father. Now it was starting to bother me. Who was this guy? Some lame private school coach trying to recruit me again?

"Ginny," my dad said, "could you play inside for a few minutes?"

He still had that strange catch to his voice. That was starting to bother me, too.

"Why?" she said.

"Just cuz, honey. You can have some screen time."

Ginny jumped up and ran inside before Dad changed his mind, leaving him and Philip standing on the stoop. They walked over to sit by the splintered picnic table in the backyard.

"C'mon over, Leo," my dad said.

By then, I knew something weird was going on. But what could it have to do with me? I flicked the ball into my arms, carried it over, and sat across from them.

"Leo, this man . . . Philip . . . is a football scout from London. London, England."

I blinked.

That was not what I expected to hear.

My dad continued, "Football is what they call soccer over there—"

"I know that."

Philip leaned forward and folded his hands atop the picnic table, the way grown-ups do when they have something serious to say. "Do you know what a scout is, Leo?"

"Sort of. Not really."

"Have you heard of the London Dragons Football Club?"

"You mean London Dragons FC?"

"That's the one."

"Um, of course. They're Premier League."

"That's who I work for. I'm a youth scout. My job is to

travel around the world to find new players who might be a good fit for the Dragons' development program."

I blinked a few more times. In fact, I couldn't seem to stop. "In America?"

Philip cracked a small smile. "Actually, no. We don't actively recruit here, not at your age. But I happened to be in town to see my sister, and she invited me to her son's game. I saw you play. I have to confess I was quite impressed."

My voice came out in a whisper. "You were?"

"You've got real talent, Leo."

"But I'm so . . . there are lots of bigger and faster kids."

He laughed. "Some of the best players in the world are the smallest players on the pitch. Maradona was barely five feet tall. Messi is tiny. That makes your talent even more intriguing. From what I saw today, you were easily the best player in a crowd of older, stronger boys. The top players in your state, too."

"The Columbus Tigers are the number one traveling team in Ohio," my dad said, which surprised me. I didn't know he knew anything about that.

"And one of the top-ranked in the country," Philip added.

"Oh," I said. "They are?"

After a moment, Dad said to Philip, "So you can tell all this from just one game?"

He gave my dad a shrewd smile. "You're a carpenter. Can you spot a good piece of wood from a bad one?"

"In a heartbeat."

"Football is my job, and I'm very good at it. I travel all over the world—Africa, Asia, the Middle East—to search for young players. I can't always predict the outcome—how a player will age, who will have what it takes to make it as a professional or even to join the Academy—but I can spot talent."

"Oh," my dad said as Philip buttoned his jacket. It was getting chilly outside.

"Leo, your dad and I have been talking about something, and he thought we should ask you together."

"Ask me what?" I glanced at my dad. He tipped his head, letting me know he was okay with all this.

Philip continued, "Did you know that all the top clubs, including the Dragons, have youth academies where they train and develop players in their system?"

"Kind of," I said.

"Messi and Iniesta and Xavi Hernandez all started in the Barcelona Youth Academy, for example. Lots of players do. But, to be fair, most of those who start at the academies don't finish. The journey to become a professional soccer player is an extremely arduous one, and it takes a lot more than just talent. But the academies are an excellent place to start."

When I looked over at my dad, I saw a proud smile on his face, as well as a sadness in his eyes I didn't understand. Maybe he wished Mom was there.

"The Dragons run a youth camp each summer at our training facility in London," Philip said. "Every year, we ask a few select players to attend. The camp is a month-long program where we determine who receives an invitation to join the youth development program, which we call the Academy."

I sat very still, not daring to breathe, wondering if I had fallen asleep and was dreaming.

"I think you've got a chance to join the Academy, Leo. We have a few spots left in our camp this summer, and I came to your house to invite you to join us."

Messi and I Talk Things Over

My voice was lost in some deep, dark forest. I could barely believe what I had just heard.

Philip pushed to his feet. "I realize this is a big decision you and your dad need to discuss. I'll be in the States a few more days if you have any questions."

"What happens if I make the team?" I blurted out without thinking. "I mean, it's in England and all. And we live in Ohio."

"It's true, you'd have to move overseas. You can't sign a professional contract until you turn seventeen, but all of our youth players receive a package worth thirty-five thousand pounds—what is that these days, fifty thousand dollars? You'd receive the best training in the world, play regular games against other youth academies, attend classes with the players, and have the chance to join the summer traveling team."

I was too stunned to think of any more questions. After he shook my hand again, my dad led Philip around the side of the house. Once he was gone, I pinched myself to make sure that had really happened.

"C'mon, Leo," my dad said when he returned. "Help me carry some wood to the porch."

We had a screen porch on the side of the house that my dad built himself, with some chairs and a hammock and a wood-burning stove. Dad hung out there a lot during the winter, sometimes to read a book, but mostly just sitting around and staring at the fire.

I struggled beneath the weight of the wood he stacked in my arms. Once we reached the porch, he started a fire and stood in front of the stove with his arms crossed. "What did you think of Mr. Niles?"

"I don't know. He's nice. Kind of hard to understand."

"And what did you think about what he said?"

"I can't believe it," I said quietly. "That would be amazing."

My dad nodded but didn't say anything.

"Can I go, Dad? To the summer camp?

It took him a few moments to respond. "I don't know, pal. It's real expensive. I'm not sure we can afford it."

I felt like a balloon someone had just let the air out of, spinning and crashing to the ground. "You have to *pay* to go?"

"The summer camp is free. But with the airfare, and a hotel for me and Ginny, and food . . . they have some scholarships, but Philip said there are no more available this year. Things are pretty tight right now, Son."

My voice was very small. "I know."

"I'm not saying *no* yet, but let me think it through, okay?"

I had the sudden knowledge that Dad wouldn't be able to find the money to take us all overseas for a month. He never complained or talked about money in front of me and Ginny, but listening to him and Aunt Janice talk, I knew we had very little savings.

"Sure. Thanks, Dad." I tried not to sound disappointed. "It's fine if I don't go. It's not a big deal. I wouldn't want to leave you and my friends, anyway."

All of that was true, except for the *big deal* part.

The London Dragon FC Academy was very much a big deal. An *enormous* deal. It was the future I had always dreamed of.

But I didn't want my dad to feel bad.

"I appreciate you saying that, Son."

He was still staring at the fire, and I noticed his hands clenched at his sides. As I turned to go back inside, I realized he hadn't looked me in the eye for the entire conversation.

And my dad always looked me in the eye.

Later that night, I went outside to catch a few crickets. I returned to my room and opened Messi's cage to feed him his dinner. He was hanging out on a fake tree and watching me with his beady eyes that stuck out from the side of his head. Messi is green and orange and yellow, fits in my hand, and loves to push up on his front legs and strut around his cage like a peacock. He's a type of lizard called a bearded dragon. The name comes from his fat throat pouch—called a beard— that blows up and turns black when he's angry. I've tried to train him to do this whenever Ginny comes into the room.

As I stroked the bumps and spiky horns along Messi's back, he flicked his pink tongue at me, over and over. He knew what was coming. I tossed the crickets inside his cage and shut it. I felt bad for the poor little guys, but it was part of Mother Nature. It wasn't Messi's fault he loved to eat live insects.

He pounced on a cricket and caught it from behind, swallowing it in a few gulps. As he waited for another, I looked at the poster of the real Messi on the wall above his cage. "I don't care that we don't have money to buy fancy things. Whatever. Who cares about that stuff? But trying out for the London

Dragons could be my big chance, and I might not get to go. That's not very fair, is it?"

Messi stopped moving as if he had heard me. My lizard and I, we understood each other. We're both a little weird, and don't look like anyone else, and he's a little small compared to other lizards, just like I am.

He flicked his tongue at me a few times, trying to tell me something in lizard language, and then pounced on another cricket.

Every day before school, I met Carlos and Dennis, my two best friends, at the bus stop at the end of our street. On Monday morning, before the bus arrived, I told them about the visit from Philip Niles.

Dennis played center midfielder on my soccer team, but Carlos was a year younger than me, and even smaller than I was. He was a really good player for his age, though, and his family went nuts over soccer. Carlos said one of his uncles played on a professional team in Mexico, but sometimes Carlos exaggerates, like the time he told me he could eat 20 hot dogs in one sitting, or that his family owns a castle in Spain.

Dennis was staring at me with his mouth open so wide our school bus could have driven inside. Carlos looked confused, then burst out laughing. "An international soccer scout . . . you . . . the Dragons . . . that's hilarious, Leo. You had me for a second."

"It really happened," Ginny said, crossing her arms with an air of self-importance. "I was there. That man had an Englishman accent and funny pants and everything. He said Leo was really awesome and should go to the London Dragons soccer camp this summer and try out for the team."

"The *youth* team," I added.

Normally, as soon as Ginny opened her mouth in front of my friends, I told her to shut it. This time, I wanted to give her a hug for vouching for my story. And while part of me wanted to shout at the top of my lungs and tell my friends what had happened, part of me felt embarrassed just talking about it. I wasn't sure why. Maybe because I didn't have the money to go. Maybe because it *did* sound ridiculous that something like that could happen to me. I mean, I was good and all, but the *London Dragons*?

Dennis was still in a daze, but Carlos's face was starting to twitch, like he had swallowed something the wrong way. He looked back and forth between me and Ginny. "You're serious about this?"

"Yeah," I said.

"That scout must be really desperate."

"Not desperate enough to ask you."

"He hasn't seen me play," Carlos said. "Are you sure he wasn't joking?"

"He wasn't joking," Ginny said. "I was *there*."

Carlos held one of his hands up. "Wait—you're really, really serious?"

I rolled my eyes. "*Yes*."

He swallowed. "You're—what the crap—I can't believe this—this is the sickest thing ever—you're awesome at soccer and all but you're not *this* good—those international players will destroy you—how did he even find you—wait are you honestly not joking around—Leo, you fart breath, this is unbelievable!!"

As the bus pulled up, Dennis whooped and slung his backpack across his shoulders. "So when are you going to London?"

"I'm not sure I am," I mumbled, staring at the bus. "Probably not."

"Probably *not*?" Carlos said.

"We don't have the money," Ginny said, matter-of-factly.

Carlos got a wild look in his eyes and started plucking at the curls of his short black hair. "Probably not? Probably *not*? You can't tell us something like that and then not go to London. You *have* to go! Sell some lemonade, or your lizard, or your sister—"

"Hey!" Ginny said.

"Do whatever it takes, Leo. We *have* to hear about this! You might meet Harry Kane or Sterling or Salah—my brother isn't going to believe this. But you're not even as good as my brother."

"He's a senior in high school."

"So? It's the *Premier League*."

Both Dennis and Carlos started laughing and hugging me in front of the whole bus. As soon as we boarded, Carlos told the entire bus what had happened, and everyone started clapping and chanting my name. I scooted down in my seat and covered my face with my backpack.

By Friday, I was growing more convinced I wouldn't be able to go to London. Every time I mentioned it to Dad, he looked sad and frustrated and said nothing had changed. I did some research and learned that a plane ticket to London cost a thousand dollars.

When I saw that, I knew it was hopeless. The only vacations we'd ever taken were to Six Flags and our grandma's house near Cincinnati. I'd never flown before. The only beach I'd visited was Lake Erie. There aren't a lot of palm trees.

That night, Aunt Janice brought over Papa John's for Pizza Friday. Dad wasn't a very good cook, so we ate a lot of pizza and fast food, but I missed Mom's spaghetti and chicken pot pie. I missed a lot of things about her. I tried not to think too much about it.

Anyway, Aunt Janice is my dad's older sister, as well as an administrative assistant to a lawyer in town. She wore thick glasses, too much makeup, always had a crossword puzzle or a book in her lap, and was my favorite person on planet Earth after my dad. Aunt Janice and Mom used to love to talk about music and travel and movies, and always made each other laugh. Now, when Aunt Janice comes over, she usually brings a home-cooked meal or a pizza, tells Dad the house was smelly, and makes sure Ginny and I do our homework.

Next to banana pancakes, pizza was my favorite food. I stuffed myself with slices of thin crust ham until my stomach felt as puffy as Messi's beard. After dinner, when I was playing FIFA, I heard Dad and Aunt Janice talking with raised voices. I left the game on, went into the dining room, and eavesdropped on their conversation. I heard *soccer* and *London* and *my job*, and it didn't take a genius to figure out what they were talking about. I moved even closer, right to the edge of the dining room. I overheard Dad say he wasn't sure where the money for the house payment would come from.

"The forbearance on the student loan is about to run out, too," Dad said.

"How much do you owe?" Aunt Janice said quietly.

"Fifty thousand. It's four hundred per month."

I knew they were talking about Mom's student loan. Dad never went to university, but she had a degree from Kenyon College. I didn't realize she still owed money—or that Dad had to pay her student loans after she died. That didn't seem fair.

Despite how badly I wanted to attend the Academy summer camp, I knew I should tell Dad I'd decided not to go. I didn't want to lose our house, and I knew how guilty Dad would feel if he had to break the news to me.

Tomorrow, I told myself. *I'll tell him tomorrow.*

"Right, Messi?" I said after I went to my room and told him all about my decision.

My lizard hopped to the highest branch on his tree and stared down at me. For the first time in a month, his beard flared in anger.

For the next two weeks, every morning I tried to tell Dad I'd decided not to go to the summer camp.

And every morning I failed.

Though I felt guilty about it, I couldn't bring myself to do it. I didn't think Dad would believe me, and I couldn't tell him that I'd overheard his conversation with Aunt Janice.

On a Saturday morning in May, the last game of the season, I played awful. I had a cold and didn't feel great, but that was no excuse for only scoring a single goal against the Bears, one of the worst teams in the league. Aunt Janice called them the Bad News Bears, and laughed her head off.

On the last play of the game, I finally got it going, and made one of my best runs of the year. I sliced through half their team, feinting and cutting, no one could touch me, and then found myself right in front of their goal. I was in the zone and stepped into the shot, but the ball hit one of the loose rocks on our patchy field that was full of weeds. The rock caused the ball to bounce up enough for the goalie to grab it.

Story of my day.

Dad made us banana pancakes and bacon for an early lunch. It started to rain, which made me feel even gloomier, despite the pancakes. Dad hadn't mentioned the summer camp for days, and even Carlos had stopped bugging me.

After breakfast, my dad made a cup of coffee and brought it to the porch. I started to head to my room when he called me over. I sat next to him while the rain slashed against the screen.

"Ginny told me you got another detention yesterday."

"She said *what*?" I said.

He raised his eyebrows. Coming from my dad, that meant I was on thin ice.

"Yeah," I said. "I did. Sorry."

"What happened this time?"

"This bully was roasting a friend of mine behind the teacher's back. I got mad, so I threw a paper airplane at his face. Mrs. Weatherholt turned around right when I did it."

"Roasting?"

"You know, throwing bombs. Insults."

"I see. You know, Leo, you didn't have a single detention before your mother died."

I looked away.

"I've given you a lot of leeway, but we have to move on. You can't stay angry forever."

"That doesn't change the fact that Wade Felder's a bully."

"*Leo.*"

"Yeah. Okay. I'll try harder."

"You favor your mother in almost every way, but I'm afraid you got my temper. It's something you're going to have to work on."

"You have a temper?" I said, surprised. I'd never seen it. Well, there was that one time when a car almost ran over Ginny and me on our bikes at the stop sign near our house. Dad ran into the front yard, yelling at the top of his voice, and started pulling that guy out of his car. I don't know what would have happened if the neighbors hadn't intervened.

"Let's call it . . . impulsive behavior. I've had a lifetime to work on it, but I was young once, too. Listen, there's something else I wanted to talk to you about. I have some news for you, pal."

I couldn't read anything from Dad's expression. But then again, I rarely could. It was probably something else about school, a note from a teacher about an assignment I'd missed.

"Are you still interested in going to that soccer camp in London?"

That soccer camp, he calls it. *It's the London Dragons FC Player Development Academy camp, Dad. That's what it is.*

I took a long time to answer. "I guess," I said, and then forced my next words out. "Not really."

"Not really?"

"You know, I just . . . it's a lot of money and everything."

His voice hardened. "Hey, kiddo—you let me worry about the money around here."

"Okay. Sorry, Dad. I just . . . I don't want to hurt the family," I blurted out.

He was quiet for a long moment. "You let me worry about that, too, okay?"

"Yes, Sir. But it's all right. I don't need to go."

"I know you don't *need* to go, but I know you *want* to go. Or am I wrong?"

I looked down at my hands. "You're not wrong."

"More than anything else in life, unless I miss my guess."

I nodded and said nothing.

When I looked up, I saw him release a deep breath, as if what he was about to say was hard for him. "I've been talking to Aunt Janice over the last few weeks. She's offered to buy your plane ticket."

For some reason, it took me a moment to realize what I was hearing. "She has?"

"Leo, if you want to go to this summer camp and try out for the team—and if you stay out of trouble at school—you can go to London."

All of a sudden, I felt light-headed.

"But you'll have to go by yourself, to a foreign country for a whole month. You'd stay at the Academy's training facility with the other boys."

He looked worried about this, but staying by myself with a bunch of other kids who are all crazy about soccer sounded like the best possible news. He started to say something else, then looked away. When he turned back to me, he cleared his throat and said, "Think about it, kiddo. I have to tell Mr. Niles by Monday, or they'll give your spot to someone else."

I had no idea he was still talking to the scout. "Okay."

"And the deal's off if you get another detention before the end of the year."

Dad patted my knee and walked out of the room. I could barely believe it. I had convinced myself I wasn't going to get to go, but now that I could . . . it was a little bit terrifying.

When I returned to my room, I stood in front of Messi's cage to talk it through. Sometimes I had trouble expressing my feelings with other people, but I could tell Messi anything.

"So what do you think? I'll be all by myself in a huge city for a whole month. A place where everyone speaks funny and the food is probably terrible. Oh, and I'll be playing against some of the best kids in the world. What was it like when you left home? Did you even notice? Do you still miss your lizard parents, or did you eat them or something?"

As I watched Messi prance about the cage, unconcerned with my problems, I remembered how much money Philip Niles said I would make if I made the youth team. Fifty thousand dollars. I knew how much Dad could use that money. It would help the family, and he wouldn't be so stressed all the time.

I'd miss my friends and my video games. I'd miss my dad and Aunt Janice and Messi—who would take care of Messi? Dad would feed him, but Messi needed me to talk to him every single day, or he got lonely and mean and tried to bite people.

I was totally nervous about this.

I'd never been away from home before.

I might fail and be embarrassed on the field.

But who was I kidding?

This was the best news of my life.

Messi stopped walking, arched his back, and locked eyes with me. I knew what he was thinking.

"Gotcha," I said, then went to look for my dad. I found him outside, checking under the hood of his truck.

"Dad, I want to go to London."

He turned, wiped his hands on a rag, and smiled.

I Can't Believe I'm Getting on a Plane to London

I managed to avoid more detentions, school let out for the summer, and the day to leave for London finally arrived.

Aunt Janice gave me her old Samsung tablet for the trip. She showed my dad how to use Skype, and Carlos told me to connect with him on WhatsApp, which he uses to text his cousins in Mexico. So at least I'd have my best friend to chat with, though there's a six-hour time difference between Ohio and London. Normally my dad wouldn't let me do something like that—he's terrified of social media and even texts—but I think he felt bad because he knew we wouldn't be able to talk very much.

When I said goodbye to Messi, he refused to look at me. I got the feeling he was proud of me for going, but would punish me anyway. I picked him up, stroked him, and fed him an extra-juicy cricket. The night before, I had given Dad and Ginny detailed instructions on how to take care of him.

He'll be okay, Leo. He's a big lizard now.

After grabbing my backpack and my suitcase, I walked out to the truck with Ginny. It felt weird leaving my house, knowing I wouldn't be back for a month. I've never lived anywhere else, or even been to summer camp.

I turned to take a long look at the worn siding, the screen porch, and the maple tree in our front yard with branches just right for climbing. I'd be missing half the summer with my friends. I was nervous and excited about staying in the dormitory with the other players. Would the other kids even speak English? Would they like Doritos and Gatorade?

After Dad walked out of the house with Aunt Janice, he locked the door and put an arm around my shoulder. "Ready to go, pal?"

"Sure," I said, walking backwards towards the truck.

Dad bought me a plane ticket from Detroit so I could fly direct to London. It took us three hours to drive to Detroit. Aunt Janice rode with us. We didn't get to see much on the way, just a bunch of shopping malls and highways that all looked the same. The airport was very crowded, with flights coming and going all over the world.

After checking in for my six p.m. flight, Dad handed me a bulky plastic bag. "I got a little something for you, kiddo."

Curious, I dug inside and pulled out a shoebox. "New cleats!"

Not just any new cleats, but rock-star red Nike sock boots with silver laces and real leather. Normally my dad takes me to a secondhand sports shop in town when I need cleats, and tells me I'm a growing boy and he can't afford a new pair of shoes every season. Which I understand. But these . . . these cleats were so smooth, and they smelled so good. I couldn't believe they were mine.

"Do these work?" he said.

"They're perfect. Thanks, Dad."

He started to pat me on the back like he usually does, then hugged me so tight I thought one of my ribs might crack.

"Okay, Dad," I said after a moment. "Kind of hard to breathe here."

When he released me, I was surprised to see a tear in the corner of his eye. The only time I had ever seen him cry was at Mom's funeral.

"Do you think you'll meet anyone famous at that academy?" Ginny said. "Like a princess?

"Um, no."

"If you do," she said shyly, "tell her I said *hi*."

"I'll tell her you said she's ugly and farts all the time."

Ginny punched me on the shoulder and started to turn away, then gave me a big hug that surprised me. "I'll take good care of Messi," she said.

I started to say he didn't really like girls, and to stay out of my room, but instead I squeezed her hand and realized I would miss teasing her.

My aunt embraced me next. All this hugging was embarrassing, and her floral perfume made me a little light-headed. It felt like being attacked by a rose bush. She let me go, placed her hands on my shoulders, and held me at arm's length. "Try to see as much of London as you can. It's a big, beautiful city full of history."

"Um, sure," I said, thinking that sightseeing was the last thing on my mind. The only thing I planned to do in my free time was play more video games and soccer.

I could tell she knew what I was thinking. "Promise me you'll try," she said. "Life isn't all about sports and PlayStation."

"I promise," I mumbled, wondering how little effort I had to put forth so it didn't count as lying to my aunt.

She drew me tight again and showered me with kisses. I really hoped no one I knew was in the Detroit airport. Ginny stuck her tongue out at me, I called her a few names, and then my dad was walking me towards the security line, where I had to empty my pockets in a plastic white box. I stuck my wallet in there, which had a hundred bucks in cash my dad had given me. Would I need to spend any money in London? Maybe I could get a signed London Dragons jersey for Carlos. Who was I kidding? I would keep that for myself.

After we found a seat at the gate, I tried to read a graphic novel I had brought, but I was too excited. I just sat there and looked at all the people while I waited for my flight, daydreaming about the Academy.

An hour later, a loud bell chimed and everyone around me stood up. At last it was time to board.

After I shrugged on my backpack, Dad put an arm around my shoulders. "I'll miss you, pal."

"I'll miss you too."

"Stay out of trouble and behave yourself at the dorm."

"Okay."

"Listen, Leo—I'm not worried or anything, but don't talk to any strangers on the plane or in the city."

"Dad, I'm not eight years old."

"I know. You're almost a grown man, but not quite. Just stick close to people you know."

"Got it covered."

"London is a really big city, pal. Way bigger than Cincinnati or Detroit or any place you've ever been. One of the biggest cities in the world."

"*Dad.* I'll be careful."

"That's what I like to hear. Love you, pal."

"Love you, too."

"And listen, when you're out there on the field . . . don't ever back down, okay? Do your best and have fun. Those are the only things that matter." He stopped walking and looked me in the eye. "I'm real proud of you, Son. And I know your Mom would be, too."

I boarded the plane with a flight attendant who would be my chaperone for the journey. As I walked down the aisle, it hit me all at once that, except for the chaperone, I was on my own. I saw all kinds of people, families and business travelers and even people in wheelchairs. The only thing I didn't see was another kid by himself. I felt alone but also kind of special.

My seat was a window seat, which I liked. I had my own screen for video games, music, and movies. This flight might be better than I had expected.

Before I stuck my backpack under the seat, I took out a few things for the journey: my graphic novel, the Samsung tablet, a pack of gum, and a small blue pillow my aunt had loaned me.

The plane had four different sections and hundreds of people on board. While the plane idled on the runway, I hunkered down and surfed through the offerings on my screen. I saw all kinds of superhero movies I wanted to see.

In the aisle seat on my row, an older lady slipped a mask over her eyes and reclined her head. I wondered why no one had taken the seat beside me. My greatest fear was someone smelly or scary-looking would take the middle seat and ruin my flight. Maybe I had gotten lucky and the seat was empty.

The last person on board was a tall teenager with a Mohawk and walnut-colored skin like my mom's. He had on ripped jeans and a bright green V-neck T-shirt, a stud earring that sparkled in his left ear, and a pile of leather bracelets on both wrists. As he approached my row, he glanced down at his boarding pass, then took out his ear buds.

"Hey Boss, are you Leo Doyle?"

"That's . . . that's me."

He hefted a duffel bag with patches all over it and stuck it in the overhead luggage rack. With an easy smile, he squeezed past the older woman, sat beside me, and stuck out a hand. "I'm Tigudzwa. Call me Tig. Philip told me you'd be on the flight, and booked my seat next to yours."

"Philip?"

"Philip Niles, yeah? The scout? You're a footballer, I hope?"

Though Tig's accent was American, he looked and talked differently than anyone I had ever met. "A footballer—yeah. I mean, I play soccer. I'm going to the London Dragons summer camp."

"Just call it the Academy Camp, Boss. That's what we all do."

"Oh. Okay. You're going too? Is it your first time?"

He chuckled. "I play for the U21s."

All of a sudden, I lost the power of speech. I stared at him with my mouth open, and, when I finally recovered my voice, blurted out an embarrassing string of words that sounded like something my little sister would say. "You *play*? For the London *Dragons*?"

"The youth squad, but yeah. Hey kid, it's nice to meet ya, but I had a late night, and I'm gonna catch some zzzs. Wake me up on the other side of the pond."

Before I could stutter a reply, he replaced his ear buds, closed his eyes, and tuned out the world.

I tried not to stare at Tig as the pilot came on the loudspeaker and said a bunch of stuff that I didn't pay attention to. Not only had I just met my first real soccer player, but Tig was easily the single coolest human being on planet Earth, period.

And I was sure he thought I was a complete dork.

When the plane surged into the sky, rumbling like a buffalo, my stomach felt as if it was dropping through the floor. Watching the plane soar high above the ground was one of the most terrifying and exhilarating experiences of my life. The people and cars below us were like ants scurrying around their little anthills, and as the Detroit skyscrapers grew smaller and smaller, the city began to resemble a drawing in a sketch book, leaving me with a funny feeling. I realized the world was far bigger than I had ever imagined. I had known this in my head, but seeing it from ten thousand feet was different.

An hour after takeoff, they fed us dinner on a tray attached to the seat. I got a Coke with ice, and the stewardess let me have an extra piece of cake. She was treating me like a child, but I didn't mind too much if I got soft drinks and extra cake. Tig slept through the whole meal.

The Atlantic Ocean was so enormous I couldn't stop staring at it. All that water! As far as I could see! After a while, I returned to my screen and played some video games—ones for noobs—and watched a Marvel movie. The sun went down over the water but I wasn't tired at all. Eventually Tig yawned and woke up.

After he took out his ear buds, he looked outside and said, "Are we close?"

"I don't know."

He checked a flight map on his screen that said we had three hours to go. "How was the food?"

"Pretty good. The stewardess said you can have yours whenever you want."

"Right-O." He looked at me kind of funny. "You've never flown before, have you?"

I shook my head.

"By the way," he said, "cool hair."

"I don't really like it. It always gets knotted."

"You serious? That golden skin and those crazy curls? I bet the little ladies love you, hey?" I felt my face grow warm, and he laughed. "Just joshing you, Boss. I know you're just a kid."

A kid? Ginny was a kid. I would be in seventh grade next year.

"Where are you from, anyway?" he said. "Do you surf?"

"Uh, no. I live in Ohio."

"You don't look like you live in Ohio."

"I don't?" I didn't feel like talking about myself, because the more Tig knew about me, the more he'd know how average and boring my life was. I said, "Are there lots of Americans going to the camp?"

"You mean North Americans?"

"Uh, yeah. I guess."

"We're it, at least on this flight. There might be one or two more at the camp. You must be pretty good, hey? How did Phil find you?"

"I think it was just luck."

"Nah, Phil knows talent. What are you, defensive mid?"

"Center forward. Striker."

"A nine?" He squinted at me. "You must be a little speedster."

"Not really."

"No?" He laughed again. "Okay, then. We'll see what you've got. I'm on staff this summer. I'll be checking you out myself."

The thought of that made me nervous, and I didn't know what to say.

"You should get some sleep," he said. "It'll be morning when we get there. The first day, it's best to stay up until nighttime if you can, and get some solid rest. Camp starts the next morning. You don't want to be tired."

Tig asked for his dinner, and we talked a bit more while he ate. I learned he was nineteen years old, from California but lived in London now, traveled all over Europe, had a girlfriend in France, liked hip-hop and candy as much as I did, was a left-footed winger, played the drums, and sometimes helped DJ at a nightclub.

Basically, he was a demigod.

After his dinner, Tig put his headphones back on, bobbed to his music for a while, and fell asleep again. I watched another movie and checked the flight path. Ninety minutes to go. I knew I should sleep, but there were too many thoughts crowding my mind, and too many good movies begging to be watched.

The plane landed just after sunrise. When the lights came on, I was so tired I felt like a zombie. It took forever to get off the plane and go through customs, the worst part of the trip by far. Tig checked his watch and said we were a little early.

I had thought the Detroit airport was big, but as we walked towards the baggage claim, I couldn't stop gawking at all the shops and people. Heathrow Airport was bigger and busier than most *cities* I'd seen. The variety of people astonished me: young and old, fat and thin, white and black and brown and everything in between.

Even a lot of the clothing was new to me. I saw people wearing robes from head to toe, some dressed like they were in a music video, some with their faces covered with black cloth, some wearing leopard print clothing and loads of jewelry and walking tiny dogs on leashes through the airport.

After retrieving our bags, we went outside to wait for the van. The weather was cloudy and chillier than Ohio at this time of year.

Tig pointed out a circle of kids close to my age. "Those must be the Mexicans and Central Americans. Phil said they're riding with us. See the tall player next to the chaperone?"

I noticed a handsome kid with dark hair who stood a foot taller than the others, almost as tall as Tig. "Yeah."

"That's Diego. He's the top player his age in all of Mexico. I saw him play in L.A. last year, and helped scout him."

"How old is he?"

"Twelve. Like you, yeah?"

"Yeah," I said in a small voice. *Twelve?* That kid looked at least sixteen. I couldn't believe he'd be in my group.

And the top player his age in *all of Mexico?*

What had I gotten myself into?

"What position does he play?" I asked, hoping to hear he played goalie, or maybe fullback.

"Striker," Tig said. "Kid's got a wicked header."

Great, I thought. *That's my worst skill. I don't think my coach back home even realizes you can use your head.*

We walked over to the circle of players. Tig introduced everyone. It turned out three were Mexican, one was Costa Rican, and the other was from a country called Nicaragua, which I knew about because they were in CONCACAF, America's qualifying division for the World Cup. They had all traveled on the same flight from Mexico City to attend the camp. Just like me, none of them had come with their parents.

They seemed like a fun bunch to be around, except for Diego, who was quiet and serious and stood apart from everyone else. Everyone spoke decent English except the Nicaraguan, Miguel. He laughed a lot, and I couldn't tell if he understood me or not.

Tig said the van was running late, pulled a soccer ball out of his bag, and pumped it up right there on the curb. "Careful with the crowd," he said, then passed the ball with his thigh to Diego, who caught it on the top of his foot and kicked it to someone else.

The sight of a soccer ball woke me up. I joined in, and we all juggled in a circle. It was a strange feeling because I'd never juggled with anyone as good as I am. Tig was the best, of course, and could do all kinds of crazy things with the ball. He popped it high with the back of his heel without looking, rolled it across his shoulders, pinched it between the back of his knee and his hamstring, then started juggling and break-dancing at the same time.

A crowd of people started to gather around us. We kept the ball in the air as we passed it back and forth, using every part of our bodies except our hands. I trapped it on my chest, used the inside of my foot to kick it high, then flicked it off my shoulder to Diego.

Tig called out some rules. Every time someone let the ball drop or made a bad pass, they had to sit. The onlookers began to clap in rhythm as we juggled, and soon it was just me and Tig and Diego left. We juggled like a symphony. I got really fancy and stuck in a few around the worlds, a side-head stall, and then a move where I stuck one leg behind the other and popped the ball up, then switched and did it on the other side. After that, I passed the ball high to Diego, who tried a fancy trap with both feet and missed. The ball hit the ground, and he looked very angry with himself as he walked to the side and sat down.

Geez, I thought. *It's just a game.*

Tig already had the ball back up. The circle of onlookers grew tighter as the two of us one-touched it back and forth with our heads, our thighs, and our feet.

"You know the crossover?" Tig asked.

"No."

"Follow me." He kicked the ball to chest-height, jumped, and while he was airborne, swung one leg all the way over the ball and kicked the ball up with his other foot, just before it hit the ground. I watched him, trying to learn the trick, and then he passed it to me in the air. Without time to think, I juggled for a few seconds and tried to do what he did. I didn't get it perfect, but I managed to keep the ball in the air.

"That's it!" Tig said, as the clapping got louder. Out of the corner of my eye, I saw all the kids in my group cheering except Diego, who looked as if he was trying to memorize what we were doing.

"Faster," Tig said, then did the trick three times in rapid succession before passing it to me.

I trapped the ball in midair, bounced it up, and did the crossover two times before the ball hit the ground. As everyone cheered for Tig, he walked over and chucked me on the shoulder. "You're legit, Boss."

Before we could start up again, a black van pulled up to the curb with the London Dragons logo emblazoned on the side. The door opened and I followed the others inside, my jaw dropping at the fancy leather seats and blue carpet, feeling as good as I ever had in my life.

The Castle, the Enemy, and the Roomie

As soon as we stepped on the bus, an adult wearing a Dragons FC sweat suit introduced himself as Coach Devon and handed everyone a breakfast biscuit and a bottle of water. The van made a stop at another terminal to pick up more players from South and Central America. It took us forty-five minutes just to leave the airport. I think it was bigger than my entire hometown.

I sat beside Alejandro, a short but stocky Costa Rican who I had juggled with in front of the airport. He had a great sense of humor. We got along well from the start.

On the ride in, most of us were too busy eating our biscuits and cutting up to notice the scenery, but I saw a lot of traffic circles called roundabouts, more cars than I'd ever seen in my life, and endless rows of brick apartment buildings with no yards or trees.

"Here's your local high street," Coach Devon said.

We were still on the outskirts of the city. Through the window, I saw a cobblestone street lined with shops and restaurants and flower sellers. The buildings looked old and kind of dingy, though I liked how close together everything was and how many people were out walking the town. I don't know if they had anything fun to do, but it seemed like a good place to explore.

A few minutes past the high street, the cars and buildings thinned, replaced by trees and parks. Soon the bus turned left and passed through a tall iron gate with the London Dragons logo. At the end of a winding driveway, we pulled into the parking lot of an enormous, gray stone building with high walls, square windows, and pointy round towers on the ends. Below the building sprawled a lawn as green as a golf course and filled with soccer fields, all with people kicking balls around.

The fields had fresh white lines and goals with crisp black netting. The half lines, center circles, corner arcs, goal area boxes, and penalty boxes were all clearly marked. I'd never seen fields that nice in my life. Giant light poles rose above the fields, and I thought how fantastic it would be to play at night under those lights.

Bleachers lined the perimeter of the complex. Behind the bleachers, a wall of trees shielded the training grounds from view. It was my dream come true, a whole little universe of soccer.

"We call this The Castle," Coach Devon called out as the van drew closer to the stone building. The driver parked between a pair of buses, close to a red-and-gold tent with a line of players my age out front. "This is your home for the next month."

Everyone on our bus had their faces pressed to the windows. I heard a lot of chatter in English, Spanish, and Portuguese, which is the language people from Brazil speak. To my ears, Portuguese sounded almost the same as Spanish, except a little more musical, as if everyone was having fun all the time.

Coach Devon stood to usher us out. "On your way in, everyone needs to visit the welcome pavilion for your room assignments. Today's a free day. Get some rest, play some pickup, take some snacks from the common room—you'll see the sign when you go inside. Except for dinner at six in the cafeteria, you're on your own until the morning."

On our own. I liked the sound of that.

Tig was sitting up front by the driver, waiting for everyone to leave. On my way out, Tig fist-bumped me. "Remember to get some sleep tonight, Boss. Tomorrow is important, because they'll sort you into squads at the end of the day. You want to make a good impression."

"What kind of squads?"

He grinned. "You'll see."

The pavilion had a sign in front marked 'Registration.' As I stood in line, I noticed a range of skin tones, body types, and ethnicities. While I wasn't the smallest player, I was close. Some of the kids were much taller and heavier than I was. They even had muscles, like some of the eighth and ninth graders I'd played against. These kids looked confident, too, like they knew they were supposed to be there. I, on the other hand, felt a little bit like I was dreaming, and that maybe a mistake had been made.

Could I, Leo K. Doyle from Middleton, Ohio, really be at a London Dragons summer camp?

Someone called out from behind me. "Cincinnati! Hey, mate!"

Cincinnati?

Wondering how there could possibly be someone who knew a city close to where I was from—maybe one of the Ohio traveling team players?—I turned and saw a burly kid with a blond crew cut standing a few people behind me, grinning and waving. He towered over the other kids in line, and had a smashed face like a bulldog. He was built like one, too.

"Hey," I replied.

"Nice trackies," he said, grinning even wider.

Huh? What's a trackie?

I looked down and remembered I was wearing my FC Cincinnati sweats, and that I'd heard players in the Premier League refer to sweat suits as a tracksuit. That must be what he was talking about. Trackies. By this time, the other people in line had started to snicker.

"What about them?" I said.

"Really?" He looked around in disbelief. "You don't even know how lame your trackies are? FC Cincinnati? Is that even a real team?"

"It's MLS," I said, which caused him to bend over laughing.

"You mean the league where European players go to die? We call it *Major League Suck* over here."

Not only did his friends laugh with him, but everyone within earshot let out a little chuckle. I wanted to disappear and start the day over with a different choice of clothing.

But nobody had ever accused me of knowing when to stay

quiet. "We've sent players to the Premier League. Ever heard of Pulisic?"

He was wiping tears from his eyes, and his grin turned nasty. "What, five in the last hundred years? How many World Cups you won over there, with all those people? What's that? Zero?"

"How many have you won?" I shot back. "One, in that same hundred years? Didn't England invent the game?"

"At least we have a chance every year, and the best pro league on the planet."

I tried to think of a good comeback. "All of our best athletes play other sports, and the MLS is getting better."

"All your best athletes play other sports?"

"That's what I just said."

"Then why are you here?"

Ouch. I had walked myself right into that one. Nor did I believe what I had said. While our biggest athletes might play other sports, that was the great thing about soccer. Players of all sizes could make the pros.

With my face turning red and everyone in line holding their sides with laughter, I debated running away to hide in my room. But that would only make it worse. Instead I held my tongue and endured the embarrassment until I reached the front of the line.

When I approached the registration table, a plump woman with a sunburnt face asked for my name, shuffled through a box at her feet, and handed me a large envelope and a duffel bag with a red-and-gold dragon emblazoned on the side.

"You'll find your room assignment and camp kit inside. Commencement is at nine-fifteen sharp tomorrow morning, on Pitch One. Be sure to wear one of the training shirts every day, and don't be late for Mr. Zepeda."

"Coach Zepeda?" I said weakly. That was the actual coach of the actual London Dragons, the one I'd seen on TV a hundred times. "Here? Talking to us?"

She smiled. "That's the one. Move along, now. Next!"

I walked away in a daze, the humiliating exchange with the bulldog almost forgotten. Giddy with excitement—would I get to meet any of the players?—I found a spot to myself on the low stone wall that encircled the Castle. The first thing I did was take off my sweatpants. It was a little chilly in the gym shorts I had on underneath, but it was better than being the butt of everyone's joke.

I opened the envelope and found a swipe card for a room, along with two sheets of paper. The first had my name and date of birth at the top, along with my dorm assignment.

The second sheet was a schedule for tomorrow.

8:30–9:10	am	Breakfast
9:15–9:30	am	Commencement
9:30–10:00	am	Group Stretch and Warm-up
10:00–1:00	pm	Athletic Testing and Drills
1:00–2:00	pm	Lunch
2:00–5:00	pm	Scrimmages
5:00–6:00	pm	Rest and Wash
6:00–9:00	pm	Pizza Party
11:00	pm	Lights Out

Nervous about the athletic testing, but pumped about the pizza party, I set the schedule aside and opened the duffel bag. Inside were three red-and-gold reversible T-shirts, a hooded sweatshirt, three pairs of white shorts, red socks, gold sweat pants, a soccer ball, and a water bottle. Every single item had the London Dragons logo printed somewhere on it, and *Leo* was printed in capital letters on the backs of the T-shirts and the sweatshirt and even the ball. Below my name were three letters: USA.

Along with my excitement from all the swag, I felt a tingle of pride that I'd be representing my country. I also felt a little dismayed, after the exchange in the registration line, that the whole camp would know, at all times, that I was from a country which got little respect in soccer. At least Tig was American. That was something. But he was much older, half British, and had already made the team.

The pickup games on the fields drew me like a magnet, but I wanted to see my room and drop my bags. After a longing glance at the games, I hopped over the wall and cut across the lawn towards the front entrance of the castle.

Both players and adults were coming and going through the tall wooden doors. Just inside was an entrance hall lined with mahogany benches. Beneath the benches were cubbies to store cleats, backpacks, and other gear. Mounted on the walls were trophies and framed photos of the Dragons playing in stadiums around the world. I pinched myself to make sure it was all real.

Signs pointed the way to different parts of the building. Straight ahead was the break room and offices. The A Wing was to my left, the B Wing on my right. The cafeteria was in the basement.

My room was at the end of the hall on the second floor. I used the swipe card to open the door. I realized I should have knocked when I saw two beds on opposite sides of the room.

No one was inside, and I didn't see any bags, so I shrugged and picked the bed against the far wall.

The room was comfortable enough, but there wasn't much to it: a table beside each bed, a long desk with two chairs built into the wall, a mini-fridge stocked with water, a closet, two dressers, and a window overlooking the forest.

Sigh. I had really been hoping for a TV. And a fridge full of Cokes and Gatorade and candy bars.

It was early in the afternoon. Dinner wasn't until six. I set my bags down and lay on the bed, suddenly very tired and overwhelmed by the journey. I was eager to get on the field and try out that sweet grass with my new cleats, but I realized how long I'd been awake. More than anything, I wanted to take a nap. Just a little refresher.

I remembered what Tig had said about staying up the first day. I worked hard to keep my eyes open, but they felt so heavy, and the pillow was so soft against my head . . .

The next thing I knew, someone was gently shaking me awake. I told them to go away and went back to sleep. This happened a few more times, I think. I wasn't really sure if anyone was there or not. I was so groggy it all felt like a dream.

When I finally woke up, I yawned and noticed a tall kid with slender tanned arms and sandy hair in my room.

"About time, roomie," he said.

I glanced out the window and noticed it was dark.

Uh-oh.

"How late is it?" I asked.

"Nine o'clock. I tried to wake you a few times. You were sleeping like the dead."

Nine o'clock? I'll be up all night, and exhausted for the first day of training.

"I'm Robbie," he said.

"Leo. You're American," I said in surprise.

"At least there's two of us. That's a first, you know."

"It is?"

"Most years there aren't any. Where are you from?"

"Ohio. You?"

"New York. Well, Long Island. Ohio has two MLS teams—are you with a development league?"

"Uh, no."

"What's your club team?"

"I play for the Beavers."

"The *Beavers*?" he said, perplexed. "Is that ENPL? USYSA?"

"It's a YMCA league."

Robbie stared at me for a few moments and then doubled over laughing. He slapped me on the back, which kinda hurt, and said, "It's good to have a roomie with a sense of humor. We'll need it here."

"It's great, isn't it? Except I'm not kidding."

"You've got to be. You can't play for a *YMCA* league and get an invite to a Premier League youth development academy."

The conversation was starting to annoy me. "Well, I did."

Robbie stared at me again, mumbled something I couldn't hear, and wandered over to his bed to curl up with an iPad. I heard the sound of a soccer game on the screen. "Who's playing?"

"Champions League. Last year's final."

"Did I miss dinner?" I asked.

"Yeah, they close it down at seven-thirty."

"Oh."

"Break room's open all night. They have a few things in there."

"Okay. Thanks."

"There's nothing very nutritious. They lower their standards in the summer."

"Even better."

Robbie yawned and said, "Don't keep me up, okay? I need as much sleep as I can get. Tomorrow's supposed to be one of the hardest days."

"It is? Why?"

"Because it's athletic testing. Didn't your coaches tell you anything? Haven't you prepared?"

"Uh, yeah. I've been . . . playing a lot of FIFA."

Robbie started shaking his head. "Do you live on the moon or something?"

On my way out the door, I said, "Who do you play for? Back home?"

"North Shore United. It's the top club in New York. I'm the center mid."

I opened my mouth to respond, but found I had nothing to say.

The break room was a simple white-walled room, but the contents were amazing. Cabinets filled with chips, granola bars, nuts, cookies, and all sorts of snack foods. Most had brand names I'd never heard of, but they looked nice and tasty. One fridge had Gatorades and waters stacked top to bottom. The other had fruit, milk, and other perishables. I debated getting my backpack, loading it up with snacks, and taking it back to my room. Instead I got an armful of chips and cookies and headed to the TV room. A flat-screen TV took up an entire wall, with a bunch of leather sofas and armchairs in front of it. The only problem was the gang of kids who all seemed to know each other sprawled out on the furniture, watching British comedies and snacking on fruit and crackers.

Why in the world would anyone eat fruit with all that delicious junk food in there?

I tried to watch a little television, but even when I could understand the actors, the jokes weren't very funny. Everyone else was cracking up like it was the funniest show they'd ever seen in their lives. No one spoke to me, and I noticed the kid with the crew cut and the bulldog face near the front. I slunk out of the room before he noticed me. Outside, I wandered around to see if anyone was playing under the lights, but the only sign of life was a chorus of frogs and crickets.

Back in my room, which I discovered had Wi-Fi, I texted Carlos on my device. He didn't respond. With Robbie fast asleep across the room, I downloaded a new game and played it for a long time. By the time I was ready to sleep again, I realized it was four in the morning.

For my first day at the Academy Camp, the most important day of my life, I was going to be utterly exhausted.

Holy Guacamole, It's the First Day of the Academy Camp

When my alarm buzzed the next morning, jerking me awake, my head felt like a pile of scrambled eggs, and my body seemed strangely heavy, weighed down by barbells. I couldn't remember where I was, and I wanted more than anything to stay under the covers and go back to sleep.

I fumbled to turn off the alarm as my eyes started to close . . . and then I realized what bed I was sleeping in, and what day it was.

The first day of the camp! My eyes popped open as thoughts flooded my head.

What sort of drills would we do? Would I see anyone famous or make any friends? What if I was terrible on the field? What is athletic testing? Would anyone pass me the ball in the scrimmage?

By the time I rolled out of bed, Robbie was dressed and walking out of the door with his bag over his shoulder. The guy was a machine. I wondered if he'd ever slept in on Saturday morning or played a video game.

The bathroom was down the hall. I had to share it with a dozen other kids. I threw on some shorts and washed my face in cold water in the bathroom sink, which helped me wake up, then brushed my teeth and returned to the room to put on my outfit for the day: white shorts, one of the Dragon T-shirts with my name and country on the back, and the Dragons FC sweatshirt. After tying on my new cleats and the battered shin guards I'd had for three seasons—I needed something from my past for good luck—I stuck my ball and water bottle in my duffel bag, and headed downstairs for breakfast.

Players and coaches packed the basement cafeteria, a large room with bare stone walls and a tile floor. I stood in line and filled my plate with eggs, bacon, and a stack of thin pancakes.

After filling my tray, I spied Robbie sitting by himself near the back wall. His shoulders were hunched and he looked unhappy, like there was a math test looming on the horizon instead of a day full of soccer. When I took the seat across from him, he said, "No one wears cleats and shin guards to breakfast."

I looked around and saw that he was correct.

"You should put them in your kit bag and change by the front entrance," he said irritably. "Cleats wear down off the field."

"Yeah, that's what my dad says. So thanks, Dad."

"Just trying to help you fit in."

"Good morning to you, too."

Robbie forked a bite of eggs. "How's the jetlag?"

"The what?"

"Jetlag—that's what happens with a change in time zone. You're probably feeling a bit out of sorts? Head's a bit fuzzy, legs a little wobbly?"

"Yeah," I admitted. "I'm also tired because I played video games all night and went to bed at four a.m."

He rolled his eyes. "Hold on." He walked over to the drink line and returned with a mug of milky brown liquid.

"What's that?" I said, when he offered it to me. "Coffee? That's gross."

"Black tea. The British drink it all the time. It might not taste great, but it will perk you up."

I stared suspiciously down at the cup. An exploratory sip revealed that it tasted a lot like milk and sugar, with a bitter aftertaste. I could tolerate it, I supposed. We ate in silence. After a few minutes, I did feel more energetic. "Thanks," I said. "The tea's working."

"Sure." Robbie stood to leave. "Good luck today."

"Let me finish and I'll go with you."

"Nah, I've got to do my warm-up drills. I've got a whole routine my coaches laid out for me."

"Oh. Okay. See you out there."

After breakfast, I headed outside and gawked at all the players on the fields. Everyone was passing balls or stretching in small groups, looking very busy. They all seemed to know exactly what they were doing, as if everyone but me had gotten a morning text about how to act. I thought Robbie was the weird one for having such a strict regimen, but maybe it was me.

Desperate for a familiar face, I looked around and saw Philip Niles talking to a group of adults. He glanced my way but didn't seem to notice me. I wanted to say hi, but I got the sense his job was to bring me here, and that was the end of it.

"Yo, Leo!"

When I turned and saw Tig, relief poured through me.

"Ready for the big day?" he said.

"I guess."

"You get some sleep like I said?"

"Not really."

He laughed. "Me either, on my first day. Stayed up all night watching music videos."

I felt a little better after his admission. "Hey Tig, how many players are at the camp?"

"Around 200 in the field. 220 with keepers."

Two *hundred*? "And, um, how many make the team?"

"They'll extend offers to eleven players to join the Academy."

My jaw slowly dropped. Eleven? I had thought maybe half would make it. Or one-third. But less than one in *twenty*? I had to be better than 95 percent of these star players from around the world?

All those pancakes felt heavy in my belly.

"But they're paying for all this food," I said. "And all these shirts and balls and bags. Why would they do that and not keep more players?"

Tig laughed and slapped me on the back. "Shirts and balls and bags—think about it, Boss. If just one of you becomes a pro one day, they can sell you for mad coin. I'm talking millions. And that's just for entry level players. Imagine a Messi or a Mbappé or a Ronaldo. I don't think they're too worried about a few shirts and bags."

"I guess you're right."

"Don't sweat it," he said, right before he started jogging towards one of the fields. "You be you."

Easy for him to say, I thought. Tig's birth certificate probably read *future international soccer star*.

I decided to juggle by myself until the commencement. Now I was so nervous my stomach felt like a troop of monkeys were swinging from tree to tree inside. Just before nine a.m., I headed to Field One with everyone else. The British call a soccer field a *pitch*, but I'll stick to *field*.

Field One ran alongside the stone wall at the base of the Castle. On the sideline at half field, someone had set up a stand with a podium. Once everyone had gathered, a man I recognized from TV walked up to the podium and grabbed the microphone, surrounded by people with clipboards and flashing cameras.

Coach Zepeda.

I couldn't believe I was standing there looking at the head coach of the London Dragons!

"Good morning, everyone," Coach Zepeda said in a soft voice that somehow commanded my attention. He was a tall, distinguished Spaniard with a pair of glasses perched on a long, pointed nose. Before he came to the Dragons and won three Premier League titles, he had played for his country's national team and coached in La Liga. The man was a living legend.

"Every year, it's my pleasure to welcome our new attendees to our summer camp. You should all feel honored to be here, as our scouts work very hard to select the best young talent from around the world. I commend you all for your hard work and dedication to the game, and I look forward to personally welcoming those who are selected to attend the Academy."

Translation: most of you won't be selected, and you will never see me again in your life, unless it's on TV.

"I wish each and every one of you the best of luck today and in the weeks to come. My advice is to leave everything on the pitch. Have no regrets when you leave, whether you make the Academy or not. The highest achievement in life is to accomplish our absolute best with the tools we're given."

Translation: some of you simply don't have what it takes. Do your best, because that's what counts.

But it won't get you a London Dragons uniform.

"Remember that being a professional footballer is about more than talent on the pitch. We're looking for character, dedication, and teamwork as much as ball skills and a world class header."

Translation: we have other reasons not to select you besides lack of talent.

"I was once just like you, a young player at an academy training camp. You might be surprised to learn I did not make the cut. How did I respond? I returned to Spain and worked even harder. It was not until my third appearance that I was selected for the squad. Don't ever give up on your dreams, and life might reward you in unexpected ways."

Translation: Coach Zepeda was so good he got three consecutive invites.

I knew his speech was supposed to be inspiring, but all I could think about was how this was my one chance at being a professional soccer player. Not only did I live in the United States, far from the eyes of scouts, but I was sure Dad and Aunt Janice wouldn't be able to send me overseas again.

Not only that, but if I didn't make the team and win the fifty-thousand-dollar contract, we might lose our house.

Nah, no pressure or anything.

Coach Zepeda spoke for a few more minutes but didn't really say anything new. I got the point: he had given us five minutes of his precious time to convince us how amazing this opportunity was, and what a privilege it was to attend the camp.

And it worked. I was star struck by his presence. More than anything, I wanted to be one of the kids selected to attend the Academy, shake Coach Zepeda's hand, and earn the chance to be an actual London Dragon. For a moment, basking in his presence, I forgot about the trials that lay ahead and how long the odds were and simply imagined what life would be like playing soccer in the Premier League, on television in front of millions of fans. My dad would never have to worry about money, and I would have the best life ever. I'd give my friends and family tickets to all the games. Messi would travel with me and move to a bigger cage and eat the juiciest forest crickets every single day. I could buy all the video games, Doritos, and soccer gear that I could ever want—

"YOUR ATTENTION, PLEASE."

A voice like the crack of a whip snapped me out of my daydream. I looked up and saw someone new on the podium: a lean man in a London Dragons tracksuit about my dad's age, with grey hair cut close to the scalp. Though not very tall, he stood as straight as a flagpole and had a square jaw that thrust forward like the prow of a battleship. He looked hard, as if every inch of him was made of iron. He reminded me of a professional soldier more than a soccer coach.

"Thank you, Coach Zepeda, for taking the time out of your busy schedule to speak to us today." The new speaker swept his gaze across the crowd like he was the king of England. "I'm

Ian Hawk, Director of the Academy Summer Camp. I'd like to welcome each and every one of you to our training facility."

Though his accent was even thicker than Philip's, he spoke loudly and enunciated clearly. "I know some of you came from very far away. I hope you all had a good journey and a good night's rest—because you're going to need it."

Uh-oh. This guy isn't going to sugarcoat things like Coach Zepeda.

"My job over the next month," he continued, "is simple. I'm tasked with finding the very best players to attend the Dragons Youth Academy. Your job is to impress me and the rest of the coaching staff enough to secure an invitation." He leaned forward on the podium. "I want to be clear right from the start that this is not your local summer camp. This is the *London Dragons Development Program*. Look around you. There are more than two hundred campers, some of the best youth players in the world, with only eleven available spots on the roster. A very small percentage of you will succeed. That is a fact."

As he paused for a drink of water, the field was so quiet I heard a pair of birds chirping. Everyone was looking at their feet or shuffling in place.

"Yes, I'm trying to intimidate you," the director continued, "because you have to learn to deal with pressure, and high expectations, and being the best of the best. The route to becoming a professional soccer player is mental as much as physical. You may not understand that yet—but I guarantee you'll understand it better by the end of this month."

A cell phone rang from somewhere in the crowd, causing the director to grimace and thrust his forearms on the podium.

His face turned bright red, and I thought his head might actually explode. "*Whose phone is that?*"

In the center of the crowd, a skinny redhead slowly raised his hand.

"Pitch Two," the director said. "Start running."

When the kid didn't move, probably too scared to react, the director leveled his iron stare at him. "*Now.*"

"He's toast," someone beside me whispered.

The crowd parted as the poor kid picked up his bag and made his way towards the back. I swallowed and vowed never to do anything that would land me on Director Hawk's bad side.

"There should never be distractions on the pitch," the director continued. "Now, let's discuss a few camp details. Starting tomorrow, you'll be divided into five squads: Komodos, Monitors, Iguanas, Gilas, and Snapping Turtles. Five of the most dangerous reptiles on planet Earth."

Well, I thought, *that's pretty awesome. Those are five of my favorites. Though technically, Komodos are a subspecies of Monitor lizards.*

"But they're still not dragons," he continued. "You have to earn that name. Now, a word about today. After the athletic testing and the afternoon scrimmages, we'll do our best to sort you into ten tiers and assemble the field squads. The best players—the number ones—will be split up, and the twos, and so on, to ensure the field squads are as even as possible. The fifth squad, the Snapping Turtles, is for the goalies. After the first week of squad training, the cuts begin. We'll send a fourth of you home, and after the end of week two, another fifty will go."

I was stunned. No one had told me they sent players home

early. I might only be here for a week? How embarrassing would that be? As if I needed any more reasons to be nervous.

"You'll stay with your squad for the first three weeks, if you make it that far. At the end of Week Three, your squad leader will submit his or her recommendation for the top remaining players. I and the rest of the coaching staff will then select four squad teams to participate in the World Cup tournament during the final week. On the last day of camp, after the World Cup finals, we'll select the eleven players who impressed us the most, and extend an invitation to join the London Dragons youth team."

He paused to let all that sink in. While the chance to play in the World Cup sounded extremely exciting, only eleven players would make the final team. The path to the top would be even more grueling than I had imagined.

Director Hawk leaned forward to deliver his parting words in a voice that seemed to resonate across the entire complex. "Good luck today, lads. Your journey starts now."

They broke us into athletic testing groups based on our surnames. I was assigned to Field 3 with a few dozen other kids whose last names fell between A and D.

Robbie, whose full name was Roberto Covitz, was in my group. So were Diego and Alejandro, two of the kids I had met at the airport. I was very happy to see Alejandro. Diego, not so much.

Our group leader, a college-age woman named Samantha, led us through the stretching. When she spoke, I was surprised to hear an American accent. Samantha had long brown hair and nice legs that made it easy to pay attention. After the warm-ups, two more instructors joined her, a man and another woman, both young and very fit, to help record results.

First up was a sprint across the field, end line to end line. We did it twice. I came in near the middle of the pack each time. Diego won all three races, and poor Alejandro finished almost last. Robbie was much closer to the front than the back.

After the long sprint came a shorter one across the width of the field. I did a little better on that one. A Nigerian kid named Dayo with really long legs won both of these races, edging Diego by a hair.

"I need to do better," Robbie said during the first water break.

"Does it really matter which squad we're in?" I said.

He almost choked on his water. "You want to be in one of the high tiers. Not only are the coaches forming impressions already, but think about it: that way there's one less talented player in a tier above you."

I thought about it, decided his argument was a little weak, and told him so.

"Trust me on this," he said. "They're judging us right from the start."

"It's not like I can make myself any faster."

Robbie dropped his water bottle on his bag. "Leo, you're annoying."

Next came sit-ups and pushups. I did pretty miserable in both of these, right near the bottom. I've always hated exercise for the sake of exercise. Give me a ball already.

Alejandro won both of those rounds. He did sixty-five pushups! Diego, Robbie, and Dayo all came in near the top.

After that, Samantha led us to a high pole on the sidelines with plastic markers every inch up to twelve feet. They tested our leaping ability by having us stand in place and jump as high as we could. Then we performed running broad jumps which reminded me of gym class. I did okay in all of these, about the middle of the pack again.

A beanpole of a kid from England had the highest vertical leap. I was surprised to see it was the kid whose cell phone had gone off during the commencement. His name was Oliver, and he had more freckles than anyone I'd ever seen. Robbie came in third on the broad jump. His technique was so good he looked ready for the Olympics. In fact, he looked good at everything he did. He probably had a private vertical-pole-thingie coach back home.

The next tests were agility-based. After the instructors placed a series of cones in a line, a foot or so apart, we had to hop, one foot to another between the cones, for ten yards and back again. Then we did another exercise I had seen in gym class: the shuttle run. The instructors set three frisbee discs on the end line, and three more ten feet away. We had to sprint back and forth, picking up one disc at a time, as fast as we could.

I surprised myself by coming in sixth in one and fifth in another. A Brazilian named José won both rounds. About my size, he had hair as dark as mine was blond, and almost as curly.

For the final two tests of the morning, we finally got to use a ball. On the first test, the instructors set up cones five yards apart, all the way down the field. We had to weave around them as fast as we could. The cones were close enough that we couldn't just kick the ball ahead and run to it. It was tiring, but much better than just running.

I shocked myself—and everyone else, I think—by coming in third. Only Diego and José had faster times.

After that, they set up the cones super close together, about a foot apart, for twenty yards. Same thing as the earlier test: with as much pace as possible, we had to dribble the ball between the cones to the end of the line and back again. They gave us three tries apiece, and only took our best time. It was tricky because every time you hit a cone, they knocked a second off. If you kicked it too hard and lost control, you had to go back to the previous cone.

Ball control was key on this one. When my turn came, I had fun with it, pretending I was Messi and the cones were defenders as I wove my way through the gauntlet. I was the last player to perform, and after I finished, they called out everyone's best score, last to first, right in front of the whole group.

I kept waiting to hear my name. When they announced that Robbie had the fifth best score, he frowned at me. I could hardly believe my ears when I wasn't in third or even second place. Surely there was some mistake, I thought, right as Samantha called my name at the very end.

I had the fastest time in the whole group.

We had a water break before the skills tests began. I didn't know what to expect: were they going to see how many times we could juggle the ball? Evaluate our street tricks?

"Nice time on the agility test," Robbie said with grudging respect as he sat cross-legged on the grass beside me. Like the day before, the weather was cool and cloudy, though I had taken off my sweatshirt. Behind us, Diego and Alejandro were sitting on a bench, talking quietly in Spanish. Dayo was juggling the ball by himself, Oliver was stretching on the sideline, and the others had clustered in small groups around the water cooler.

"Thanks," I said.

"But only nine pushups? You need to get stronger."

I glanced away, irritated. He unwrapped a performance bar and took a bite. "Back home, I tested first in almost everything," he said.

"You have tests like this on Long Island?"

Robbie looked around as if someone might be listening. "So far, there's no way I'm a one or a two. Maybe not even a three."

At first his comment confused me. Then I remembered the coaches were using the athletic testing groups to help sort us into tiers for the squads.

"Plus," Robbie continued, "we have to impress the coaches double here, because we're American."

I was just as nervous as he was, and probably in the bottom half of the athletic testing, despite my agility tests. But I didn't need to be reminded about how hard it all was every single second. "Robbie, have you ever played a video game?"

He looked caught off guard. "Sure. I have FIFA."

"Okay, that barely counts since it's a soccer game—anything besides FIFA?"

"A few," he mumbled.

"Which ones?"

"Fortnite?" he said weakly, after a moment.

"What's your favorite skin?"

"Uh . . . okay, I've seen it, but I haven't actually played it."

"You need to chill out," I said. "Find another hobby."

"You need to concentrate more on soccer."

"Really?" I said, standing as I flicked the ball in the air with my feet and started juggling. "Alejandro, trade me!" Without further warning, I sent the ball high in the air in his direction.

Just before the ball hit the ground, Alejandro caught on. He lifted his own ball over to me, then just managed to trap my ball with his foot before it hit the ground and started juggling. I popped the ball off my back and caught it on the top of my left foot. We passed our balls back and forth in the air a few times, never letting them hit the ground, and I started juggling in a circle around Robbie, and even bounced it off his head and back to my feet. This caused the other players to laugh, but Robbie jumped up and stalked off with his ball.

"I was just playing," I called out, but he didn't turn around. "Geez," I muttered. "Take a joke."

Out of the corner of my eye, I saw Samantha walking over with a clipboard in her hand, trying to bury a smile. "Break time's over!" she called out.

Clowning around helped me relax. I grabbed my ball and followed everyone back to Field 3, where Samantha and the other coaches had set up cones around the goal for shooting drills.

I was excited. I've scored the most goals on every team I've played on for as long as I could remember, and I kicked harder than anyone I knew, despite my small size. Plus, shooting drills were the most fun. Who doesn't like to blast a half-volley high in the corner and make the net ripple?

For the first drill, we lined up ten feet outside the penalty box, right in front of the goal. One of the coaches passed the ball to us from the side and let us shoot from wherever we wanted, while another coach played goalie. The pass was always right on the edge of the box. A decent range shot.

After a few warm-up rotations, Samantha started calling out a destination before the pass. 'Top right,' or 'bottom left' or 'on the ground down the middle.' Then they made us shoot from the outside corners of the box, using our right foot on the right side and the left on the other. The whole time, they observed us and jotted down notes. Being under constant surveillance was nerve-wracking.

After the shooting drill was over, I congratulated myself for my performance. I could shoot with both feet and I was pretty accurate during the drill. I shot the ball as hard and as well as I was capable of.

But plenty of other kids were better. Some of them *much* better. They shot like robots, pounding the ball into the side netting over and over. Diego's foot was a cannon. He kicked the ball with more velocity than any kid my age I'd ever seen. He shot harder than most of the kids on the Middleton *High School* team. I would be terrified to be in the goal if Diego was shooting.

By the time the drill was over, I was thoroughly convinced I was one of the worst shooters in our group.

And I'm a center forward.

On the way to the next station, Samantha jogged over to walk beside me. "How much training have you had, Leo?"

"What do you mean?"

"Do you play for a club team?"

"No," I said quietly.

"Do you have a private coach?"

"Does YouTube count?"

She chuckled. "Okay, well, how long have you been playing football?"

I told her I'd been playing my whole life, in the backyard and the neighborhood park and the YMCA leagues. No club teams, private coaches, or even special summer camps.

She jotted down a few notes, patted me on the back, told me to keep up the good work, and wandered off. I was pretty sure she was about to tell the other coaches they'd made a mistake and shouldn't have invited me. I wondered if I would even be put into a squad tomorrow. They might just send me home.

Except for the dribbling and passing tests, which I thought I aced, the rest of the morning only reinforced my notion that I was an impostor. It wasn't that I was bad at trapping, corner kicks and set pieces, volleys, shielding, defense—okay, I was bad at defense. I admit it. I'd rather do math homework and eat liver-and-egg sandwiches for a year than play defense. Just give me the ball and let me score.

But my point was, I was *good* at all those other skills. Really good. Better than anyone back home. But these kids?

They were spectacular. In the zone. On a whole other level. Their feet were always in the right position, they knew the drills without having to ask questions, and they rarely missed a trap or a half-volley or made a bad pass.

By the end of the morning session, the only thing I wanted to do was go back to my room and call my dad. Tell him how these kids were bigger, stronger, faster, and better than I was. Tell him it was a really great experience but that I missed home and just wanted to spend time with my friends.

Except I couldn't do that. I wasn't a quitter, and my dad *needed* me. I had to give it my very best shot, no matter the outcome.

I tried not to despair as we broke for lunch and I walked alone back to the Castle. My calves and thighs ached. My new cleats had caused blisters to form on the soles of my feet.

And we still had three hours of afternoon scrimmages.

I wondered how I'd manage to finish out the day, not to mention the week. The one thing I knew for sure?

That if I wanted to make it past the first cuts, I had to show them something amazing.

ENTRY #7

Scrimmages and Screen Time

On the way into the cafeteria for lunch, one of the workers handed me a paper box and a glass and told me to choose any drink I wanted from the fountain. No soft drinks, but there was Gatorade and fruit punch.

I found a seat by myself and hunkered down with my ham and cheese baguette, which tasted better than it looked. The lunch box also contained a pack of potato chips, an apple, a stick of cheese, and carrot sticks.

The cafeteria was much quieter than at breakfast. I noticed a lot of people sitting alone or in groups but not talking. Everyone seemed a little wary of their neighbor, as if we'd all just realized we were in competition for a few coveted spots with every single person in the room.

No one sat next to me. I was glad for the time to myself, but my lack of sleep was starting to hit me. Deciding I needed some sugar, I drank three glasses of fruit punch and grabbed a banana pudding off the dessert tray. While there were plenty of adults in the room, eating at their own table, no one was watching us, as far as I could tell. I could hardly believe my luck, and went back for another banana pudding.

After lunch, deciding to save my remaining energy for the field, I crashed in a chair in the break room. This time everyone was excited about a game on TV called cricket. I had no idea what was going on, and after a few minutes of watching, I decided the game was about as exciting as watching a couple of real crickets rub their legs together.

On the way back to the field, my stomach started to hurt. Maybe I shouldn't have gone back for seconds on the pudding. The day had warmed up, and I ran into Tig lugging a bag of balls over his shoulder. He was wearing a pair of gold Dragon sweats that hugged his ankles, a Brazil tank top, and a leather necklace. Smooth as always.

"How goes it, Boss? Slay some baby dragons this morning?"

"Hardly," I said.

"I bet it's not as bad as you think."

I wanted to spill the beans about my lackluster athletic testing, but I didn't want Tig to think I was a loser or a complainer. "It was tough."

He laughed. "It's supposed to be. This is the Academy, eh? Were you at lunch? You could hear a pin drop. Everybody's shell-shocked by all the talent. They're used to being the best player on their club team, probably in their whole city. I remember my own tryouts like they were yesterday."

"Some kids don't seem that affected. Like Diego."

"Maybe they're over-confident. Or maybe you can learn something from them. It doesn't really help to get down on yourself, does it?"

I thought about that. "Someone told me this morning that no American has ever made it through. But you did."

"My mum's British. I lived in London until I was ten, and I have a British passport. So technically, I'm a Brit. But I went to middle and high school in the States."

His answer deflated me. "Oh."

Another coach called Tig's name and waved him over. "Don't sweat it," he said as he walked off. "Someone has to be the first. Just show off those sweet skills I saw at the airport."

For the scrimmages, they split us into twenty teams with eleven players each. The teams seemed randomly selected. The only person I knew on my team was José, the Brazilian midfielder from my testing group who had won the first agility test. I felt adrift among all the strangers, but once our team assembled, José and I slapped hands, and I liked his infectious smile.

We learned there would be five games played at the same time, on five different fields, while the other teams watched on the sidelines. Every fifteen minutes, the teams would switch out, and the players on the sideline would take the field. Despite how tired I was, my adrenaline kicked in. Forget practices and drills. I lived for games!

My team played in the first wave of games, on Field Two. Coach Tanner, a chunky Englishman with a green visor, handed out blue pennies and told us we'd be playing a classic 4-3-3 formation. That meant four defenders, three midfielders, three forwards, and of course a goalie. No one asked me what position I played, and I was disappointed when the coach checked his clipboard and stuck me at right midfield.

What?

My entire life, I'd played center forward, or striker as they called it over here. Occasionally I'd slide to center mid, if I really needed to take over a game, but never on the outside. I didn't know the position very well. I knew I was supposed to move the ball to the wing and play some defense—ugh—and that was about it. As soon as the game started, I felt lost.

Back home, my teammates would look for me at once, or I would pick on a weaker player and steal the ball, or just wait for the other team to shank a pass. Now I found myself running up and down the field without ever touching the ball, tiring myself out without contributing to the game. It was the opposite of how I liked to play. I preferred to pick my battles and wait for the ball to come near me, then strike like a cobra.

The pace was incredibly fast, much faster than in any game I'd ever played, so fast it almost made me dizzy. Back and forth went the ball, knocking around from player to player, sideline to sideline. The passes were crisp and hard and accurate, and decisions had to be made in a split second. It was almost like playing a different game.

No, I told myself.

It's not a different game. It's just soccer, played at a much higher level than I'm used to. Every kid here is better than the best kids from the fancy club teams back home. You just have to adjust, Leo.

I took a deep breath and dove in. On my first touch, a pass from José at center mid, I trapped the ball, turned to survey the field, and saw my tall and lanky forward, a Danish kid named Sven, streaking down the right wing. I sent it to him on the ground, slipping it past the fullback—only to have it intercepted by the center back, who came out of nowhere to collect the ball.

My first pass, and I gave it away!

It got worse from there. The other team realized how bad

I was at defense, and took advantage. They ran plays on my side, passing and dribbling around me as if I was standing still. I grew increasingly frustrated as José and my fullbacks had to bail me out again and again.

None of the coaches were saying anything—they were just letting us play and taking notes. Javier, a lightning-fast French winger with earrings and bright green hair, scored the first goal for the other team, a heat-seeking missile just outside the penalty box.

After the goal, we huddled at midfield. "C'mon guys," José said in heavily accented English. "We must do better."

So far, José had been our best player. His first touch was amazing, and he released his passes very quickly, as if he was thinking three steps ahead.

Sven, the Danish right winger, spoke English as well as I did. He told our center back to pick up Javier as soon as he crossed half field. "He's their biggest threat," Sven said. "We're doing okay in the midfield—" I noticed he avoided looking at me as he said this "—but we have to tighten up on defense and advance the ball."

The ref blew the whistle to restart the game.

Sven was wrong. Javier wasn't the main problem. He might be the biggest *scoring* threat, but their center back, a scarily large German named Hans, was terrorizing our offense, interrupting everything we tried. He was a human vacuum cleaner, sucking up our passes every time we crossed half field.

"Get wide next time," I said to Sven. "I'll find you in the corner."

He looked dubious and didn't respond. I couldn't blame him.

My teammates didn't want to give me the ball, and it took

a long time before I received another pass. I trapped the ball and dribbled past the center line, drawing the attention of their left mid. Sven ran towards me, calling for the ball. Even my own team thought I was timid and would give the ball up right away. I faked the easy side pass everyone thought I was going to make, flicked the ball to my right to avoid the mid-fielder bearing down on me, then chipped it long and hard down the sideline. Sven turned and sprinted by his defender, who couldn't switch directions in time, and chased the ball down in the corner. It was a beautiful pass, and slowed down just enough for Sven to reach it.

By trying to anticipate my pass, Hans had overcommitted, and now he had to race to cut off Sven, who had the ball and was cutting straight for the goal. Hans arrived before Sven could get off a good shot, but Sven dropped a nifty pass back to the top of the box, where José was streaking in with a de-fender on his shoulder. José reached the ball a step ahead of him and rocketed it at the goal.

Bam! Top corner! The goalie's outstretched fingers grazed the ball but he missed the save.

1-1. Tie game.

Moments later, the ref blew the whistle, signaling the end of the half.

"Sweet pass," Sven said, as we headed off the field to watch the next set of teams.

I played it cool but felt a rush of pride. I had contributed to our goal, an assist to the assist. It almost made up for my poor performance during the rest of the half.

During the break, I grabbed a bottle of water from the coolers on the sideline, then roamed the fields to watch the other teams. Since everyone's name and country initials were printed on the backs of their jerseys, I started learning who the best and worst players were, their home country, and their style of play.

Most of the Germans played the same way: physical, sharp passes, very little dribbling. The Brazilians were creative with the ball and fun to watch. The Mexicans had excellent foot skills, and Diego might be the best player at the whole camp. I watched him score two goals in rapid succession: one a long run down the center that led to a beautiful shot in the bottom left corner; the other a header on a corner kick where Diego simply rose higher than everyone else and blasted the ball in the side netting. It was almost unfair.

I kept moving, checking out the players I already knew and trying to get a handle on the others. Robbie was handling himself well at center mid. Alejandro was the right fullback on his team, and I saw him make a powerful tackle. The speed of Dayo, the Nigerian forward from my morning group, gave his defenders fits.

On Field 4, I watched a scrawny, pimply Polish winger named Sebastian fly past his defender time and again. Sebastian was the speediest kid my age I'd ever seen. He didn't have the best touch, but he just kicked the ball ahead and beat everyone to it.

On the other side of the field, a wily Canadian fullback named Simon was frustrating the opposing forward, an Egyptian named Mahmoud with a wicked cross.

There was Charlie, an Australian keeper who filled up the goal with his bulk and could punt the ball past midfield.

Sergi, a Spanish midfielder with catlike agility who always managed to be near the ball.

A slight kid from Zimbabwe—I had to ask one of the coaches what country ZIM stood for—was impressing the crowd with his aerial kicks and boundless energy. His name was Garika and his shoes were so worn they flapped as he ran.

One of the best all-around players was an Argentinian center back named Mateo, who liked to win the ball with bruising slide tackles. His red hair surprised me. Wasn't Argentina in South America, where everyone had dark hair?

It went on and on. So many players and styles. I forgot about myself and marveled at all the talent. Finally the whistle blew and I was back on the field. I thought we'd play the second half of the first game, but instead we moved to a different field to play a different team.

This time, the coach stuck me at left mid. I played even worse. Though I could kick with either foot—that was one of my strengths—I just wasn't used to the position. We lost 1-0, and I struggled the entire fifteen minutes. I was never in the right place and always behind the game.

"It's okay," José said to me as we walked off. "You're not a midfielder?"

"You can tell?"

He put an arm around my shoulder. "Relax. Don't commit so much on defense. You're really quick but you give everything away. Hold your ground. Don't stab at the ball. Make them work to get past you."

"I've never had to play defense."

"Let the game come to you. Ease into the flow. Be one with the chem—what is it called? Chemistry? No—the alchemy."

At this point, I had no idea what he was talking about. The alchemy? Was this some kind of mysterious Brazilian wisdom?

The next two games passed by in a blur. Again the coach played me at the two outside midfield positions. Goals were hard to come by, and we tied both games: 0-0 and 1-1. Our lone goal was scored by our center back on a free kick.

For the last game of the day, they finally let me play forward. Unfortunately, I was on the left wing, my least favorite of the forward positions. Still, it was better than midfield. I had returned to my natural habitat!

My excitement faded when we lined up on the field and I noticed the fullback on the other team: the beefy English kid with the crew cut who had embarrassed me in the registration line.

Brock, his jersey read. England.

Great. My defender for the last game was the strongest, meanest kid in the whole camp, and he already had it out for me. When I looked his way, he stared right at me with a huge grin. Not a happy grin, but a hungry shark-smirk that said he was looking forward to chomping right through me.

Well, he'd have to catch me first.

After the whistle blew, the game played out in midfield for a while, and then José sent a ball sailing towards the left corner, on my side of the field. I felt a burst of adrenaline as I streaked down the sideline. This was my chance! I kept even with Brock as the ball was kicked, staying onside. I expected to easily outrun him. He was too big and heavy to be that fast.

Oh, how wrong I was. He paced me step for step, and we arrived at the ball at the same time. I tried to stick a leg in and poke the ball to the side, but Brock didn't bother making a play on the ball. He rammed his shoulder straight into mine, causing me to fly off my feet and land out of bounds.

No whistle. It was a legal play, shoulder-to-shoulder contact within playing distance of the ball.

He had just outmuscled me.

Knocked me flat in front of the whole camp.

I grimaced and pushed to my feet. After he collected the ball and sent it downfield, he looked at me with his smashed bulldog face and said, "Why don't you go back to America? That's where the amateurs play."

"Hey, Brock?"

"Yeah?"

"Why don't you go break a few mirrors?"

"Huh?"

"Think about it."

Before he could figure it out, I dashed away, but things got worse from there. First off, I learned that I really didn't know how to play winger, not at this level. I kept misreading passes from midfield, and when I finally managed to cross a ball, it sailed over Sven's head on the right side.

Our center forward for most of the day, Kaito, had not been very effective. He was a nice Japanese kid with slippery ball skills and a wicked knuckleball shot, and he could dart forward like a mongoose. On paper, he was a rock star. But all day he failed to do the one thing that strikers had to do: score. The coach had moved him to midfield for the final game, and, for some reason, chosen Conor, an Irish fullback, to play striker.

Conor was even less effective than Kaito. The other team's center back was not as good as Brock, but he wasn't having any trouble keeping Conor in check. The Irish player had a good shot and was great in the air, but he couldn't get open to use his strengths.

I couldn't, either. Brock wasn't giving me room to breathe. He knocked me off the ball every time I touched it. When the referee gave the five-minute warning, I grew nervous about my performance. This was the last game of the day. I had tanked most of the athletic testing, and had failed to distinguish myself in the scrimmages, except for my pass to Sven that had led to a goal.

The worst thing of all was that I hadn't had a chance to showcase my strengths. I was a center forward, a scorer, not a midfielder or a winger.

Towards the end of the game, I smelled an opportunity. Sven was dribbling the ball hard down the right wing, looking for space. I followed him on the opposite sideline, just as I was supposed to do, in preparation for a long cross.

Except Sven hadn't crossed the ball to me all game. I wasn't great in the air, and Brock was so much bigger I had little chance of heading the ball over him. Everyone on the field knew this.

So I decided to mix things up. As Sven worked his magic to get open in the corner, I cut hard inside, crowding our center forward's space, confusing the defense. Brock stayed put to guard the far side of the goal, since our left midfielder was racing in as well.

As I suspected, Sven crossed the ball in the center, right to the top of the box. It was a hard and swerving ball, difficult to control, and Conor's first touch got away from him. The center back moved to retrieve it—except I arrived before him, which took him by surprise. Since I'd been shadowing

Conor, doubling up in the middle, his poor touch landed right at my feet. It was a daring, lucky break, but who cared—I had a chance to make a play!

The center back scrambled to cut me off. The smart thing to do was slip the ball to the side and hope a teammate was making a run. Out of the corner of my eye, I saw a blue penny streaking towards me, and a defender right with him.

Passing to my teammate was the safe play. But I was a center forward. I didn't always do the smart thing. Sometimes, I was selfish and just wanted to score. My instincts took over as the center back flew in for the tackle. I faked a pass, causing his bodyweight to shift. Then I rolled the ball to the side with the bottom of my right foot, causing him to lurch again. I cut back hard to the left, scooping the ball with the inside of the same foot, then pushed the ball a few feet past him. I was free, and the move caused him to twist around so hard he lost his footing and fell on the ground.

For one glorious instant, there was nothing but air between me and the goalie. Space in the box to shoot: the moment center forwards dream about. I hit the ball in stride, connecting perfectly, smacking it hard to the upper left corner . . .

Right into the outstretched fingertips of Charlie, the Australian keeper. Somehow, he had dived all the way across the goal, and managed to knock the ball a few inches wide.

I couldn't believe it. It was a killer shot. No way anyone back home could have stopped that. Not even a high schooler. Charlie must have picked a direction and guessed—that was the only way he could have saved it.

But save it he did.

"Leo!" Someone barked from the sideline. "You were out of position!"

I looked over to see Director Hawk glaring at me, standing as still and rigid as a marble statue. His arms were folded, and his mouth was set in a thin, hard line.

Soon after, the ref blew the whistle.

Tie game. 0-0.

I hung my head as I walked off the field, stunned I had missed the shot, ashamed about the only words the director had said to me all day.

On the way to the sideline, someone slapped me on the back. I turned to see Sven taking off his shirt. "Hey," he said, with a big grin on his sweat-soaked face. "Don't worry about the shot. That was a great hit, and Charlie made a once-in-a-lifetime save. He's the best keeper in the camp. But everyone saw that center back fall down after you diced him. That move was *sick*, Leo."

Before dinner, I stood in the shower for a long time, letting the steaming water soothe my tired muscles. Back in my room, I applied some padded adhesives called Moleskin to the soles of my feet. Robbie had given me the Moleskin for my blisters. He had a whole bag of ointments, wraps, tape, gels, and supplements. My dad, on the other hand, had sent me off with a stern warning to eat my fruits and veggies. Which I was ignoring.

Robbie had left early for dinner. I threw on some clothes, played a few video games, and headed to the cafeteria around seven-thirty. The pizza party was in full swing. Dozens of open boxes were lined up on a table, and everybody was chowing down. Drinks were stacked in ice-filled coolers on the floor.

I grabbed four slices of pepperoni and headed to one of the tables, happy as a squirrel in spring, my tough day a bad memory. I loved pizza. I *lived* for it. This pizza was a little different than back home, with thinner crust and pepperoni that wasn't thick or greasy enough for me. But it was still pizza.

As I stuffed my face and watched the rest of the kids mingle, I noticed some social groups starting to form.

The Alpha males had flocked together: big kids who looked two or three years older than the rest of us, and liked to talk loudly and belch and crush soda cans with their bare hands. Brock seemed to be their leader. Charlie, the Australian keeper who had saved my shot, was right beside him.

Sometimes the players from one country, or who all spoke the same language, hung together: the Italians, Argentinians, and Spanish, for example. A posse of Central Americans had taken over one table. A tribe of cooler-than-cool kids, like Javier, the French winger with the green hair and earrings, stood in the corner and snickered at a joke that was too good for the rest of us. On the far wall, a trio of pretty boys with gelled hair and designer clothes were bent over someone's phone, doing their best Ronaldo impressions.

I wondered where I belonged. The only other American, Robbie, was part of yet another group I definitely was not a part of: the players who oozed confidence and seemed like they were born to be here. Diego, José, Sven, and a dozen or so other members of this privileged clan had gathered in a circle by the pizza table. They wore pro-looking warm-ups from their club teams, and had the best cleats and gear. Robbie hung with them, laughing and fist-bumping, though I knew on the inside he was a nervous wreck and just fronting.

After a while, Alejandro strolled in. He saw the Central American players gathered together, hesitated, then walked over to join me after he got his pizza. Somehow just seeing each other made us laugh. Dayo wandered over next, and then freckle-faced Oliver. Garika, the Zimbabwean, looked a little lost as well, so I waved him over. More and more players hesitantly approached our table, some of whom were the only kids from their country or who didn't speak English or who just looked out of place for some reason. I realized that I, too, belonged to a tribe: the group for kids who didn't have one.

And that was right where I belonged.

Later that night, I called my dad for the first time since leaving home. I'd sent him plenty of texts to let him know I had arrived and was okay. Ginny, I was sure, had helped him figure out the Skype app. My dad thought a microwave was complicated technology. He always talked about the good old days when there were only three TV channels and no cell phones or devices. It sounded like a horror movie to me.

"Hey kiddo," he said, once the call went through.

"Hi, Dad."

"How are you?"

"Good."

"Just good? Not great, or best ever?"

"Just good," I said.

"Okay . . . I bet you've got a lot to tell me."

"You could say that again."

I heard shuffling on the other end, and Ginny let out a squeal. "Hi Leo! Have you met anyone famous yet?"

"I met Coach Zepeda."

"Who?"

I rolled my eyes. "I also met Meghan Markle."

"You *did*?!"

"That was a joke, Ginny."

"Oh."

I heard Dad whispering in the background. "Tell him you miss him and love him."

"Eeeww, no," she whispered back.

"Your sister loves and misses you very much," Dad said in a louder voice. "So how is it, kiddo?"

"It's, um, hard."

"I can only imagine."

"Everybody's *really* good, Dad. I mean, these kids are amazing. I've never played against anyone like them. At least not my age."

"Did you expect anything different?"

"I guess not."

"You should be really proud just to be there."

"I guess."

"You're doing a lot of guessing."

"I just . . . I'm not sure I belong."

"I doubt that, Leo. You're really, really good."

"Maybe back home I am."

"*Leo.* You just concentrate on yourself, and don't worry about them. You hear me?"

"I have to worry about them. They're the competition. There's over two hundred kids here, Dad. And only eleven make the team."

"Philip Niles is a professional scout. He wouldn't risk his

reputation—his job—if he didn't think you deserved to be there. The rest is up to you."

"Maybe he just needed someone at the last minute."

"Believe in yourself, Leo. And listen, it doesn't matter if you make the team or not. I don't care a whit about that."

He might not, but I did. And whether Dad admitted it or not, our future might depend on whether or not I made the Dragons.

"I mean it. When you come home, I want you to be able to say you gave it your very best shot. That's all we can do in life. Deal?"

"*Okay*, Dad."

"Did you do anything good today? A shot or a pass or something?"

I thought back on the day. "Yeah. A couple of things."

"Glad to hear it. Don't forget about them. You can play with those kids, Leo. I know you can."

They were nice words to hear, but they didn't mean very much, because everyone knows your parents always think you're the best at everything.

We chatted for a while longer. It was really good to hear his voice and I was sad when it was time to hang up.

"Hey Dad—is Messi okay?"

"He's great. I'm sure he misses you."

"Make sure to watch him eat his crickets, okay? He gets grumpy if he doesn't get to show off."

"I will, Leo," my dad said gravely.

⚽ ⚽ ⚽

I was feeling really homesick after I hung up with my dad. It was late, and I should probably have gone to sleep, but I still hadn't adjusted to the time change. My body wanted to sleep but my mind was going in a thousand directions, thinking about everything that had happened and worrying about tomorrow.

Feeling the need to talk to a friend from back home, I sent Carlos a text, though he was probably at someone's house or playing soccer in the neighborhood.

To my surprise, he texted back almost immediately.

Leo! Wuzzup! What's it like over there?

Though it was kind of weird to be texting with someone thousands of miles away, I knew Carlos so well it felt like he was in the same room.

> The weather is colder here. I'm tired because of the time change. My room is a little small, and I have a roommate from New York.

Leo?

> Yeah?

I don't care about any of that crap. How's the SOCCER? At the LONDON DRAGONS training camp?

I thought for a second.

> You know how we go see the high school team play sometimes?

Sure.

These kids aren't as big as the high schoolers, but they're better. *Way* better.

No surprise, doofus. They're probably, like, the best in the world. How did you get invited, anyway? Was it a joke like I thought?

Maybe.

Are they laughing at you? Megging you all the time?

I had an assist to an assist in a scrimmage and I got first place in a dribbling competition. But it's pretty tough.

No goals?

I almost scored once. You wouldn't even believe the save this keeper made.

Loser. Just try not to get kicked out or anything. And remember every single detail so you can tell us about it when you get home.

Don't worry. I'm writing everything down in a journal. Even this conversation.

That's weird.

Get over it.

U seen anyone famous?

Just Coach Zepeda.

Coach Zepeda?!? For realzzzzz? You met him?

He spoke to us before the camp began.

He's coaching you???

I just told you—he spoke for a minute and then disappeared with some other VIPs.

Oh. U met any Dragons?

Nope.

Why not? I want some autographs. My brother wants some, too.

I'll try.

Hey I gotta run. We're about to have a game. Try not to stink the place up too much, okay?

Thanks for the support.

Don't mention it.

After Carlos signed off, I couldn't help but grin. The fact that he roasted me a bit was comforting. That was just Carlos. No matter what happened in life, I wanted him to treat me the same as he always did. If he started acting like I was special or singing my praises like my dad, I knew I'd *really* feel lonely.

Feeling better, I crawled into bed and did my best to get

some sleep. Across the room, Robbie was lying on his back with a black cloth over his eyes to make sure he wasn't disturbed by a single trickle of light.

With a sigh, wishing I had someone fun for a roommate, I turned on my side and tried to clear my head—except I couldn't stop thinking about the morning and what squad I was going to be on. Would any of my new friends join me? What if I didn't know anyone? What if my coach didn't like me? What if Brock and his club of morons were assigned to the same squad as me?

My goal of being a professional soccer player still seemed as far away as the moon. I told myself to calm down and take it one step at a time. First I had to make it past the cuts at the end of Week One.

As the digital clock on the desk changed to eleven-thirty, and only the faint chirp of crickets outside broke the silence, I found myself missing my mom more than I had in some time. For my entire life, whenever Ginny or I had trouble falling asleep, Mom would sing lullabies to us and stroke our backs to help us relax.

Knowing that would never happen again made me feel small and alone, and very far from home.

Slowly but surely, the clock crept closer to midnight.

Spiky Green Iguanas

After seven hours of sleep, I woke the next morning feeling refreshed. I was ready to hit the field and prove myself, take on the world and come out on top.

Then I pulled the covers off, rolled out of bed, and realized my body was reading a different book than my mind. My blisters had doubled in size, and my legs ached so bad I wondered how I would make it through the day. I groaned, looked over to see if Robbie was feeling the same, and realized he was already gone. Of course he was. He was probably doing wind sprints up a set of stairs somewhere.

I limped down the hall to the bathroom. After a hot shower, my muscles loosened up a bit. I stuck some more Moleskin on my blisters and wandered down to the basement for breakfast. The cafeteria was buzzing, and I quickly saw why. On the wall to my left, the squads were posted, with kids crowding in to see where they had landed.

Just as Director Hawk had said, there were four field squads for the summer camp: Komodos, Monitors, Iguanas, and Gilas. After scanning the rosters of the first three, my stomach started to churn when I didn't see my name listed. Had my worst fears come true? Did I perform so miserably yesterday that I wouldn't even be assigned to a squad? Sent home on a plane by myself?

When I saw my name halfway down the fourth roster, all the tension poured out of me. I was an Iguana. An official member of a London Dragons Academy summer camp squad.

I might have preferred the Komodos—those were some ginormous, dangerous lizards—or even a Gila, which has potent venom. But I had always liked iguanas. They have spiky ridges down their backs and can grow quite large, around six feet long. Similar to Messi's beard, they can make their bodies appear bigger by lowering the dewlap under their chins. Iguanas do have venom glands but, like most lizards, the delivery system is much less potent than a snake's, and harmless to humans.

Now that I knew my squad, I started pondering the characteristics that iguanas and I shared. Like me, iguanas are very quick, have sharp teeth they will use when threatened, and are known to strike without warning. They're also a little lazy, which is not my best character trait, but I can't deny it. Now that I thought about it, iguanas are born center forwards. They lurk around until it's time to strike, then close in fast and hard. All lizards have superpowers, and iguanas are known for being able to regrow their tails if they get cut off. I wasn't sure how that applied to me yet, but I filed that fact away for the future.

So I was a spiky green Iguana.

I could get used to that.

Like the other kids, I scanned my roster and was relieved to see some familiar names. My first choice of all, Alejandro, was on the Iguanas with me. So were Robbie, José, Oliver, Sven, Javier, Kaito, Garika, and Dayo. I had lucked out with so many friends.

The squad leaders were listed at the bottom of the rosters. My excitement grew when I read that Samantha was assigned to the Iguanas. The only person I would have preferred was Tig, but glancing at the other groups, I didn't see his name listed.

My only disappointment was that Brock, my arch-enemy, was also an Iguana. That stung. I would have to deal with that loud-mouthed brute all day long.

"So you're a six?" Robbie said, coming up to stand beside me. "That's higher than I thought you'd land."

I remembered the coaches had ranked all the players from one to ten in order to sort the squads fairly. "Uh, thanks, I guess. Though how do you know my number?"

"Not counting the keepers, there's two hundred players ranked one to ten, separated into four squads. That's fifty players per squad, and five of each ranked number. You're the twenty-eighth player listed on the Iguanas. That means you're a six."

I did the math in my head, and looked at the roster again. "Maybe they just wrote our names down based on when we signed up. Or something else random."

"Do you believe that?" Robbie said with a chuckle. "They don't come out and say it, but everybody knows they list the names by rank. They *want* you to know. My coach back home has the inside scoop."

A six, I thought. If what Robbie said was true, then he was right, a six was higher than I thought I'd be ranked.

But it was still miles from the top.

I glanced up again and saw that José, the Brazilian midfielder, was the first player listed on the Iguanas. Impressive, but he deserved it. Sven was fifth—so also a number one. Javier and Dayo were right below him. Brock was the thirteenth player listed, and Robbie the fifteenth.

"Congrats," I said to my roommate. "You're a three."

Robbie gave me a sharp glance, as if trying to decide if I was roasting him. "Congrats? I'm fifteenth. The bottom of the threes. Overall, that means I'm ranked about sixtieth out of two hundred players. That's not even close to the top eleven."

He wandered off with a scowl on his face.

I've got to find a way to loosen this guy up, I thought. *It's like they gave me a worrywart adult for a roomie.*

Before I joined the breakfast line, I glanced at the board again. All the goalies were in a separate squad called the Snapping Turtles. Charlie was the first keeper listed. Plenty of kids I didn't know yet were listed near the top of the field player squads. My eyes roamed higher, to the very first names. Mateo and Hans, both excellent defenders, headlined the Monitors squad. Sebastian, the Polish speedster, was the number one Gila. And of course, it was no surprise to see Diego, maybe the best player in the whole camp, and certainly the center forward I had to beat out for the top eleven, leading the way for the Komodos.

I ate breakfast with some players from my squad. We clowned around the whole time, and it was nice to feel the camaraderie, as well as forget about the ranking system. I know Director Hawk warned us we would have to learn to deal with pressure and high expectations, but that was a dirty trick, letting the whole camp see everyone's rank. I felt bad for the kids close to the bottom. Alejandro was an eight, but he didn't seem bothered. Maybe he was keeping it all inside. That's what I would do.

On each of the breakfast tables, a stack of fliers detailed the schedule for the next week. I took one and studied it.

7:30–8:30	am	Breakfast
9:00–9:30	am	Warm-up
9:30–12:00	pm	Morning Training
12:00–1:00	pm	Lunch
1:00–3:30	pm	Afternoon Training
3:30–4:00	pm	Break
4:00–5:00	pm	Scrimmage
5:00–6:00	pm	Clean Up
6:00–7:30	pm	Dinner
7:30–?	pm	Special Activity
11:00	pm	Lights Out

Special Activity, I wondered? What was that?

Happy to be on a squad, I couldn't wait to get started, as long as my body cooperated. I was as stiff as a telephone pole, and the bottoms of my feet hurt to the touch.

After breakfast, I grabbed my ball and bag and headed to the fields with Robbie. The Iguanas were assigned to Field 4. It was the furthest one from the Castle, which Robbie speculated was because our group was the least talented in the eyes of the coaches. I rolled my eyes and asked him if he thought the eggs they gave us for breakfast had any special meaning.

Samantha met us on the field, wearing cleats and a large brace on her left knee. She was juggling with Tig, and I was surprised to see her keeping up with him—around-the-worlds, shoulder rolls, all kinds of fancy moves. We all stopped for a moment as we approached the field, wide-eyed at their talent.

"Don't be shy," Samantha called out. "Everyone grab your kit bag off the bench. Put on one of the pennies, it doesn't matter what color. Take three laps with your ball to warm up, then meet me over here to stretch."

Our field did not have bleachers. On the sideline, just below the stone wall at the bottom of the hill, was a line of drawstring nylon bags imprinted with our names and the Dragons logo. I found my bag and opened it. Inside were two pennies, one red and one gold. On the front was a picture of an iguana thrusting up on its front legs, its back lined with the distinctive ridge of spikes.

After jogging around the field three times, we all spread out in front of Samantha and Tig. When they stopped juggling, Tig leaned in to whisper something in her ear. She laughed, and he took her hand as they parted, letting his fingers trail away. She watched him jog off the field, then turned to us and smiled.

"Come in closer," she said. "I don't bite."

If you did bite, I thought, *you would lean forward and bob your head as a sign that you're angry, like a proper iguana.*

"Hi Robbie, Alejandro, Leo. Nice to see you again. For everyone else, my name is Samantha. I'm from the States— Atlanta, Georgia. I'll be your squad leader for the next three weeks. I sincerely wish you could all stay with me the entire time, but, well, Director Hawk has told you how it works. That said, I don't want you to stress about the cuts."

"Yeah, right," Robbie whispered beside me.

"It's true they're going to happen," she continued, "but I personally feel that if you're stressed, you won't play your best. And my job is to make sure that I and the other coaches see you at your best. Okay?"

No one responded.

Samantha frowned and held open her palms. "*Okay*, Iguanas?"

We gave her a shout of affirmation.

"Good," she said. "Now stretch with me, and I'll tell you how the first week is going to go."

She sat on the ground and led us through a series of stretches as she talked. I winced at the first one, a butterfly to stretch the groin. I could barely push my knees down.

"You've seen the schedule, and we'll stick to it. For the first week, every day we'll focus on one or two basic skills, until the last day, which is a catch-all. Today is trapping and passing. For most of the day, we'll run a series of drills emphasizing these skills. I'll try to make it fun, but sometimes, drills are just drills. When it comes to football, or any skill, repetition is the key to success. Knowledge is, too. There's a right way and a wrong way to do things. Now listen, I know Ronaldo or Neymar might do things differently, or use fancy tricks, but trust me, they learned how to do it the right way first. You have to know the rules before you can break them. *Capisce*?"

She laughed when she saw our confused looks. "Capisce means, does everyone understand? I picked up some Italian when I played for Juventus."

Wait—Samantha used to play in Italy? For one of the best teams in Serie A?

I wondered how this was possible, since she couldn't be much older than Tig. Maybe she was joking.

When we were done stretching, Samantha stood, rolled her ball back on her instep, and flicked it high in the air. "Juggle with me," she said. I copied the trick she used to get the ball in the air, and did my best to follow along as she used her head, thighs, and feet to keep the ball in the air.

"Good, Leo," she said with a smile. "Everyone should juggle however feels natural, though I do want you to try new things. It's okay if you drop the ball. This isn't a test. Your ball should be your best friend on the field. Just like with any friend, you have to cultivate that relationship. Spend time with your friend. Listen to them. Understand them. If you're kind to your friend, your friend will be kind to you."

Out of the corner of my eye, I caught a glimpse of the other kids. Everyone looked comfortable with the ball—far more than the best kids back home—but the only other person doing fancy tricks without dropping the ball, like me and Samantha, was José. I noticed Samantha scanning the group as she talked. She wasn't even looking at her ball.

"A few more things before we start. No, keep juggling please, and just listen. I know this is the first time away from home for most of you. It's a lot to take in. I'm always here if you need advice about anything, or just need to talk. You should enjoy the experience, but remember you're here to focus on football. To do that, you have to take care of your body. Make sure you get enough sleep, at least eight hours a night. Don't eat too much junk food or load up on soft drinks. It will hurt you on the field, I promise."

What was she talking about? I play better after a Coke and a candy bar.

She talked for a few more minutes about nutrition and a

few other things, like using mindfulness to not get stressed about the cuts. I lost interest and started focusing on my juggling, trying out a new trick I'd seen on YouTube. I almost had it right—

"Leo!"

I looked up to find Samantha staring at me. All the other kids had their balls at their feet. Sheepish, I let my ball hit the ground and put my foot on it.

"Thank you," she said. "Now, our two skills for the day are passing and trapping. I like to group these together and call them First Touch. In my opinion, this is the single most important skill in soccer. Whether it's a one-touch pass, or a trap and a shot, or a trap to gain space, your first touch is the primary skill that separates the pros from the amateurs. Watch some tape of Messi, or De Bruyne, or any of the very best players. They're always thinking three steps ahead, and their first touch puts them in a position to succeed. I'll be working on your first touch over the next three weeks, so this is just an introduction. But get that into your head: it all starts there, and you should know exactly what you're doing and where you're going before you receive the ball."

I had never thought about my first touch in that way. Sure, I knew it was important, but Samantha talked about it like it was a religion.

"Dayo," she said, "can you kick your ball straight up for me, as high as you can?"

He flicked the ball up and punted it high in the sky above Samantha. I thought she was going to let it hit the ground and step on it, like I would have done, but instead she caught it on her instep, straight out of the air, and the ball stuck there as if she had glue on her foot.

The entire squad of Iguanas, myself included, was speechless.

"Give it a shot," she said.

I looked around the group, wondering if I was the only one who thought her trap looked impossible. Robbie had turned pale and was staring at his ball as if it had chicken pox.

With a shrug, I picked up my ball, kicked it as high as I could, and tried to imitate what Samantha had done. The ball bounced off my instep twenty feet away.

No one else did any better, not even José, and Samantha laughed. "That was a bit cruel, I know. That's not even useful in a game. But *this* is." She flicked her ball up and punted it into the sky herself, even higher than Dayo. This time, instead of catching it, the ball bounced softly on the top of her foot, as if it had hit a pillow, and landed a foot in front of her.

"From here," she said, "I can dribble or make a pass, whatever I want. It's a better trap—a better first touch—than stopping the ball with the bottom of your foot. If the ball is under your foot, it takes more time to move the ball into a playable position. That's just one example of how advanced trapping can lead to a better first touch, and make you a better player. Now, let's pair up and do some drills."

Robbie glanced my way almost guiltily before hurrying over to José, but the Brazilian midfielder had already paired up with Dayo. Alejandro picked me up in a bearhug from behind, making my choice easy. After losing out on José, Robbie turned to Sven and then Javier, looking for the best player available, but everyone had a partner. Robbie stood in the center of the group, glum when he realized that Garika, the Zimbabwean with the shoes that barely fit, was the only player left.

For the rest of the morning, we did some basic drills with our partners while Samantha walked around to observe and offer pointers. She was an excellent teacher. I learned more about trapping and passing in those two and a half hours than in my entire life. I learned how to make my foot soft yet hard at the same time when trapping or receiving a pass, a trick Samantha called the Water Foot. I learned to point my plant foot in the direction I wanted the pass to go, which everyone else seemed to know already. There were lots of little details I soaked up like a sponge, and she encouraged us to always keep our heads up and watch the game unfold when the ball was at our feet.

During the morning session, my muscles loosened up, only to stiffen again at lunch. When I walked to our table carrying a plate full of mac and cheese and Swedish meatballs, Alejandro laughed and told me I looked as if I had just finished riding a horse for the first time.

Most of the kids sat with their friends at lunch, instead of with their new squads. I didn't have to choose, and it was nice getting to know everyone better. I learned that Kaito and Oliver liked video games as much as I did. Garika, though a bit shy and wide-eyed, was easy to get along with. A scout had spotted him playing in a public park, which made me feel better about my own lack of formal training. Not everyone had to play on fancy club teams, like Robbie seemed to believe. Garika was ranked near the bottom of our squad, however, and his game was very raw. Like me, he had a long hill to climb.

Sven, Robbie, and José sat at a different table with the other Club Kids, the name I gave the players with the best credentials and all the right gear. Javier surprised me by sitting at our table instead of with the other cool kids. He barely said a word until he learned I had a pet lizard, which caused him to give me a barely perceptible nod. For him, this was a shout of approval. He revealed he had a pet boa, and I asked him if the boa had green hair and earrings like him. This caused him to stare at me for a moment, then roll his eyes and say something in French. I didn't blame him for being annoyed. Javier was a sophisticated city kid from Paris, and he really was cooler than the rest of us.

But I was still going to roast him.

After lunch, the drills got harder. We did all kinds of complex maneuvers that I imagined the pros, or at least the youth teams, used during practice. The morning session was all about correct technique, while the afternoon session was more about putting what we had learned into practice. We wove down the field with one-touch passes, trapped super hard balls in the goal that Samantha kicked, and did drills that forced us to trap the ball and react quickly to choose a passer.

The final drill of the day was the hardest, but also the most fun. Everyone knew this drill. Even players from Middleton, Ohio with basketball coaches. To start, Samantha divided us into groups of five and formed a square with the cones ten yards apart. Four players stood at the cones and passed the ball around the perimeter of the square while the fifth player, a defender in the middle, tried to steal the ball.

The other players in my group were Dayo, Sven, Brock, and Julian, an attacking midfielder and one of Brock's closest friends. Julian was tall and slim and blond, with a nice touch on the ball. He wore his hair slicked back and reminded me of a young Harry Kane, except for the annoying smirk that never left his face.

The drill started out fine. Samantha let us hold the ball as long as we wanted, and use as many touches as we needed. It was pretty easy to keep the ball away from the defenders, except when Dayo was in the middle. He was so fast he gave you almost no time to trap the ball, and had good defensive instincts for a forward.

"Three touches only," Samantha called out after a few minutes, forcing us to use our skills with a defender bearing down on us. Sven was in the middle. Though a gifted right winger, his defense was as bad as mine. He couldn't get the ball, and grew so frustrated he started walking, causing Samantha to raise her voice for the first time.

"Never quit on the ball, Sven! Not even in a drill!"

With a burst of effort, Sven intercepted a pass from Julian, putting the British player in the middle.

"Two touches!" Samantha yelled. "Make your first one count!"

The pace of the drill picked up. I was doing well, controlling every pass, putting my first touch exactly where I wanted it. I even got cocky and sent a few passes behind my legs, or scooped them through the air. After I sent a volley towards Dayo, he trapped it with a knee and volleyed it back. I trapped it and, as Julian came flying in, I stepped over the ball, faking a pass to my left. Julian bit hard and stumbled. I clowned a bit, simulating a yawn as I took my time passing the ball to Brock on my right.

I heard Julian mutter something nasty under his breath, but Brock did something even nastier. When my pass reached him, he sent the ball back to me with lots of pace. Julian was still right beside me, and I had no time to recover. Brock should have passed it to Dayo or Sven, but he wanted to set me up. I tried to flick the ball to the side before Julian reached it, but he came in hard with a slide tackle. He got the ball, but also my legs, and I crashed to the ground.

Samantha called out from across the field. "Julian—stay on your feet! Okay, everyone, one touch only for the last few minutes."

Julian offered a hand to help me up. When I tried to take it, he retracted it, causing me to fall back down.

Brock snorted. "Loser Yank. Your turn in the pot."

I jumped to my feet, trying not to show how much the slide tackle had hurt or how embarrassed I was. I could already feel a knot forming on my thigh. By this time, Samantha had wandered over, and I was forced to endure more humiliation as she watched me chase the ball around the circle in vain. Everyone knew I couldn't play defense. Still, one touch passes with pace in a small area are hard to control, and I was quick. Julian made a pass to Brock that wasn't as crisp as it could have been, and I closed in, sensing a kill. No way could Brock get off a pass in time.

Nor did he try. Right before I reached him, he whipped around and threw his heavy body into mine, hitting me in the stomach so hard with his hips that it knocked the wind out of me. He made a stab at Julian's pass before it sailed by him.

"Guess I'm in the middle," Brock said, as I took a knee and struggled to regain my wind.

"Brock," Samantha said evenly, "take three laps around the field, and then do fifty pushups."

"What? The ball was within playing distance. Fair contact."

"No. It was not. Fair contact is shoulder to shoulder, not ramming someone in the stomach as hard as you can. That's called a yellow card." She pointed at the edge of the field. "Get going." She turned to me. "Are you okay, Leo?"

Dayo ran over to help me up as Julian watched with a smirk. "I'm fine," I said. "No big deal."

Samantha watched me for a moment before she blew her whistle. "Break time, everyone. Be back in thirty!"

During the afternoon break, I collapsed with my water bottle under the closest shade tree I could find. When my friends stopped by to check on me, I waved them off. Although Julian's slide tackle and Brock's blow to my stomach still hurt, the main problem was my legs. They were gone. Toast.

It seemed no time at all had passed when Samantha blew her whistle again. I walked slowly back to the field, hoping my legs didn't cramp. My only consolation was that some of the other players looked as tired as I felt. Not many, but some.

Samantha divided us into ten teams of five for the small-sided scrimmage. Using tiny goals with no keepers, each team played four others, ten minutes per game, with short breaks in between.

I don't know how I made it through the scrimmages. It's hard to hide in five-on-five, but I did my best to conserve my energy, and passed the ball as soon as I got it. Samantha even complimented my one-touch passing, which made me laugh. I was just trying to survive.

José and Robbie were both on my team. José seemed to

have an unlimited source of energy, like he had a power source under his shirt, and Robbie was in top shape from all his conditioning. I didn't know the other two kids on our team.

I can't even remember how our team did. I think we tied three and won one. Though I wanted to deal out some payback to Julian and Brock, I couldn't muster the strength. After Samantha blew her whistle at the end of the final game, I collapsed to the ground and stared at the sky, too exhausted to move.

When I finally made it back to my room, Robbie tossed me a small jar as I limped to my bed.

"What's this?" I said.

"Icy Hot. Rub it on your legs tonight and in the morning. It will help."

"Thanks."

"Sure. I've got plenty."

"And hey, thanks for holding up the fort in the scrimmage," I said. "I'm sure you could tell I was out of gas."

Robbie had already showered and dressed for dinner. As he opened the door to leave, he paused and said, "We're competing with each other, Leo. Don't you know that? I just didn't want our team to lose. We aren't friends on the field, okay? I don't want to be mean, I just don't want you to take it personally."

"Robbie?"

"Yeah?"

"Don't take it personally when I make the Academy and you don't."

He laughed and shook his head. "Leo, if you even make it to the World Cup, I'll eat my shirt."

"Better steal some chocolate sauce from the cafeteria. Cotton doesn't taste very good."

After he left, I took a long shower and tried not to let Robbie's words get to me. Instead I wondered what the cafeteria would serve for dinner, since I had rarely been so hungry in my life. Even more, I wondered about the mysterious Special Activity marked on the schedule for later that evening.

Stars, Skills, and Sore Legs

Towards the end of dinner, after I was stuffed full of shepherd's pie, Director Hawk sent a chill down everyone's spine when he stood at the head of the coaches' table and raised a hand for silence. Within moments, the cafeteria was so quiet I could have heard a bird fart.

"Congratulations on finishing the first day of squad training," Director Hawk said, though his tone did not sound like he was complimenting us. More like he was sorry we were all still there. "I'm sure you all have sore legs, so make sure to get your rest tonight. Now, in just a few minutes, you'll be attending your first Special Activity of the summer. The evening Specials are a tradition at the London Dragons summer camp. Every night during the first three weeks, and on Sundays, our rest day, we'll provide a different activity for everyone to attend. The Specials are meant to encourage camaraderie among the players, as well as introducing our foreign players to British culture. Our hope is you'll find them fun and rewarding."

I had serious doubts as to whether Director Hawk and I had the same definition of *fun* and *rewarding*.

"As soon as you're finished with dinner," Director Hawk continued, "I'd like all of you to retrieve your balls from your room and gather in the entrance hall. You won't need your cleats. When everyone is assembled, Coach Tanner will lead you to the indoor practice facility."

Retrieve our balls? Indoor practice facility? Were we going to scrimmage again? He said we didn't need our cleats, but maybe we weren't allowed to wear them in the indoor facility.

On a normal night, I would have welcomed more soccer, but I badly needed to rest my legs. No way could I play another game. My stomach churned with worry as I returned my tray and headed to my room.

"Where do you think we're going?" Alejandro whispered, as everyone gathered in the entry hall with Coach Tanner, the short, heavyset man with a kind face who had coached one of my scrimmages.

"I hope we aren't playing after that meal," freckle-faced Oliver said after a belch, in his thick British accent. "I'm so full of shepherd's pie I have potatoes in my toes."

"Quiet, please," Kaito said. "We do not want to anger the director."

Coach Tanner led us through the courtyard on the rear side of the Castle to a building we had not yet visited. As soon as we entered, I realized the smaller stone structure had been transformed into an indoor soccer facility. The emerald turf glistened under the lights, bleachers surrounded the perimeter of the field, photos of players lined the walls, and championship pennants hung from the rafters.

A gigantic projector screen had been set up in the center of the field. Coach Tanner ushered us forward, telling us to find a seat. I released a sigh of relief as I sat at the rear of the crowd with my friends and leaned my back against my ball. Maybe we wouldn't have to play after all. When everyone had taken a seat, the lights turned out, causing a ripple of excitement. I had no idea what to expect, but I hoped we didn't have to sit through one of those awful British comedies.

A spotlight came on, illuminating a man standing in front of the projector screen. I gasped when I saw him. It was Frankie Dylan, one of the most famous Dragons to have ever played. He retired a few years ago, after leading the Dragons to three Premier League titles and a Champions League victory. Frankie was a central midfielder who flowed like water around the field and had a bazooka for a right leg. He had won Premier League player of the year at least twice.

I couldn't believe he was standing right there in the flesh, about to talk to us!

"Welcome," Frankie said, and I was surprised by his short stature. He wasn't any taller than Coach Tanner. "Congrats to all of you for receiving an invitation. You may not know this, but I too once attended the Dragons summer camp, and came up through the youth teams. I'm a Dragon through and through!"

This caused a roar of approval from the crowd. I joined in with the clapping and shouting, proud to be included, knowing I would be a Dragon for life no matter what happened.

When the applause died, Frankie said, "I know what it's like to sit where you're sitting, and how anxious you feel about the summer. When I retired, I made a vow to give back to the game however I could. Every year since, Director Hawk has graciously allowed me to lead the summer camp through a film session."

After Frankie finished his speech, the spotlight dimmed and the projector came to life, showcasing two teams taking the field in front of a massive crowd. Frankie introduced the game as the one in which the London Dragons had defeated Real Madrid in the Champions League final. Once the game started, Frankie paused the game every few minutes for behind-the-scenes commentary. Sometimes he gave strategy pointers, or told us what he had been thinking at the time, or even made funny comments about the other players. I soaked in every single word, riveted to the screen.

It took three and a half hours to finish the game, but the time flew by so fast I barely noticed. At the end, we all gave Frankie a standing ovation, and then Coach Tanner asked us to form a line if we wanted Frankie to sign our soccer balls.

If we wanted him to? Was that a joke?

I hurried to join the line, and stood starry-eyed as Frankie Dylan shook my hand, asked for my name, and scribbled his signature on my ball in permanent black marker.

I left the indoor facility in a daze. Just before the stairs to my hall, a hand slapped my shoulder from behind. "Hey Boss."

I turned at the sound of Tig's voice, wincing as a stab of pain shot down my leg.

He frowned. "You okay there?"

"Yeah. Just a little sore."

"A little?"

"Maybe a lot."

He chuckled and patted me on the arm, more softly this time. "You'll make it. Lots of rest and water, okay?"

"Okay," I said, not sure I would even make it through the next day.

"Hey, I've heard people talking about your slick move in the scrimmage yesterday."

I blinked. "You have?"

"Keep it up, and listen, I wanted to give you another piece of advice. Samantha's easy to like, yeah?"

"She's really nice."

"Stay on her good side, because your group leader is the key to success. You have to impress all the coaches eventually, but she'll be your biggest advocate when it comes time to make the cut." He clicked his tongue. "So be sure to keep a good attitude, okay?"

"Sure. Thanks. Hey Tig, is Samantha . . . your girlfriend?"

He gave me a conspiratorial wink. "Something like that, Boss."

Day Two of Skills Week.

Everything hurt.

Calves, quads, hamstrings, glutes.

Even my toes were sore.

C'mon, Leo. You can do this. It's the London Dragons summer camp.

As awful as I felt, I was excited about another full day of soccer. With a groan, I rolled out of bed and slathered Icy Hot on my aching legs. The icky stuff smelled like peppermint medicine and made my nose wrinkle. I got dressed and applied more Moleskin to the blisters on the soles of my feet.

Knowing how long the day would be, I didn't clown around with the ball after breakfast. Instead I showed up just in time to take three slow laps around the field and stretch. I had never taken stretching seriously—that was something adults had to do—but my leg muscles felt as if they were going to snap in half, like rubber bands stretched too far. Even worse, today was shooting and place kicks. Two skills designed to push my legs to the limit.

The morning session began with two shooting lines from the edge of the penalty box. Despite how sore I was, I pushed through and performed close to my best. That still put me near the bottom of the pack. Not good for a striker. My only consolation was that I could use both feet almost equally. Only José was as bipedal—that means good with both feet—as I was.

The squads had borrowed the goalies for the day. Unfortunately, we got two of the best: Charlie the Australian, and Koffi, a scrawny kid from the Ivory Coast, a country known for producing strong players. Koffi was so tall he could reach up and wrap his fingers around the crossbar.

As we shot, Samantha walked around and made notes on a clipboard. Sven had the strongest foot of the group, with Dayo and Julian close behind. Sven was a winger, and Dayo a center forward, but Julian was a defensive midfielder, making his shooting prowess even more impressive. Robbie and José, our center midfielders, both had solid shots which almost always landed on target.

For forwards, Kaito and Oliver had surprisingly mediocre legs, though both were crafty and able to bend the ball. Alejandro and Brock could kick almost as hard as Sven, but had issues with control. Among my friends, the only player with a worse shot than mine was Garika. Half of his attempts sailed wide or over the goal, and his approach looked awkward.

Samantha blew her whistle and lined us up for penalty kicks. I wondered why she had not given us any pointers like the day before. Every now and then, she would make a comment, but mostly she just took notes.

I had fun watching Charlie and Koffi try to stop our PKs. Charlie, the hulking Australian keeper who had blocked my zinger on the first day, had an almost supernatural ability to guess where people were shooting. Javier shouted in French and waved his hands after the second time Charlie laid out in a dive and reached his kick with his fingertips, sending it just wide. After the save, Charlie grinned and clapped his hands, then hunkered down like an ogre in the goal mouth. He stopped all but one of my shots, a lucky blast that rippled the side netting. I had better luck with Koffi, because I figured out he had a hard time with low balls. I used push passes to the corners and beat him every time.

I caught Samantha frowning and scribbling in her notepad, probably because of my poor form, but hey, I had scored. Wasn't that what counted?

We took a water break and moved on to place kicks outside the penalty box. After shooting from various angles, we added in a wall. Kaito, Oliver, and Javier excelled at these drills. I marveled at how they could make the ball dip and curve towards the goal like puppeteers yanking on a string. I vowed to learn the skill.

When Brock's turn came to shoot, I was in the middle of a three-person wall with Alejandro and Julian. Brock's shot hit me square in the chest.

"He has terrible aim," Julian said. "He might hit your face next time. You should go stand over by the coach."

"You'd love that, wouldn't you?" I shot back. "That way I can't take your spot on the team."

Julian sneered. "Keep dreaming."

I gritted my teeth and stood in the wall again. Brock's next shot soared high overhead, and his third one went straight at Alejandro's face. The stocky Costa Rican lowered his head and let the ball hit him. It bounced far away and must have hurt like crazy.

"Is that it?" Alejandro said. "My grandmother kicks harder than that."

The players waiting in line to kick laughed, causing Brock to turn bright red and stomp off to retrieve his ball. The next time his turn came, Samantha was watching. Brock hesitated as if deciding what to do, then tried to bend the ball around the wall and failed. For some reason, he glared at me as he walked off the field, as if I had caused him to miss.

During lunch, I sat with my friends as Brock and his crew laughed and pointed in our direction from the next table over. Alejandro was right beside me. I knew he could see them, but it didn't seem to bother him.

"Doesn't it make you mad?" I asked.

"What?" he said, between mouthfuls of his ham and cheese sandwich.

"Those idiots over there. They think they're better than us."

"So? Do you think that?"

I waved a hand. "Of course not. That isn't the point. They won't even roast us to our face."

"Why does it bother you?"

"It just does. How come *nothing* bothers you?"

Alejandro finished the last bite of his sandwich, and wiped a spot of mustard off his mouth. "Costa Rica is a beautiful country. We're very . . . how do you say . . . successful . . . compared to other countries in Central America. But many of us are still poor. I come from a small village. I love my home, but I take a bus an hour each way every day, so I can attend a school in the city that teaches English and has a good football team. My parents have given up everything for my education and my dreams, just like my grandparents, who do not have running water or electricity, gave up everything for them. I'm at the summer camp of the London Dragons. It's an incredible honor. What is there to be unhappy about?"

"Not making the team? Jerks like Brock and Julian?"

Alejandro shrugged. "I will do my best, Leo. If I make the team, it will be a great adventure. If not, I'll have a good life in Costa Rica. I've already been accepted at a private school in San José," he said proudly, "on full scholarship."

As I congratulated him, I realized that, while every kid here came from a different place than I did, and we might speak different languages, and look different, and eat things that seemed funny to others, we all had homes and families, friends and enemies, the same hopes and dreams.

Well, I thought darkly as I glanced at Brock's table, *we're almost all the same.*

I wished I could be as carefree about making the team as Alejandro. Robbie took life way too seriously, and that wasn't me either, but I wanted with all my heart to be a London Dragon and help my family.

Was there a good middle ground?

Could I still be myself and do what it took to succeed?

⚽ ⚽ ⚽

You know that feeling towards the end of a hard game, when you've been running nonstop for an hour-and-a-half and your lungs are about to burst and your legs are on fire and you don't know if you'll be able to finish without collapsing?

That's how I felt *before* the afternoon scrimmages.

This time, I didn't have José and Robbie to lean on. Kaito and Garika were on my team, along with two players I didn't know very well. While Garika had boundless energy, he was a defender, and did not control the flow of the game like José or even Robbie. Kaito and our other teammates gave me some good passes, but I was too gassed to do much with them. It was embarrassing. I was a liability, and we lost all four games.

"You going to make it, Leo?" Samantha asked as I collapsed on the field for the second day in a row, right after the final whistle.

Too tired and hurting to speak, I could only nod.

"Hang in there," she said before walking away to meet Tig, who was waiting for her on the sideline.

The Special that night was an ice cream party on Field One, with every topping you can imagine. Chocolate chips, butterscotch, fudge sauce, whipped cream, cherries, all my favorites. I took pride in building an ice cream cone bigger than anyone else, and got lots of compliments on the size of my creation. My stomach didn't feel so good when I finished, but it helped take my mind off the pain in my legs.

After the party, lots of kids stuck around to hang out on the field. A few even started an impromptu game. Normally I would have joined in, but I was so exhausted I said goodbye to my friends and went straight back to the Castle.

My legs started to cramp as I climbed the stairs to my floor. I limped all the way down the hall, unsure if I was going to make it, and collapsed on my bed. I was so tired I forgot to turn out the lights.

The next morning, after Robbie left for breakfast, I stood in front of the mirror for a long time, wondering how I could possibly make it through the day. To make matters worse, the skill for today was defense. The absolute worst part of my game.

I remembered something my mom used to say, whenever I had a tough time with something in school. *It's not your failures in life that matter, Leo, because everyone fails at something. The most successful people in the world often fail the most. What matters is that you get out of bed the next day and try again.*

I never fully understood her advice until today, when it was literally hard to get out of bed. *Okay Mom,* I said to the mirror, right before I started to dress for the day.

This one's for you.

Reeking of Icy Hot, I grimaced my way through the morning jog and the stretches. As Samantha talked about the principles of defense, I could sense the excitement from the center backs, fullbacks, and wing backs, who finally had a chance to showcase their skills. Brock was grinning and cracking his knuckles, as if he couldn't wait to get on the field and put some forwards on their backs.

"Forwards don't get a pass on defense," Samantha said, when she noticed that not all of us were paying attention. "It's a team effort. There are specific skills to learn, just like any position, but the other half of defense is effort. You have to *want* the ball more than the other player, just like when you're trying to score."

Though I still detested defense, I learned a lot that morning. How to play help defense with my teammates, and how good center backs can orchestrate a defensive scheme using all ten field players. I had always thought defense was simply about taking the ball from someone trying to beat you, but I learned that defense took place all over the field, at every position, with and without the ball.

I thanked my lucky stars we did very little running that morning, instead working on positioning drills and simple two v. ones. After lunch it got harder. Samantha varied up the drills. We played two v. two with a roving defender, a four-on-two overload drill, and a 'clear the box' drill with Samantha sending in crosses from each side of the field.

After the break, we turned to one-on-one drills, but always with a quirky addition. Samantha made the attackers start off with their backs to the ball for one drill, or made you dribble to the left, or kicked a ball high in the air to make you fight for it. We also worked on shielding. I thought I knew how to shield, but the defenders knocked me off the ball so easily, even skinny Garika, that I realized I wasn't nearly as good as I thought.

As expected, Brock had a very good day. He was the best defender on our squad. Garika performed well too. He was fast and agile but had trouble with physical play, especially against larger forwards such as Sven. Time and again, the skinny Zimbabwean got knocked off the ball by a shoulder, causing Samantha to shake her head and tell him to plant his feet, lower his hips, and stand firm.

When it came time to scrimmage, my legs felt so wobbly I wasn't sure I was going to make it. A few of my friends noticed and patted me on the back. A Hungarian kid named Jakub had to drop out for the day due to cramps, and I felt guilty for being relieved I wasn't the only one having trouble. But I knew there would be no excuses when it came time for the cuts at the end of Week One. In fact, watching the way Samantha frowned as Jakub limped off the field, I had a feeling the coaches had little sympathy for tired legs.

Instead of the typical scrimmages, Samantha divided us into ten teams: five offensive, consisting of strikers and attacking midfielders, and five teams for players with a defensive mindset. Could the attackers score against a defense-heavy squad? Could the fullbacks and defensive midfielders punch through a goal against the forwards?

This time, Sven and Oliver were on my team, along with a pair of midfielders. For our first match, we faced off against a squad that included José, Javier, and Alejandro.

I remembered what Robbie had said to me. *We can't be friends on the field, okay?*

Back home, I had no problem playing against my friends. That's what friends were for, right? Roasting each other and trying to outdo each other on the field. Making the London Dragons was serious business, but soccer was still a game, and during the scrimmage Alejandro and I *did* have fun with each other. I beat him once or twice, and he stole the ball from me once or twice, and each time we laughed or slapped each other on the back.

As usual, José made the difference. He was the best two-way player in the squad, maybe in the whole camp, and he put his side ahead with a pass that threaded the needle through our defense and found Javier right in front of the goal. The French winger tapped it in for an easy score.

Towards the end of the game, I stood with my hands on my hips near the opponents' goal, too tired to run back when the ball was cleared. But the long ball went right to Sven, who decided to give me a one-touch pass before the defense could settle. Alejandro was right on my back, between me and the goal. Too close, in my opinion. If I had any gas left, I would have flicked it to my right and run around him. But I was simply too spent. Instead I saw Oliver charging in on the right. With my back to the goal, I lifted the ball into the air with the side of my foot, then volleyed the ball in Oliver's direction.

It was not the prettiest bicycle kick, and I crash-landed on my back. But I managed to turn my head in time to see Oliver's gangly body flying through the air. He dove forward, further than I thought was possible, and caught the ball with his head just in time. It bounced once and slipped into the goal.

I stayed on my back, too tired to move, as the whistle blew and my teammates whooped in celebration. A tie against that team was a huge accomplishment. As José passed me on the field, he shook his head. "Leo, Leo, Leo. My lucky American friend. Admit it, you had no idea where that kick was going."

"Of course I did—backwards."

⚽   ⚽   ⚽

The last scrimmage of the day was the hardest. We had to play a team led by Brock and Julian. My legs felt like cement blocks when I tried to run, and now I had to finish the day against those two jerks? My only consolation was that Brock looked pretty exhausted also, huffing on the sidelines before the game started, his face red and splotchy.

Right when the game began, Sven shocked the other team with a bullet from the right wing that struck the center of the goal from fifteen yards out. That put us ahead 1-0. The game settled down after that, until Julian put a nifty spin move on Oliver that left him flat-footed near the goal.

1-1.

I could sense the time winding down. Just a few more minutes and this torturous day would be over. Even though Samantha had warned us against jaybirding, I lingered near the opponents' goal, too tired to run back. Sven crossed a wicked ball from the right that Julian mishandled. The ball dropped right in front of the goal, and the two closest players were Brock and me.

Both of us were exhausted, but I wanted to score on Brock as badly as he wanted to stop me. Just like me, Brock summoned every ounce of energy he had left and broke for the ball. I wanted to scream in pain as I willed my feet to keep moving and my legs to churn forward.

He arrived a step ahead of me. Just as I expected, he flung his back to me, trying to catch me with his hips again and knock the wind out of me. This time I anticipated it and didn't rush in. I avoided the dirty trick, but his bulky body was still in the mouth of the goal, between me and the ball.

"C'mon Leo," he taunted. "All you have to do is poke it in."

The ball was inches from the goal line, sitting there like a cookie on the countertop, waiting to be snatched. In the corner of my eye, I noticed Samantha had wandered over to watch.

I grunted and tried to get past him, but it was like trying to push through a brick wall. Sven had run over, but the little goal was so small there was no room for another player. This fight was between me and Brock.

"The clock's ticking," Brock said, putting a foot on the ball as he leaned his back against my chest to keep me away.

I tried to go around him, first on one side and then the other, but he held me off with his arms. They were down at his side in a legal position. Brock was just bigger, stronger, and a better shielder than I was.

With a last-ditch effort, I tried to slide to reach the ball, whipping my leg around his. He shifted his hips in time to block it, and the only thing I accomplished was landing on my side with a grunt. With both teams watching, Samantha blew the whistle to end the match as I laid on the ground, staring at the mouth of the goal and the ball right in front of it.

"Better luck next time," Brock said, stepping over me to walk to the sideline.

When I returned to my room, the most dejected I had felt since arriving in London, I collapsed onto my bed, put some headphones on, and listened to some music so I wouldn't have to talk to Robbie.

Halfway through a song, my phone pinged. I looked down and saw a text from Carlos.

Leo? You there?

I hesitated, then decided to reply.

> Just finished playing for the day.

How did it go?

> I'm so sore and exhausted I can barely walk. I'm just trying not to cramp out or pull a hamstring.

Making excuses already?

> It's so intense you wouldn't believe it.

How did you think it would be? Easy? I'm shocked they haven't sent you home yet.

I stared down at the phone, trying to be angry at his comments, but my scowl turned slowly into a grin.

> I met Frankie Dylan.

Shut up. I don't believe you.

> Truth.

Wait—for real? U have proof?

> He signed my ball.

Whoa. Now that's what I'm talking about! Can I have it?

> No, but I got you some swag. A London Dragons practice penny.

A *penny*? Am I your best friend, or your sister? You can do better than that. I want a signed jersey, and not some knock-off.

I grinned again.

> I'll see what I can do.

You better. So when are the first cuts?

> The end of this week. Four more days.

Seriously—how do you think you're doing?

> I don't know. It's weird. Everyone is so good at their positions, and I'm not even sure where I fit in.

What are you talking about? You're a center forward.

> In Middleton, yeah. But here, I'm not the fastest player, and my shot is kind of weak, and I can't head the ball very well, and I just don't know. There's this guy Diego, he's like the best striker his age in all of Mexico. He's really, *really* good. A born center forward.

Yawn. Just go out there and play. Stop worrying about everyone else.

> Funny. That's what Tig says.

Who?

> This guy I know. He plays for the Dragon FC youth team.

Stop trying to impress me. He probably doesn't even know your name.

> Whatever. I have to go eat dinner. Catch u later?

Maybe, if I'm not grinding Rocket League.

At dinner, I learned the Special for the night was popcorn and a movie. The movie was *Black Panther*, which I had seen twice and loved. I looked forward to chilling with my friends and a bag of buttery popcorn at my side.

When I returned to my room after dinner, digesting the two hamburgers and fries I had eaten, I laid down on my bed to rest my legs. The mattress felt so nice and soft, and I glanced at the clock. 7:10 p.m. I had twenty minutes until the movie started. I was so exhausted I let my eyes close, and hugged the pillow to my chest. *I'll just rest for a second,* I told himself, not wanting to miss a minute of the movie.

The next thing I knew my alarm was going off, and the morning sun was shining through the window.

ENTRY #10

Superheroes and Video Games

I turned to look at the clock. 7:15 a.m.

I had slept almost twelve hours.

"You okay, roomie?" Robbie said. He was already dressed and packing his bag. "I thought you might be dead."

Expecting to feel worse than the day before, I was surprised to find that when I rose out of bed and stood, my legs felt a little stronger and less sore. Not a lot, but a little.

This was a huge relief. I wasn't going to continue on a downward spiral. It might be hard, but if I could hang in there until Sunday, the end of Week One and a free day, I felt that I could make it through.

If I didn't get cut.

"Any idea what today is?" I asked Robbie.

"Last year they did crossing, heading, and throw-ins on Day Four. If it's the same today, we'll probably have lots of set pieces. My coaches made me work on these for months. We practiced plays used by Liverpool, Barcelona, and Bayern Munich."

"Oh yeah? Me too."

"Really?" Robbie said, surprised. "Which ones?"

"The ones they have on FIFA."

Robbie snorted and reached for the door.

For breakfast, I gobbled down a plate stacked with eggs, pancakes, sausages, and blueberries. After washing it all down with a glass of orange juice, I returned to my room to grab my ball and bag, then headed to the field for warmups.

"Where were you last night?" Alejandro asked, as we took our laps around the field.

"I crashed early. Did you like the movie?"

"*Black Panther* is one of my favorites. I've seen it five times."

"You have?" I said, surprised.

"Did you think we've never seen movies in Costa Rica?"

"Kind of."

He laughed and shook his head. "My friends and I take the bus to San José all the time. Mall San Pedro has a huge cinema right by the university. We've seen all the Marvel movies."

"Marvel's okay," Oliver said, who was running behind us with Dayo, "but I prefer DC."

I started to choke. Alejandro patted me on the back, and we exchanged a look of disbelief. "Are you crazy?" I said. "That can't be possible. Maybe you don't have Marvel movies in England."

"I've seen them," Oliver said with a shrug. "I just like DC better. They have all the classics."

"Exactly," I said. "Which is why my parents prefer them."

Alejandro started plucking at his curly black hair. "Are you kidding me? Thor, Hulk, Spidey, Captain America? *Wolverine*? Marvel would totally crush DC."

Oliver threw his hands up. "Crush Superman, the Flash, Batman, and Green Lantern? I don't think so."

"Which one is Silver Surfer?" Dayo asked.

"Marvel," I said. "Why?"

"He is my favorite."

When we saw he wasn't joking, Alejandro and I laughed so hard we started to cry. "Silver Surfer?" Alejandro said. "Who follows him?"

"I love the Fantastic Four."

Javier was jogging close behind and sped up to join the conversation. "When you little boys grow up, I suggest manga and anime. Naruto and Demon Slayer are far superior to this silly Batman, Superman, or X-Men."

"Whatever, dude," I said. "I think your green hair has scrambled your brain."

Even Robbie laughed at that, though my poor roommate looked confused by the conversation, as if he'd never seen a superhero movie.

The argument continued after we finished the run and gathered to stretch with Samantha. "What's all the chatter about?" she asked.

"Marvel versus DC," I said.

"Oh," she said, nodding sagely. "Clearly it's DC. I'm a Storm and Jean Grey fan, but you can't beat Wonder Woman."

She let us continue arguing while we stretched, and was just as knowledgeable about pop culture as the rest of us, which made me like her even more.

For the first half of Day Four, Samantha evaluated our form on headers, throw-ins, and corner kicks. I had never been taught how to do any of these things. I had simply learned as I went or watched the pros and tried to copy them. Who knew throw-ins had actual techniques beyond planting your feet and heaving it as far as you could? Samantha told us the top Premier League teams had coaches who did nothing but teach throw-in technique and strategy.

Compared to everyone else, I was even worse at heading than at shooting. I had always just jumped and tried to hit the ball without bashing in my nose. Samantha taught me all about tightening my neck and stomach and using my core for power.

After the morning session, Samantha lined everyone up behind the penalty box and made us hit the crossbar three times before we left for lunch. We were supposed to use the form we had learned for crosses and corner kicks, but that wasn't working out too well for me. José, Sven, and Robbie had already finished the drill. I didn't want to be last, so I started kicking the ball like I always did on crosses, something between a shot and a pass that seemed natural. I was the next player to hit the cross bar three times.

"Leo!" Samantha said, waving me over as I started to run off the field.

"Yeah?" I said, expecting a high five.

"I'm letting you go," she said, "but your form is terrible. It got you through this drill, but it won't get you invited to join the London Dragons."

She turned back to watch the other players, leaving me to jog off the field, hurt and troubled by her words.

As Robbie had predicted, we spent the afternoon running through set pieces. Samantha discussed the different strategies used by different teams. My head started to spin from all the information. Who knew soccer was this complicated? I tried my best to keep up, but I kept getting lost in the drills, which made Samantha even more annoyed with me.

By the last game, my legs felt like wobbly rubber bands that might snap at any moment. Our opponent was a strong team featuring Brock and José. Brock decided to make my life miserable and mark me the entire time. Whenever he reached the ball first, even if he had a good pass, he held the ball and shielded me off, just to make the point that I couldn't get the ball from him.

When the final whistle blew, I passed by Samantha on my way off the field. "You have to fight through it, Leo," she said quietly, before congratulating the squad on a good practice.

Earlier in the day, Samantha had asked us all to wear one of our London Dragons practice shirts to dinner. She never told us why, but in the cafeteria that evening, Director Hawk informed us that, instead of dinner and a Special, we were going to serve food at an orphanage as ambassadors for the London Dragons.

The coaches shepherded us towards a line of Dragon FC buses waiting outside the Castle. The inside of my bus had fancy leather seats with screens attached, and I wondered if these were the real buses the players used for away games. We all played with our screens and chatted as the buses drove us to an orphanage thirty minutes away. The three-story building was as big as the Castle, though the dreary gray walls and lack of windows made me feel as if I was about to enter a prison instead of a home for children.

Our coaches took us through a side entrance and down a stone hallway that reeked of mildew. When we entered the dining hall, even more basic than my school cafeteria back home, the children broke into a huge cheer, as if we were rock stars. Some of them were older than us, which surprised me. I realized that, to them, we sort of *were* rock stars. I had never felt so popular or important in my life than when those kids stood and cheered wildly as we filed into their humble cafeteria.

The cooks had prepared fish and chips for everyone. We only had to serve the food, which relieved me, because I had no idea how to cook. Chips, I learned, meant French fries in England. What we called potato chips, they called crisps.

The kids in the orphanage waited patiently at their tables while we players went through the line. The cooks handed each of us two plates of fish and chips and garden peas that didn't look anywhere near as inviting as the food in the Castle. I took my two trays and found a seat at one of the long wooden tables, next to a little girl about Ginny's age. Her name tag read Lily. I don't know why I chose her, except that she looked lonely, and it seemed like the right thing to do. When Lily took her tray from me and looked up with a shy smile, I felt gooey inside, and realized that doing something nice for someone made me feel even better than before, when everyone had cheered as we entered the cafeteria.

A light rain greeted me as I headed to the field the next morning. The focus for Day Five was dribbling and ball control. *Finally*, I thought, *a day made for me.*

The session started well. Samantha praised me in front of the group for my juggling skills, and said everyone should strive to become as comfortable as me with their ball.

After that, we dribbled through a mazelike series of cones up and down the field as fast as we could. Samantha made us use both feet, change directions, and turn on a dime. Throughout the drills, José and I had the fastest times in the group, though I usually edged him by a hair.

Next up was a one-on-one drill with Samantha playing goalie. She divided us into two lines, offense and defense, then rolled the ball out to the offense and challenged them to score however they could. She told us to be as creative as possible.

On my first turn, I one-touched her pass from twenty yards out before my defender could set up. It even caught Samantha by surprise. My shot sailed into the upper right corner, just above her outstretched fingers. The players hooted as I trotted off with a smile.

"Very cheeky, Leo," Samantha called out.

I learned a lot about the other players that day. Sven and Kaito didn't do as well in the one on one drill as I thought they would. This was partly because the defenders were so good, and partly because it's always hard to beat someone one on one, especially with no one to fake a pass to.

Because Dayo was so fast, he had success with his principal form of attack: kicking the ball past people and running to it. Samantha made it harder for him by coming out of the box, but he scored a lot of goals. On the other hand, Robbie and Julian both struggled against good defenders, though they and everyone else scored easily on me and Oliver. I tried to implement the defensive skills I had learned but I still wasn't comfortable against this level of talent.

None of the defenders had success on the attack except for Garika, who was fast and had good moves for a center back. His problem was that he could never finish the shot. During one attempt, his shoe came off and flew over the goal. Everyone laughed until Samantha silenced us with a shout, but Garika didn't seem embarrassed as he ran to retrieve his shoe.

José was his usual solid self. He never used flashy moves, but was almost impossible to steal the ball from. He just held on to it patiently, like a master chess player waiting for his opponent to make a mistake. Inevitably, his defender would step the wrong way or leave José a tiny opening to shoot, and the Brazilian would pounce like a tiger and sneak a clever shot past Samantha.

Javier, the French attacking midfielder, had some really sweet moves. Almost as sweet as mine. Like me, he pulled out trick after trick, nutmegging people left and right, flicking the ball above outstretched legs, and spinning around defenders.

Alejandro performed well all day, but only Brock consistently got the better of the forwards. Both Julian and I had trouble with his size, and the English bulldog was just as fast as we were. He tackled *hard*, making everyone think twice about challenging him. I kept expecting Samantha to call a foul or tell him to tone it down, but she never did.

During the afternoon, we played keep away in smaller and smaller spaces, combining ball control with shielding. Samantha introduced us to some new moves that impressed me, including a step-over that left Julian flat on his back when he tried to defend her. I thought I knew how to dribble, but when I watched Samantha go to work, I realized I was still at the bottom of the mountain looking up.

In the scrimmages, my legs felt decent for the first time

all week. I managed to shield off a few players, drawing praise from Samantha, and I scored two goals as well, one of them after I beat Julian off the dribble. Everyone on my team high-fived me except for Brock, who had not bothered to conceal his annoyance with playing on my team.

It was my best day by far, and it got even better when I learned what the evening Special would be. I could barely believe my eyes when I walked into the cafeteria and saw the flyers on the tables.

PlayStation FIFA Tournament

Single Elimination

7:30–10:30

As soon as we saw the flyer, Alejandro and I whooped and fist-bumped each other. A FIFA tournament? Had I died and gone to heaven?

The smack talk began during dinner. Everyone was throwing bombs and roasting everyone else, bragging about how good they were at FIFA. After we finished eating, everyone filed into the indoor practice facility, where the staff had set up thirty-two desks with monitors, PlayStations, and two chairs. I couldn't believe they had that many devices. At the front of the room, an easel and whiteboard were set up with brackets for 256 entrants. This was more players than we had at the camp, and a quick browse of the whiteboard told me the coaches and staff had added their names to the mix. I almost laughed out loud. Adults who wanted to challenge us in video games? Bring it on.

I laughed even harder when I saw that Robbie was my first

opponent. Everyone had to play their roommates first. It was a cruel trick—especially for Robbie.

Coach Tanner gathered everyone together and called for quiet. "Listen up, Dragons! This is a single-elimination tournament. Lose once and you're out. Since we have limited PlayStations, the first three rounds will only be played to half time. After that it's full length games. Feel free to stick around and cheer each other on, because you kids are going to need it. We coaches feel confident that victory shall be ours! Oh, there's one more thing: at the end of the tournament, the winner will face last year's victor for the title of Ultimate Summer Camp FIFA Champion. Last year's winner has held the title three years in a row, and is considered by many to be unbeatable. So good luck to you all, and let the best Dragon win!"

I wondered who the secret champion was as my fingers twitched in anticipation. I could barely wait to get started.

"Do you want to go ahead and concede?" I asked Robbie as we sat down in front of the monitor and grabbed our controllers. "It will save you some embarrassment."

"You're that confident?"

"I'm not going to beat you, roomie. I'm going to destroy you."

"I know you think I never do anything besides practice," Robbie said, "but I play FIFA, too. You might be in for a surprise."

I only smiled.

According to the rules, a coin flip determined who chose the first team. This was a big deal, since the version of FIFA they had was a few years old, back when Barcelona had Messi, and everyone knew Barcelona was the best.

Robbie won the toss. As I expected, he chose Barcelona. I

calmly selected Arsenal, which caused him to laugh. "What're you doing, Leo? You can't beat Barcelona with Arsenal."

I liked to use Arsenal when I was clowning around with weaker players, just to prove I could win without a superteam. I also liked Arsenal because they had one of my favorite players, Bukayo Saka. He's very young and FIFA didn't rate him highly enough in my opinion.

After five seconds, I knew Robbie was a noob. He had trouble completing a pass under the slightest amount of pressure. I scored two goals in the first minute, and another within moments. Robbie frowned and grew very quiet, but I kept pounding him, merciless on the attack.

The halftime score was eighteen to zero. I scored six times with my goalie on a full field run. The devastation was complete.

"Whatever, Leo," Robbie said, fuming as he slammed the controller on the table. "You didn't tell me you were like a pro or something."

"You didn't ask."

What happens when you put a group of ultra-competitive soccer players in a room with a bunch of PlayStations and hold a mass FIFA tournament? Pandemonium, that's what. All over the room, kids and adults were shouting at the screens, pounding the tables in victory, and wailing with the agony of defeat. After the first round, which took half the players out of the tournament, everyone stayed around to cheer on their squads and friends, making the room even noisier.

I dispatched my next two opponents with ease, winning by more than ten goals each time. The tournament was down to thirty-two players, and now we'd be playing full games.

My next opponent was Samantha. It shocked me that she

was still in the tournament. I'd never met anyone over eighteen who could hang with kids. She won the flip and chose Tottenham. I asked her why.

"Harry Kane, natch. He's such a cutie. Get ready to lose, Leo."

I stuck with Arsenal, toyed with her for a while, then blasted a shot from Saka into the corner from thirty yards out.

"Since you're my squad leader and all," I said, "I won't embarrass you."

I kept to my word. The score at halftime was only 2-0. Samantha was pretty good, much better than my first three opponents, but nowhere near my league. I let her score once in the second half, then held the ball as the clock ran out.

"You did great," I said, patting her on the back.

"Leo," she said, her eyes flashing as she bent down to whisper in my ear, "if you ever take it easy on me again, in anything, I'll make you run laps until your legs fall off."

Up next was Diego. I was nervous at first, since Diego was so good at real soccer. I won the flip and chose PSG, just in case. I could score all day with Mbappe and Neymar. Diego chose Piemonte Calcio, which was Juventus in disguise.

A crowd of people gathered behind us to watch. Diego proclaimed he was going to abuse me with Ronaldo, his favorite player.

Diego was very good. Much better than Samantha. I was impressed by his skills and wondered when he found the time to play.

But he wasn't as good as me. Not even close. I showed him no mercy and played as hard as I could until the very end. The final score was 9-1. The crowd behind us cheered at the end of the game. No one wanted Diego to be the best player on the field *and* in the video game. Diego snarled in disgust and walked off without shaking my hand. I threw a few bombs his way to make it worse.

Eight players left. Three games to go. All the coaches and staff had been eliminated. In the quarterfinals, I reverted back to Arsenal to dispatch Alejandro 5-1. After the game, he picked me up in a bear hug and told me I better win the tournament for the Iguanas.

I faced off against Simon, the Canadian center back, in the semis. I had no idea how he had made it that far, because I beat him 7-2 without breaking a sweat. All of the Iguanas were gathered around me now. When I looked up, I saw Hans, my opponent in the finals, walking towards me.

Hans was the largest kid in the camp, even bigger than Charlie. He sat down heavily beside me as cheers broke out for both sides. Hans played for the Monitors, and had a reputation as one of the best center backs his age in the world.

"So it is America versus Germany, *ja*?" Hans said. He won the toss and chose Bayern Munich. "Perhaps you would like to choose an MLS team and represent your country?"

I was reckless, but not *that* reckless. I didn't like his confident smirk, so I chose Arsenal again, to make a point.

"The Gunners?" Hans said with a chuckle. "No forward ranked above ninety against the best goalie in the world?"

"Hans?"

"Ja?"

"Watch and learn."

Competing chants of Iguanas and Monitors arose as the game started. Alejandro massaged my shoulders as if he was my trainer. Hans scored first, earning a penalty kick when David Luiz fouled Lewandowski. Hans was right, my defense was going to have a hard time against Bayern's smooth attack. Still, as the game wore on, I figured out his style of play, and managed to adjust. He had the better players, but I knew the game so well I was able to pass the ball around too fast for him to keep up.

I won the game 4-1. Graceful in defeat, Hans solemnly shook my hand as a roar of victory rose up behind us. I slapped hands with my friends and joined in the *Iguanas* chant as Coach Tanner wrote my name at the top of the board and called for quiet.

"Congratulations, Leo. We're all impressed and left wondering just how many hours of FIFA you play a day. But an even greater challenge awaits. Are you ready to face last year's winner—the last *three* years' winner—in your quest to become Ultimate Summer Camp FIFA Champion?"

Curious, all the players quieted, including myself, as the coaches and adults in the room began clapping in tune. Did Director Hawk or one of the other coaches have a hidden talent? A son or daughter they brought in as a ringer?

My eyebrows rose when Tig strolled into the room like a Roman gladiator, thrusting a FIFA controller above his head as the adults went wild and chanted his name. Tig was wearing ripped jeans, flip flops, and a PlayStation T-shirt that read Born to Play.

Of course it was him.

A huge grin creased Tig's face as he joined me by a monitor in the center of the room for the final game. "I like you, Boss, but I can't show you any mercy tonight."

"It's hard to show mercy when you're losing," I said.

The coin toss fell to Tig. He chose Man City. "Good luck stealing the ball from David Silva and de Bruyne," he said. "I'm going to control the midfield and wear you down."

I hesitated, sensing Tig would not be as easy as my other opponents. I gave in and chose Barcelona.

It was a tough battle. Tig was the real deal. Although the coaches and adults, especially Samantha, made a lot of noise, they were drowned by all the players, who had united together to pull for me. It lent my tired fingers a burst of adrenaline. This was my tenth game in a row, and Tig's first of the night. How was that fair? No wonder he had held on to the title.

The halftime score was 3-3. As Tig had promised, he controlled the midfield and scored with long-range bombs and crosses. I, on the other hand, turned my forwards into dribbling machines, using short passes and special moves to find the goal.

One minute to go in game time. The score was still tied, 5-5. The room was so loud I couldn't hear the announcer. Both Tig and I were on our feet, hunched over our controllers, giving it everything we had. We had wowed the crowd with skill moves like the advanced rainbow, triple elastico, and sombrero flick. Near the end of the game, Tig's goalie made an incredible save, and everyone thought it was going to overtime—right before I intercepted the outlet pass at half field with Messi.

Man City had some of the best midfielders in the world—but I had Lionel Messi. I drove straight for the goal, beat every defender Tig threw at me, cut to the right of the goalie at the last second, and slipped the ball into the corner.

Game over.

As the players went wild, Tig stared at the screen in disbelief, then threw an arm around my shoulders. "I haven't lost at FIFA in three years."

"Sorry to break the streak."

"Hey, at least we're keeping the title across the pond. Now go apply yourself on the field like that, and maybe you'll join me on the team one day."

Tig's parting comment and my two goals in the scrimmages that day had sent me soaring towards the moon, brimming with confidence. But my performance on the final day before the cuts sent me crashing back to Earth.

Day Six was a catch-all. Volleys and half-volleys, complicated set plays, advanced passing and trapping, a whole assortment of skills. Samantha ran us through a series of drills, some of them repeats from earlier in the week, and took so many notes I thought her pen might run dry. While my legs felt even better than the day before, I was lost in some of the drills, and I never stood out.

The looming cuts had me on edge. During the scrimmage, I scored one goal and had an assist, but when we played Brock's team, he owned me on defense again. I thought he might have some respect for me after my FIFA victory, but he targeted me even more. He pushed me in the back and pulled on my jersey when Samantha wasn't looking, talking trash the entire time, telling me I wasn't good enough to make the cut. I went right back at him, but too often ended up on the ground after another dirty play.

When the final whistle blew, signaling the end of the week,

Alejandro caught up with me and leaned on my shoulder, breathing hard. "Nice work, Leo."

"You too."

"I guess we'll discover our fate tomorrow."

"I think you're in for sure."

His face brightened at the compliment, which I had meant, but I walked off the field with the troubling feeling that I hadn't performed at my best. My tired legs had given me trouble all week, I had let a bully push me around, and I was so afraid of failure I had failed to play with abandon and take risks on the field.

Despite a few bright spots, I had my doubts as to whether I would get another chance to prove myself.

Look Kids, Big Ben!

Eager and nervous to learn my fate, my stomach fluttering like a bird had gotten loose inside it, I walked slowly to the cafeteria for breakfast on Sunday. I didn't want this magical ride to be over, I didn't want to disappoint my friends, I didn't want to tell my dad we had missed out on fifty thousand dollars because I wasn't good enough to make the team. I knew I was being unreasonable, and acting more like Robbie than myself, but I couldn't help it. I had never wanted anything so much in my life.

The cafeteria was quieter than I had ever seen it. My friends and I barely talked as we ate our breakfast. To make matters worse, Coach Tanner announced the first cuts would not be revealed until the evening. Instead the summer camp staff had planned a field trip to central London, and they wanted everyone to enjoy the excursion. Some of the kids sighed in relief at the delay. I just wanted to get it over with.

Today was a free day, so the London trip was not mandatory. I wanted to stay in my room and rest my tired legs. But my friends seemed excited about the field trip, and I kept hearing Aunt Janice's words in the back of my head.

Try to see as much of London as you can. Promise me you'll try.

If I went to the city, at least I could keep my promise to my aunt.

After breakfast, we all piled into the plush Dragon FC buses again. I sat next to Alejandro and across the aisle from Kaito and Oliver. A professional guide at the front of the bus began describing the history of the city. I had to strain to understand his accent.

For the first part of the trip, we left our little neighborhood and traveled down a highway choked with traffic. I ignored the scenery and the guide and cut up with my friends. But as we entered the heart of the city, and saw more and more buildings and people crowded together, the laughter and conversations on the bus faded away. My dad was right, this city was far bigger than Cincinnati or Detroit. It was so big I had trouble wrapping my mind around it.

Everyone crowded to the windows to watch the city unfold. I saw block after block full of people, street markets, huge stone buildings, parks, cathedrals, museums, landmarks, a whole world unlike anything I had ever seen.

The guide got my attention when we passed the Tower of London, a castle on the bank of the River Thames which housed the crown jewels, as well as a dungeon where they used to torture political prisoners. Dungeons? Treasure? An actual castle in the middle of the city? Now we were talking.

We crossed the river Thames on a fancy bridge. The guide kept pointing out landmarks, such as St. Paul's Cathedral and the Royal Opera House, which I knew my aunt would love. She and my mom used to visit Cincinnati to see the opera, but thankfully, my mom loved all kinds of good music and not just classical, which I found as boring as the news.

I saw a sign for Liverpool and wondered if the team played nearby. The London streets turned narrower and curvier as we drove into the West End. My jaw fell open when we passed through Piccadilly Circus, which wasn't a circus at all, unless you count the hordes of people, the dizzying whirlwind of traffic in the roundabout, and the blinking neon signs advertising clothes, movies, cell phones, and anything else you could imagine.

Our bus parked nearby, and we rushed outside to explore. I had thought Javier's green hair and earrings were strange, but in Leicester Square and Piccadilly, the rest of us stood out more than he did.

To my surprise—I never thought buildings would interest me—I couldn't stop staring at the golden spires of Parliament, which looked like a fairy tale and dwarfed any structure I had ever seen. My favorite sight of all was Big Ben, a clock tower attached to Parliament that rose above the city like a giant candle. I didn't understand it. Why did they need a clock that big? Maybe they had built it simply because it looked nice.

Which, I thought, was a pretty good reason.

We walked around in a daze, ignoring the guide as we chatted and laughed with each other. After lunch in Covent Garden, we licked ice cream cones as we watched a street performer on stilts perform magic tricks for the crowd.

We popped into the British Museum, which seemed a little dull compared to the streets of London—until we entered the Egypt exhibit and saw real-life mummies. Their shriveled flesh wrapped in bandages was even spookier than in the movies.

The highlight of the day was the London Eye, a Ferris wheel so enormous we could see the entire city from the top of it.

Darkness had fallen by the time we piled into the buses for the return journey. I didn't want the day to end and had almost forgotten that, when we returned, we would learn whether we made the first cut. As the bus left Central London, I turned to stare at the lights of the city for as long as I could, realizing I would never look at life in the same way again.

When we pulled into the parking lot of the Castle, Coach Tanner announced that we would find envelopes in our rooms, letting us know if we had survived the first week.

"Good luck," I said to Alejandro and the others, but even my Costa Rican friend's smile seemed forced.

"I can't wait until the morning to find out who made it," Oliver said. "That's torture. Text me as soon as you know." He was bouncing on the balls of his feet, his freckled face bright with anticipation.

As we parted, I felt almost as much worry for my friends as I did for myself. It would be hard not to see a single one of them around anymore, especially Alejandro.

When I entered the room, Robbie was sitting on his bed with an open envelope and a big smile on his face. I didn't need to ask if he had made the cut. "Yours is on the desk," he said. "They were under the door when I came in. Listen, I'm going to the break room to meet some of the guys. Come down if you want."

"Sure. Okay."

"Hey Leo . . . good luck."

"Thanks."

As soon as he left the room, I hurried to the desk and picked up the sealed envelope with my name on it. I tore open the envelope and took out a slip of white paper. With trembling hands, I read the handwritten message from our squad leader.

Congratulations Leo! You made the First Cut.

Samantha

I sat on my bed and held the piece of paper in my hands for a very long time. I was legit. Philip Niles wasn't tricking me, or desperate to fill a roster spot. I might have a long way to go, and I had no idea how to convince the coaches I was a better striker than Diego, but I had made the first cut.

Deep breaths, Leo. *One day at a time.*

I lay on my back on my bed, exhausted from the long day in London, not to mention the rest of the week. Before I knew it, my eyes had closed, and I fell asleep wondering what challenges Week Two would bring.

War Games

After a solid night's sleep, I was the first player from my squad to arrive on the field. My legs felt almost back to normal. I took a moment to breathe in the crisp air and appreciate my surroundings.

The smell of chalk dust and freshly cut grass.

A meadow of emerald-green fields laid out like a carpet in front of the Castle, just waiting to be played on.

Morning dew on my fingers as I bent down to adjust my shin guards and tighten my cleats.

On the next field over, I noticed Diego and Hans taking warmup shots on Charlie, the Australian goalie. None of the other players had made it to the fields yet. I flicked the ball in the air and began to juggle, practicing some of my favorite tricks and trying a few new ones. I felt more like myself than I had since I stepped off the plane.

"You're up early, Leo."

I looked up to see Samantha setting her bag and clipboard on the sideline. Along with her shorts and long-sleeved Juventus shirt, she had on teal-and-white shoes with orange cleats. The British called soccer cleats *boots*, which I thought was funny. My dad wore boots, not soccer players.

Samantha clapped and opened her hands. I lifted the ball to her, and we began juggling. "Listen," she said, "I'm glad you're here, because there's something I wanted to ask you."

"There is?" I said. "What?"

She hesitated. "I don't want you to take this the wrong way, but the decision to keep you was a close one."

I trapped the ball with my thigh and volleyed it back to her, trying not to show my disappointment. "Why shouldn't I take that the wrong way?"

"Because I believe you're much better than you've shown so far."

I wasn't sure what to say in response to that. I'd been trying my hardest.

She continued, "But my feeling won't get you to the World Cup. I have to convince the other coaches. I, too, need to see improvement. Here's the thing, Leo: you're one of a handful of kids at the whole camp who haven't received advanced training in their home country. You have incredible instincts, but you lack basic skills."

"I do?"

"To make it through the next few weeks, I think you need a renewed commitment. I love your personality, and the way you play the game, but you have to buckle down. Tig and I have talked about this, and we'd both like to help you. What do you think about meeting us for an extra hour at night? It's my job to bring out the best in my squad and, while everyone is welcome, I think you and Garika would benefit the most."

Still juggling, she glanced over as more kids started filing onto the field. "Let me know by the end of practice. Tig and I have plans later tonight, so we'd have to start during the pizza party. Oops! That's the Special tonight. I wasn't supposed to let that slip. Mum's the word, okay?"

"I don't need to think about it," I said. "I'm in."

She smiled. "Great! We'll see you at 7:30."

Before I could thank her, or ask how to find her and Tig later that night, Alejandro ran over to pick me up in a bear hug. "Leo! I thought you were cut for sure! I mean, I didn't think you should have been, but I didn't hear from you . . . why didn't you text anyone?"

"Oh," I said, still trying to process what Samantha had told me. "Sorry about that. I just didn't want to be disappointed—wait! You're still here. That means you didn't get cut!"

His face split into a wide grin. We whooped and celebrated as more players arrived. I scanned the crowd and saw Oliver, Javier, Dayo, Garika, and of course Sven and José. Unfortunately, I saw Brock and Julian also.

With a sigh of relief that my friends had made the cut, I noticed they all looked as happy and as confident as I felt, ready to take on the world.

Or as confident as I had felt before Samantha dropped her bombshell. I tried to put her words out of my mind and focus on the positive, but I kept hearing *the decision to keep you was a close one.*

"Wait," I said to Alejandro. "Where's Kaito?"

Alejandro pressed his lips together and shook his head.

"Oh no," I said. "But he was *good.*"

"Everyone here is good," Alejandro said. "Haven't you noticed? People are talking about how the forwards are especially strong this year. I mean, just in our squad, there's Sven and Dayo and you, and of course you all have to deal with Diego . . ."

Samantha called us over. My step was heavy as I thought about Kaito's slick moves and the wicked bend on his shot. I wondered why they had cut him so early.

"Gather in, everyone," Samantha said, waving us closer. "First of all, congratulations for making the cut. I know we're all sad for our friends who are going home early. But losing and not making the team is part of life. There will always be someone better than you, or a team you don't get invited to join. All you can do is try your hardest so you can live without regret, both on and off the field."

"How many players were cut?" Robbie asked.

Samantha eyed him for a long moment, as if annoyed. "Twelve from this squad," she said, "and fifty field players in total. Another fifty will go home at the end of this week, and another sixty after Week Three. That will leave one full team from each squad for the World Cup. At the end of the tournament, the coaches will select ten field players and at least one goalie to join the Academy."

We knew this already, but Samantha looked slowly around the group, letting her words sink in.

She clapped her hands. "Now. Put that out of your mind, and let's talk about Week Two. Each day we'll start out with some basic drills, building on what we've learned. After that, we'll work in some more complex maneuvers and simulations the Dragons coaching squad has developed for the Academy. We call them war games. I think you'll find them challenging and fun. As before, we'll end the day with a few scrimmages. Any questions?"

José held up a hand. "Do we get a FIFA rematch? I want to take Leo down."

Samantha smiled. "I'll see if I can requisition a PlayStation for the break room."

We all clapped at that, restoring the positive mood.

As promised, we began with some of the same drills from Week One, though instead of focusing on one particular skill we ran through them all before the morning break.

After everyone had some water, the war games began. During the break, Samantha had set up four cones ten yards apart, forming a square. She divided the players into four groups and placed each group in a line behind one of the cones. Then she asked Javier to stand in the middle of the square with his ball.

"When I blow my whistle," she said, holding a stopwatch in her hand, "the front person in each line—all four at the same time—will try to take the ball from Javier. That's four on one. Javier, your job is to last as long as you can, however you can. Let's see those moves."

Javier put a foot on his ball and ran a hand through his green hair. When the whistle blew, four players sprinted right at him. Javier spun away from the first player who arrived, but the second attacker kicked the ball out of the circle before Javier could recover.

"Two seconds," Samantha called out.

"But what is it I am supposed to do?" Javier complained, flinging his hands in the air.

"Next," Samantha said. "José, you're in the middle."

As the players on the four corners streamed towards the center of the square, the talented Brazilian midfielder faked a move to the right before they arrived, drawing two people away from the ball. Then José cut hard to the left, beat one player, and managed to last a few seconds before the other players converged.

"Good," Samantha said. "Five seconds."

José's record stood for most of the first round, until Brock got in the middle and managed to shield all four players by hovering over the ball and spinning around it. He also roared at them like an ogre, causing them to think twice before they moved him off the ball.

"Six seconds," Samantha said when someone poked the ball away. "Way to be strong, Brock."

When my turn came, I waited calmly until the attackers converged, and then, right when they arrived, I flicked the ball high over their legs and into one of the corners. Before they could recover, I sprinted to the ball, held it against the cone with my toe, and shielded the ball from the first player who ran over. Though I was trapped in the corner, only one player could knock me off the ball at one time. Or so I thought until Robbie ran around the cone and kicked the ball away from the other side.

"Hey," I said. "He was out of bounds!"

"Everything except a foul is legal," Samantha said with a smile. "But Leo won the first round. Eight seconds!"

On the second run, the players got more inventive, but so did the attackers. Shielding seemed to be the key, but no one could hold off four players at once. My record held for the whole round. For the third and final round, Samantha mixed it up by kicking the ball out at various spots. This made it a race to the ball, and harder to evade the first attacker, but if you could beat that first person, you bought yourself some time. José and Javier both beat my record by a second by darting into free space and shielding off two attackers until the rest arrived.

"Okay Leo," Samantha said, "you're up last. Can you re-take the crown?"

I looked up to see who my attackers would be. Brock, Julian, Garika, and one other player. *Great. Three of the best defenders in the squad.*

Samantha kicked the ball out between me and Julian. I sprinted over and arrived just before him. I stepped over the ball, freezing him, but instead of trying to dribble, I did a quick rainbow, flicking the ball into the air. When it came back down, I volleyed the ball as high as I could.

Everyone froze, unsure what to do. The ball seemed to linger in the air forever. When it finally descended, I concentrated and kicked it again, higher this time. Even I was surprised when the path of the ball stayed true and didn't sail off into one of the other fields. This time, when the ball came back down, Brock shielded me off while Julian trapped the ball and kicked it away.

"Twelve seconds," Samantha said, shaking her head but unable to hide the grin that had crept onto her face. "Leo has a new camp record."

We did variations on that drill until lunch, adding in more people in the center and more attackers from the outside. In the afternoon, Samantha split us into two teams for a scrimmage, nineteen players per team. She also brought over two goalies. I was excited at the thought of a full team scrimmage, and assumed she would pick a starting ten on both sides, and use the rest as subs.

Instead she told us all to take the field at the same time and organize ourselves however we wished. What? Nineteen players per side? I drifted towards the center forward spot, along with Dayo and two others. Before we had figured out how to use so many players, Samantha kicked a ball onto the field—and then she kicked another.

"Two balls!" she called out. "No corners. Everything that crosses the end line is a goal kick. Same for a goal—the keepers will throw the ball out to keep the game moving. Good luck, and score however you can! The losing team runs wind sprints!"

As soon as the game started, chaos reigned. Everyone was doubled up on their positions, and the fact that two balls were in play threw everyone off balance. No one knew which ball to follow or how to organize.

"What is this crap?" Robbie said as he ran by me to chase a ball. He was on my team, playing in the midfield with Javier and six other players. To his credit, Robbie tried to take charge and organize us, but no one listened.

It was kind of fun, running around the field like chickens with our heads cut off, but it was also frustrating. The Beautiful Game had turned into an ugly free-for-all that barely resembled soccer. By the time Samantha blew the whistle for a water break, each side had managed to score two goals, mainly when the keepers were distracted by another ball zooming at them.

"This is mad," Oliver said, as we held our sides to catch our breath from running all over the field. "What's Samantha trying to prove?"

"She's trying to weed us out, obviously," Robbie said. "See who rises to the top, even with thirty-eight players on the field."

"I suppose you're right," Sven said, holding his water bottle over his head so he could dump water on his blond hair to cool off. "Though I don't see what this has to do with football."

It was the hottest day so far, although the temperature and humidity did not approach the sweltering summer days back home. As I wiped sweat off my face with my shirt, everyone argued back and forth about strategy. Some players thought we should overload the offense, or the defense, or the midfield. I called everyone together as I walked over to Koffi, our goalie for the scrimmage. "I have an idea," I said.

As Samantha blew the whistle to start the game, Robbie tossed his water bottle to the side. "Got to go."

"Just kick the ball down the field," Dayo said, "and let me run to it."

"Wait," I said. "This is quick, and Dayo has the right idea. Whoever gets the ball next—er, either one of the balls—I want you to kick it back to Koffi. Then do the same with the next ball. There's no rule against the keeper having both balls, right?"

"Leo," Robbie said, "that's ridiculous. What are you trying to do?"

I turned to Koffi. "I want you to kick one ball out of bounds as far as you can, then kick the second ball down the right side of the field. Then I want every single field player besides Garika and Alejandro to sprint to the right. We'll overload that side of the field before they figure out what's going on."

Samantha blew the whistle again. "Now, Iguanas!"

"Okay?" I said as I jogged onto the field.

Although Robbie muttered that my idea was ridiculous, the players agreed to try it out. Right after kickoff, Sven took the ball and passed it back to Alejandro. Half the opposing team chased the ball, but Alejandro passed it back to Koffi.

The Ivorian goalie held the ball at his feet and took his time, surveying the field, waiting for the other ball.

I stole a pass near midfield and kicked the ball all the way back to Alejandro again. When he passed the second ball to Koffi, our keeper kicked it straight out of bounds as everyone on our team except Garika and Alejandro crept towards the right side.

Tired of waiting around, the other team's forwards surged towards Koffi. He toed the ball forward, then kicked it far down the right side. Since our team knew exactly where it was going, we sent nearly all of our players sprinting down the right flank.

Our plan wouldn't work if the other team took possession at midfield. In fact, we would all be out of position, and the plan would fail spectacularly. Knowing this, I fought hard to reach the ball and managed to trap it beneath my foot. I didn't even look up. Instead I turned and kicked the ball further down the right side, towards the corner flag.

When I did raise my head, I saw Dayo reach the ball first, with nine or so of our players trailing him. The defenders near the ball were overwhelmed. Our team used short passes to get around them and approach the goal. Imagine a full soccer team in the penalty box, bearing down on the goalie!

Dayo received the ball again near the penalty spot, and blasted the ball in the corner. Everyone whooped and clapped me on the back as we raced back to defend our goal. The other team cried foul, but Samantha shook her head and smiled.

The trick didn't work a second time, and both teams started overloading their defense to clog the penalty box, making it very hard to score. That goal after the water break turned out to be the last one of the day. We won 2-1. My teammates congratulated me as we drank water and watched the other team struggle through their wind sprints. After we assembled again, Samantha announced that instead of dinner and a Special Activity, there would be a pizza party at 7:30.

"Your luck's going to run out one day," Robbie said as we walked off the field.

"If you prefer to run sprints," I said, "why didn't you join the other team?"

Later that evening, instead of heading down to the pizza party, I sat on my bed dressed to play. For dinner I had gone down to the break room to scrounge for some food. Normally I wouldn't complain about potato chips and chocolate chip granola bars, but I loved pizza more than anything. I felt sorry for myself, wondering if I really needed extra time to practice, or if it would make a difference. All I wanted was to sink my teeth into a gooey slice of pepperoni pizza, talk to my friends, play a few video games, and go to bed.

I heard a knock at my door.

For a moment I ignored it, sitting in bed with my hands on my knees, dreaming of a plate full of pizza and a soft drink to wash it down. My legs were tired. My blisters had turned white and started to peel.

The knock came again, more loudly this time. "Psst—hey Boss," I heard Tig say. "You ready to roll?"

Night School

When I opened the door, I saw Tig standing in the hallway in his Adidas slides, a pair of lime green linen shorts, and a button down shirt with sleeves rolled to the elbows. Although he still had his leather necklace, earrings, and wrist bands, he looked more dressed up than I had ever seen him.

"Were you asleep or something, Boss?"

"No, I just . . . it took me a second."

"You ready? Grab your ball and let's go. Sam and I only have an hour."

I got my ball and followed him into the hall. "Do you two have a date tonight?"

He winked at me. "We're meeting some friends in the city."

"How old is Samantha?"

"Twenty-one."

"And she's already played for Juventus? In Serie A?"

Tig took the stairs two at a time. "She got called up at eighteen. A real prodigy before she got injured. She was one of the best players in America, on track to start for the national team."

"She got injured? That's why she wears the knee brace?"

"Yeah. Tore her PCL in practice and was never the same."

"PCL? What's that?"

"The ligament in the back of the knee. Like a torn ACL, only worse. Poor girl. I can't even imagine . . . ."

We were both quiet for a moment, sharing Samantha's pain. To an athlete in their prime, nothing could be worse than a career-ending injury. When we reached the foyer, Tig took me out the back door and into the fading daylight. I assumed he was headed to the indoor facility, but instead he led me down a stone path that circled around the building, to yet another outdoor soccer field, this one behind the Castle and out of view. There were no bleachers, but the field was lined and surrounded by lights.

"What's this?" I said.

"Just another training pitch. They don't advertise it, but you can play here all night if you want."

"Really?"

"Boss, as long as you're playing football, the coaches will never say a word." He took the ball from me and kicked it behind his leg onto the field.

"Sam should be here any minute. She's bringing Garika, too."

Like me, the Zimbabwean defender had no formal training, and was a raw talent in need of some coaching. As we walked onto the field, I said, "Tig?"

"Yeah?"

"Thanks."

"For what?"

"I know you didn't have to come out here."

He stopped in surprise. "You think I'm doing this for you? Have you seen the legs on my girl? I mean, c'mon kid . . ." He laughed and slapped me on the back. "I'm just joshing you. Yeah, she asked me to help out, and I'm not sure about Garika because I haven't seen him that much, but I agree with her about you. Like I said, you've got real talent. Listen, Leo, all the pros have world-class technique. But so do thousands of other really great players. What sets the best apart is fitness, athleticism, the proper mindset, and game intelligence. You have to *want it*, Leo, and you have to put in the time." He wagged a finger. "Game intelligence is a little different. Part of it, sure, is developing a feel for the game after playing for a long time. I'm talking thousands of hours on the pitch, maybe tens of thousands. You know those superstars Brazil is always producing? Most of them never played organized football as kids. They just played with their friends, every day, as hard as they could. And believe me, in the favelas, it isn't easy to win on the playground. The other half of game intelligence is pure instinct. You don't know how to shoot the ball properly, Leo, but you've got some of the best natural reactions in the camp. You make things happen. You're *creative*. You can't teach that. I'll take you over a kid with perfect technique and no imagination any day of the week."

As I thought about what he said, Samantha and Garika walked onto the field. The Zimbabwean was grinning and bouncing on his toes as he always did. I wondered if he drank a lot of British tea.

Samantha was dressed in a sleeveless green top and a skirt with a slit on her thigh that made her toned legs seem even longer than usual. At first, I didn't realize why she looked so different, and then I noticed she was wearing makeup. I stared at her with my mouth open, startled by how beautiful she was, before I realized what I was doing and looked away.

"Hi Leo," she said. "Glad you could make it."

"Hey," I said, and fist-bumped Garika. I wondered if any

of our friends knew about this training session. I had been too embarrassed to mention it.

"Before we get started," Samantha said, setting down a small black handbag and a duffel bag, "Tig and I have something for Garika."

Curious, I edged forward to get a better look as she opened the bag. "What shoe size are you?" she asked him. "Forty? Forty-one?"

"Forty," Garika said. "Why?"

She pulled out a pair of red and black cleats that barely looked used. "Try these," she said, tossing them to him.

The Zimbabwean caught the shoes and held them gingerly in his hands, as if they were made of glass. "What are these?"

"Shoes," she said with a smile. "Some of the Dragons buy new boots every year, especially if there's a jersey change. We have a whole box of old ones, and give them away at the end of the year. Tig and I got permission to raid the youth teams' stash. Go ahead, see if they fit."

Garika looked dazed by the offer. After thanking her profusely, he bent down to yank off his cleats, which looked even more worn after a week of summer camp. On one of the sides, the bottom had separated completely from the top, and I could see his foot poking through.

As Samantha and Tig stepped away to talk in private, smiling and holding hands, I sat in the grass with Garika as he loosened his cleats. "I'm glad you're out here, hey?" he said. "So I am not the only charity case."

"Ha. Same here. I guess we don't have the right training."

"But aren't you American? Where are you from? New York? Los Angeles?"

"Middleton, Ohio."

"Where is that?"

"Exactly."

Garika laughed. "I'm from Harare, the capital. It's a big city, yeah, but not like London."

For some reason, I had thought Garika was from some tiny village with no electricity or running water. I guess we both had made faulty assumptions.

"We weren't always poor," he said as he tightened his laces. "Both my parents are doctors."

"*Doctors?*" I said in disbelief. "But aren't all doctors, like, rich? Even in Zimbabwe?"

"Not anymore," he said. "Things are not good right now. But come," he said, hopping to his feet and reaching out a hand to pull me up. "Let's learn this game we apparently do not know how to play."

"How do they feel?" I said.

He lifted his feet one at a time and flexed his toes, his grin expanding. "Like pure gold." He gave Tig and Samantha a thumbs up.

Samantha kicked off her heels, and Tig stepped out of his slides. "Follow us," she said.

"You're playing barefoot?" I said. "What if we step on you?"

Tig chuckled. "We're not playing. *You* are."

When we arrived at the nearest goal, Samantha asked Garika to be the keeper as she placed the ball on the penalty spot. "As I've said, both of you lack some basic skills which the other players have. I can't take time during the day to teach you. It's not fair to the others. Today we'll work on shooting, which as a striker, Leo, you desperately need. And Garika, well," she rolled her eyes, "it'd be nice if you hit the goal once in a while."

We all laughed as she stepped back and told us to watch Tig's form as he took a shot. Garika didn't even have time to move as Tig cannoned the ball barefoot into the side netting.

"What did you see, Leo?" Samantha asked.

"Uh, a goal?"

"Such a quick wit. What else?"

"I don't know."

"You shoot. Garika, step out of the goal and watch him."

I did as she asked. My shot was nice and hard, but nowhere near as powerful as Tig's.

"Leo lands on the other foot," Garika said suddenly. "Tig lands on the same one he shoots with."

"Very good," Samantha said. "Tig also points his toe down, brings his shooting knee up, plants his off foot for direction, and uses his core for power. Watch again, Leo."

I did, and she was right. Tig did all of those things, time and again, with perfect form each time.

"Now you try," she said.

For the next hour, Garika and I shot penalty kicks over and over on each other, while Tig and Samantha corrected our form. We only had two balls, so we had to chase a ball every time we missed. I realized that, for all of my life, I had just been running up to the ball and kicking it. No one had ever taught me how to shoot with proper form. I had no idea so many mechanics were in play. It was awkward to shoot the way they taught me, even after practicing over and over. I supposed it would take a while to learn, and I had my doubts whether it would improve my game in time to make a difference. I voiced my concern, and Samantha agreed. "You're probably right," she said, "if you don't practice enough."

The sun had sunk far enough below the tops of the trees surrounding the field that it was getting hard to see. "We should bolt," Tig said to Samantha.

She checked her watch and agreed. "We'll turn the lights on for you," she said to me and Garika. "Just turn them off whenever you leave. The switch is by the pole next to the stairs."

Garika and I looked at each other. "How long can we stay?" I asked.

"As long as you want."

After Samantha and Tig left, Garika and I stayed for hours, practicing more penalty kicks and then just having fun, juggling and playing one on one. It was sweet to be under the lights, and we started crossing corners to each other, pretending it was the last few seconds of a Premier League final and we had one chance to score a goal.

By the time we left, all the lights in the Castle had winked off, and the only sound we could hear, besides our labored breathing, was the chirp of crickets in the woods.

When I returned to my room and eased the door open, Robbie turned over in his sleep and mumbled something I couldn't understand. I crept past him and checked the time. Twelve-thirty. Oops. Maybe Garika and I should have left earlier.

On my bed, I found a box of pizza with a note.

Where were you tonight? I saved you some food.

Alejandro

When I opened the box, I found it full of pepperoni pizza. Except for a missing slice, Alejandro had scored a whole pie! I had almost forgotten how hungry I was, and wished I knew Garika's room number.

I didn't bother taking the pizza downstairs to warm it up. Instead I sat right there on my bed and ate the entire thing. After a burp, I set the box on the floor beside me, drank a glass of water, then collapsed on my back and went to sleep.

Week Two and the Fantastic Four

The next morning, I had a hard time waking up, and my legs ached again. I groaned as I pushed out of bed and stumbled to the bathroom. When I checked the time, I realized I had missed breakfast. How could I play until lunch without fuel?

After dressing as fast as I could, I threw my gear together and raced downstairs. I arrived in the dining hall while the staff was still cleaning up, and managed to snag an egg biscuit and an orange juice. By the time I laced up my cleats and made it to the field, my squad was on the field stretching.

Samantha glared at me as I ran over. "You're late."

"Sorry. It won't happen again."

"I know it won't. Three unexcused tardies and you get a plane ticket home."

Brock and some of the others snickered.

When I looked up at Samantha, I didn't see a trace of sympathy in her eyes, and I realized how serious she was. I wasn't getting any special treatment from her. In fact, since she was helping me at night, I realized she was going to hold me to a higher standard than everyone else. All at once, I realized I had let her down, and felt guilty. "I'm really sorry," I said again, in a quiet voice.

"This isn't a rec league, Leo. This is the London Dragons Academy summer camp. Most kids would give anything to be here. It's an incredible honor and should never be taken for granted. That goes for all of you," she said in a hard voice as she glanced around the group.

Every player in the squad, even Garika, was staring at me. I had never wanted to disappear under a rock so badly in my life. In the past, I would have shrugged off a tardy at school, not to mention my soccer team. No one cared if you were late for practice in the YMCA League. But I had just let someone down I cared about, and who was trying to help me. Not only that, I had jeopardized my dreams for the future.

My legs felt leaden during the morning session. This frustrated me, since I had just started to feel like myself again. In one of the afternoon drills, I walked back to the line instead of running. I didn't think Samantha was watching, but she was, and she yelled at me. Again I had let her down. By the time the day ended, I doubted she would ever want to talk to me again, not to mention train me at night.

Before she left the field, she walked over to where I was sitting by myself, struggling to take off my cleats. My thighs were on the verge of cramping, and the soles of my feet hurt to the touch.

"Are we on tonight, Leo? Or do you need some time off?"

Though I didn't hear any anger in her voice, it wasn't warm and friendly, either. It was all business, the kind of voice adults use when they're disappointed with you. Samantha's bag was slung over her shoulder, and she looked impatient, as if she had somewhere to be.

"I'll be there," I said. "I'm sorry again about today."

"You don't have to apologize. You won't hurt my feelings. But you do have to decide whether this is truly something you want."

One of the other coaches called out to her. She shrugged her bag higher on her shoulder and walked off to join him.

The Special that night was a dodgeball tournament in the indoor practice facility. Coaches versus players. I loved dodgeball, and the thought of trying to tag Coach Tanner with a bouncy rubber ball sounded like so much fun. But I knew I had to choose between the Special and meeting Samantha and Tig for a night session. I only had enough juice in my legs for one or the other.

It might sound silly, but I almost chose dodgeball. I was on the verge of going to the Special and telling Samantha I didn't want to continue the night sessions. If I skipped dodgeball, wouldn't I be just like Robbie, choosing hard work over fun?

All of my life, I had taken the easy road. To be honest, I was proud of that fact. I liked to cut up and have as much fun as possible.

But this was different. Joining the Academy was something I truly, desperately wanted—and I realized that to have a chance at reaching my goals, I had to change my ways. For some reason, I thought of my pet lizard, and what he would have said. Messi would think I was stupid for even debating the decision. He would tell me to stop complaining and go get what I wanted. All of it. That's what a real lizard does.

With a deep breath, instead of heading to the gym for dodgeball, I laid on my bed listening to music until it was time to meet Samantha. I didn't have to like it, or brag about how disciplined I was. I made a vow, right then and there, to put in as much time as it took to increase my skills and be the best player I could be—but also never to let it change me. I didn't have to be Robbie, I didn't *want* to be Robbie, and I was never going to stop having as much fun as possible.

But I could admit that maybe the old Leo needed a few tweaks to achieve his dreams.

Okay, I could hear Messi saying as he strutted around the cage. *I guess I can live with that.*

At the night session, neither Samantha nor Tig said a word about my late arrival to practice or my lazy performance. We focused on heading, and Samantha broke down the basic form. She taught me where to position my feet, how to tighten my neck and core before I made contact with the ball, and where to direct the ball on goal.

The night after that, she and Tig led us through the basic defensive stances, and how to read an attacker's intentions by watching his body language. Both Garika and I listened intently. I learned more in that hour about how the mind of a defender works than I had during all my years of playing soccer put together.

Garika and I continued to stay and practice long after Tig and Samantha had left, trying to implement what they had taught us. The night sessions continued to take a toll on my legs, and the new skills seemed awkward at first, but with repetition they gradually took hold, and I began to see improvements during the day.

At breakfast on Friday, Garika and I decided to tell our friends where we had been at night. Samantha had said from the start the training sessions should not be a secret, and I knew my friends were suspicious about my absence at some of the Specials.

"Night sessions?" Alejandro said, after we told them. "Aren't you too tired for that?"

"It's tough," I admitted, and exchanged a look with Garika. "But Samantha thought we needed the work."

"Your shot is pretty weak," Oliver said between bites of the breakfast sausage he liked to eat with baked beans. He was the skinniest kid in camp but ate like a starving wolf in winter. "You have an awful header, too. But yeah," he said brightly, "I've seen you getting better!"

"Uh, thanks?" I said.

After a moment, Alejandro said shyly, "Do you think Samantha would mind if I joined you?"

"You're serious?" I said, excited by the prospect.

"I might join too," Oliver said, "as long as I don't have to miss dinner."

Sven heard us talking and wished us good luck, but did not offer to join. Javier, who had decided to grace us with his presence that morning, sniffed as if the conversation was beneath him. I knew Robbie would feel the same, and hadn't even bothered to tell him. He never asked where I was at night, and probably assumed I was playing FIFA in the break room.

Before the morning session began, I asked Samantha if she minded the other players joining us. She said of course not. In fact, she told the whole group they could join. No one else seemed interested in giving up their free time or missing the Special. When Garika and I met with Tig and Samantha later that night, Alejandro and Dayo joined us, but Oliver never showed.

"I can use the extra work," Dayo said after the night session ended. "I don't want to go home early."

Back home, Dayo played for the top youth team in Lagos. He said his home city was even bigger than London, although I couldn't imagine how that could be true.

"It was fate that you two decided to join us," I said when we finally left the field together. "Isn't it, Dayo? Because now we're a good number."

Everyone looked confused for a moment, but then Dayo laughed. "Yes, this is true. Now I can be the Silver Surfer."

"That's right," I said with a grin. "We're the Fantastic Four."

The wargames had continued throughout the week. While I didn't understand the principles behind many of the drills, they were always exciting, and challenged us mentally as much as physically. During the scrimmages, Samantha added in another ball on two more occasions, so that by Friday we had to scramble around the field with four balls in play. It taught me to be aware of the entire field at all times, and forced us to invent new hacks and strategies to win the games.

When the final whistle blew, signaling the end of Week Two, I collapsed on my back with my hands over my head, dripping in sweat, relieved and exhausted and happy all at the same time. Though my thighs throbbed and my calves ached, it wasn't as bad as before, and patches of tough skin had replaced the blisters on my feet. I knew the worst was over, at least when it came to conditioning. I had played all day and throughout the evening, every single day over the last week, and managed to survive.

I could only get stronger from here.

"Listen up, Iguanas," Samantha said, waving us over. "I have a few announcements."

Alejandro offered a hand to help me up. I groaned and grabbed my water bottle on my way to the huddle.

"First off, there's no Special tonight. After dinner is free time. I'll be unavailable as well, so all of you should rest up and enjoy your evening." Her eyes twinkled as if sharing a secret joke with someone, and I suspected she had another date with Tig.

"When do we find out who's cut?" Robbie asked.

Irritation flashed in Samantha's eyes, but then her expression softened. "I know that's on everyone's mind. I just wanted to enjoy a few moments together, and tell everyone how much I've enjoyed coaching you. It's been a challenging two weeks. Each one of you should be proud of the effort you've put in. In fact, Director Hawk and the coaches have decided to reward that effort with a swimming party at the local pool tomorrow. When you return tomorrow night, you'll find out who will be staying and who will be going home."

Someone Tries to Drown Me, and I Open Another Envelope

After lunch on Sunday, I put on my swim trunks and met my friends in the parking lot outside the Castle. We all piled into one of the buses and sat in the back, laughing and cutting up as the driver took us to the lido, which is what the British call a local swimming pool.

A lido? Why do they use all these weird names for things? Why not just call it a swimming pool?

It was a hot summer day, the warmest so far in London. Before we left the bus, the coaches gave us a speech about respectful behavior in public, but as soon as we filed through the entrance gate, we all whooped with glee, dropped our bags on the concrete tables beside the pool, stripped off our shirts and shoes, and jumped into the water.

The lido was similar to my public pool back home. A square of clear blue water that smelled of chlorine and looked as big as a lake once you were inside it. In the deep end, three diving boards begged to be used and abused. Parents lounged in beach chairs, trying to read books while kids shouted and played in the packed pool.

Inside the wall surrounding the complex, I spotted a snack shop, two tennis courts, a tetherball on a pole, and a grassy area filled with kids playing soccer. I grinned at the thought of some of us joining the game, and I couldn't believe that I wanted to play more soccer after such a long, hard week. But right now, I was happy to enjoy the cool water and hang out with my friends.

Not long after we arrived, Charlie, the Australian goalie, stood up in the water and roared, "Cannonball battle!"

He waded to the side of the pool, climbed out, and led a mad rush to the diving boards. Half the team followed him, including me and my friends, overwhelming the local kids.

Charlie set a high standard by jumping off the high dive, tucking his knees, and making a splash that resembled an erupting geyser. He even sprayed the lifeguard in her tower chair. Brock went next and rocked the pool even more. By the time fifty of us or so had finished the first round, the waves were lapping over the edges. We moved on from cannonballs to all kinds of crazy jumps. Alejandro made us laugh with a spread-eagle belly flop off the low dive. I cringed at the *splat* he made, and was relieved when he climbed out with a grin on his face, his entire torso as red as a tomato.

I cracked everyone up with something I called the *angry principal*, a jump where I sat cross-legged in midair off the middle-dive, scowling with my arms folded all the way until I hit the water on my bottom. Garika one-upped me by racing off the high dive and continuing to run in midair, his arms and legs flailing all the way down. Oliver tried the same thing, but tipped too far forward and crash-landed on his face.

After an hour on the boards, I convinced my friends to start a chicken fight in the shallow end. I had to teach them the game, which involved climbing onto the shoulders of a partner and trying to knock the other pairs down any way you could. I hoisted myself onto Alejandro's shoulders, since he was stronger and heavier, and together we stalked the pool, looking for victims. We took down Oliver and Garika with ease, then Dayo and Robbie, and Sven and José. Every time I was about to fall, Alejandro would steady me, or trip one of the other players underneath the water. It was all in good fun until I saw Julian hop onto Brock's shoulders, and I knew there would be trouble.

"Let's take those jerks down," Alejandro said.

"Absolutely," I said. "Be strong, my faithful steed."

Brock waded towards us, pawing through the water with his huge mitts. "I hear you're going to night school, Leo. That's what you get for learning to play in rec leagues."

Julian beat his chest and howled. "I hope you know how to swim, because you're about to go down."

"Bring it," I said, right as Julian and I locked fingers high above the water.

Though not as big as Brock, Julian was taller than me, and outweighed me by ten pounds. But I held my own, shoving him forward as much as he shoved me. We teetered and almost fell multiple times before recovering our balance. I switched my grip and yanked on his arm, trying a different tactic, but he grabbed my neck and pulled me close. We wrapped our arms around each other and fought hard to unbalance the other team as Alejandro and Brock worked furiously to steady us. Finally Julian and I fell into the water at the same time. I didn't have time to hold my breath, and I started to swim back to the surface—right as someone yanked me down from behind and held me underwater with a hand on my neck.

Confused, thinking Alejandro might be playing with me,

I opened my eyes underwater and saw a pair of black trunks and two thighs as thick as concrete blocks.

Brock.

I squirmed from side to side, trying to escape, but his grip was as strong as iron. The water was shallow, only four feet deep, but that wouldn't help me if I couldn't stand up. I doubted any of the lifeguards or adults had noticed. There were far too many people in the pool. All I could see were legs and torsos in every direction.

I didn't have much air left. Was Brock evil enough to drown me right in front of everyone? If so, then he might get away with it. He might even be able to swim off without anyone realizing what had happened.

I reached behind my neck to peel his hand off, but I couldn't break his grip. I bent my knees and tried to use my legs to kick off his torso, but he simply pushed my legs away and kept holding me down. I started to panic. My dad had taught me a few nasty things to do to an attacker, but I couldn't concentrate long enough to remember them. Just as I started to feel light-headed, Brock pulled me up, smacked me hard on the back a few times, and gave me a worried look.

"Hey, Leo? You okay? It looked like you couldn't breathe down there."

I gulped in huge mouthfuls of air. Out of the corner of my eye, I saw the lifeguard rise up in her chair. Before I could retaliate, Alejandro stepped forward and shoved Brock hard in the chest, causing him to fall on his back in the water. When Brock tried to get up, Alejandro pounced on him and shoved him under, holding him down with both hands.

The lifeguard blasted her whistle. Julian grabbed

Alejandro and pulled him off Brock. I went after Julian but someone held my arms from behind. I turned, furious, and saw that it was Robbie.

"Let it go, Leo," he said quietly.

When I whipped back around, I saw Charlie with an arm around Brock, helping Julian hold him back from Alejandro. More players poured in to separate us as lifeguards rushed over, blowing their whistles and ordering us all out of the pool. Our coaches raced towards us as well, and I had never seen them so furious.

"What happened?" asked Coach Tanner, glaring at Alejandro and then Brock. By the way the lifeguards were holding them back, it was clear they thought those two had caused the trouble.

"Brock tried to drown me!" I shouted, stepping forward. "It was his fault!"

"We were playing a game," Brock yelled back. "Leo got upset when he lost!"

"Who started the fight?" Coach Tanner said. "I want to know right this second."

I swallowed and glanced at Alejandro. "Brock did," I said. "But I pushed him back."

"Both of you," Coach Tanner said, "stay apart the rest of the day. And the moment we get back, you're going to see Director Hawk."

The incident with Brock ruined the rest of the party for me. I didn't want to play soccer or tetherball, and the cheeseburgers and fries from the snack shop tasted like cardboard. Alejandro felt awful that I had taken the blame for him, and begged me to tell the truth. I wouldn't hear of it. He had only been trying to protect me. At first I worried Brock would try to retaliate against him, but even he and Julian were not stupid enough to make the coaches any angrier, and kept to themselves the rest of the day.

Later that evening, after we returned to the Castle, I found myself sitting in Director Hawk's office, the last place on Earth I wanted to be, along with the last two people I wanted to see there: Brock and Director Hawk.

As always, the camp director was dressed in a London Dragons tracksuit zipped to the neck. After Brock and I sat down, Director Hawk leaned across the wooden desk and planted his forearms on the surface. "It's been a very long day. I've been on the phone with management for hours discussing transfer options. And now, instead of having a Sunday roast with my family, here I am, still in my office, dealing with two misbehaving children."

Brock raised his hand. "I didn't start the—"

"Quiet!" the director thundered. A vein pulsed on his forehead, right beneath the iron-gray line of his crew cut. "Did I grant you permission to speak?"

Brock squirmed in his chair. I would have enjoyed his discomfort if I wasn't terrified I would be next. "No, Sir," Brock said.

"This is not a discussion, nor will it ever be. Too many players arrive here thinking they're special, and end up leaving for the very same reason. How can I recommend you to the youth team if you can't behave yourselves during summer camp? Are the two of you promising young men hoping to become pros one day, or spoiled lads in need of discipline? Well?" he said, when we didn't answer. "Which is it?"

"Young men," Brock said, looking straight ahead. "I mean, young men, Sir."

"Young men," I agreed. "Very promising young men."

The director thrust his jaw forward and leveled his stare at me as if trying to decide if I was being sarcastic. A bead of sweat dripped off my forehead and rolled down my cheek. It tickled, but I didn't dare reach up to wipe it away.

"I've sent players home for lesser infractions," he said finally. "In fact, I'd send you both home right now, were it not for the intervention of the coaches, who asked me to give you both a second chance." He leaned back in his chair, and his jaw tightened even further, if such a thing were possible. "But hear me, lads, and hear me well. This conversation will not be repeated. If either of you so much as arrive a second late for practice, or utter another angry word to each other on the field, I will personally drive you both to the airport."

When I trudged back to my room with my head down, Robbie was nowhere in sight. I noticed an open envelope and a piece of paper on his bed. I knew what it was at once, and I couldn't help peeking.

As I suspected, Robbie had made the second cut.

Still rattled by the incident with Brock, my heart was heavy as I walked to the desk to pick up another envelope with my name on it. It would be a fitting end to my worst day at camp if I were sent home as well.

I carried the envelope to my bed, tore it open, and unfolded the slip of paper inside.

> *Congratulations, Leo. I'm sending you through to Week Three. I can tell your hard work is paying off, but there's a long way to go. Keep it up.*
> *Samantha*

A mixture of emotions flowed through me: relief that I had made the cut, excitement about Week Three, shame that I had landed in Director Hawk's office, fear that I would be sent home if I slipped up again, and pure rage at Brock for putting me in that boat to begin with. What did he have against me, anyway? He practically tried to drown me!

I kicked my feet up and laid on my back, planning to spend the rest of the night in the same position, listening to music and playing on my device. A few minutes later, a text came in from Carlos.

So? Week Three?? Did you make it through???

I debated ignoring the text, then decided it might help my mood to talk to a friend.

I made it.

Whoa. Really?

Did I stutter?

> You're gonna make the world cup, Leo.
> I know it.

> I hope so. But it's gonna be so
> hard now. Everyone is so good.

> Didn't I tell you to stop whining? Listen,
> I know there will be some great swag if
> you make it that far. So don't screw it
> up.

I decided to give him the condensed version of the incident in the pool, to get it off my chest.

> There's a bully here who won't
> leave me alone.

> Bruh. A bully? Picking on *you*?

Back home, I was a soccer star. No one had ever picked on me before. Plus, I'd been kind of angry since my mom had died, and everyone at school knew I had a temper.

> This English kid named Brock
> has it out for me. I don't think he
> likes Americans. Though he never
> bothers Robbie for some reason.

> Why is he such a loser? Is he jealous?

> I don't think so. He's a really good player. But he almost got me kicked out today for fighting. If it happens again, they'll send me home.

> You can't let him keep bullying you, because you're Leo K. Doyle and I know you won't do that, but you also can't jeopardize your place on the team.

Carlos always had a knack for seeing to the heart of a problem.

> Exactly.

> So? What are you going to do about it?

I propped my back against the pillow and considered the question I'd been thinking about all day.

> I don't know.

Here There Be Dragons

"Congratulations on making it to Week Three," Samantha said as we gathered for the next morning session. "We're down to ninety-six players in the camp, which means only twenty-four Iguanas are left. I know this is bittersweet news, because a lot of familiar faces are no longer with us."

During the jog around the field, I had been relieved to see Alejandro, Garika, and most of my closest friends. Only Oliver was missing, and Alejandro had confirmed my fears: our gangly, cheerful, freckle-faced British friend hadn't made it through. Knowing most of us would get cut eventually, I had already exchanged contact information with all of my friends, and vowed to stay in touch.

Kaito, and now Oliver. A part of me was relieved that two forwards were no longer in the competition, though I felt guilty for even having the thought.

"You should be proud to make it this far, but don't get complacent," Samantha said. "It only gets harder from here. We had a difficult time deciding who to keep, so you're going to have to truly stand out to make the World Cup."

Robbie raised a hand. "What's the schedule for this week?"

"Ah, Sir Robbie," Samantha said with a smile, "always beating me to the punch. This week will look a lot like the last one, with one big exception: during the scrimmages, you'll be playing against the other squads."

This caused a ripple of excitement.

"The coaches need to start evaluating you in comparison to the other players at your position. It isn't the World Cup yet, so nothing's set in stone, but I, too, need to start thinking about my final eleven."

Her words rang in my ears as we began the day with a passing drill.

Final eleven.

Somehow, the closer I drew to the finish line, the harder securing an invitation to the Dragons youth team seemed to be. Half the camp had been cut, but the smaller numbers only seemed to reinforce how talented all the remaining players were. I was getting better, I knew, but I would never be as fast and strong as Dayo and Diego, or kick the ball as hard.

I took a deep breath and vowed not to worry about it. There was nothing I could do except play my best. My next goal was making the World Cup, and to do that, I would have to work harder than I ever had.

As Samantha had promised, Week Three proved to be the most difficult one yet. The morning drills were faster and more tiring. Samantha made us run wind sprints before lunch. As she led us through the cool-down stretches, she talked to us about nutrition again, and how our diet directly affects our performance on the field.

"Leo," she said, as my attention wandered during her speech. "Are you listening?"

"Uh, yeah," I said.

"I've noticed you have a, shall we say, certain affinity for potato chips, sodas, and desserts. Especially snack cakes and chocolate cream pie."

Some of the other players snickered, but I was quite proud of my good taste in food. "Don't forget Orange Fanta and Reese's Pieces," I said. "Those are my favorites."

She rolled her eyes. "I know it's fun to eat whatever we want when our parents aren't around—trust me, I like junk food too—but just be careful you don't let it affect your play. To compete at the professional level, and play your best for an entire ninety minutes, you have to put the right foods in your body. These do not, ahem, include sodas and snack cakes before games. So just think about it, okay?"

"Sure," I said, since I saw no harm in doing what she said. *There*, I said to myself. *I just thought about it. Moving on now.*

After lunch, Samantha set up two gameplay areas, each with four miniature goals spaced an equal distance apart and arranged in a diamond shape. She called it the Four Kingdoms game, divided us into teams of six, and told us that each team had two goals to defend and two goals to attack.

It was a fun but challenging drill. I would have struggled when I first arrived at camp, because everyone had to play both offense and defense. But my defense had steadily improved after the night sessions. I wasn't about to start throwing down slide tackles all over the field, or trying to strip the ball from Javier, but I had quick feet, and I knew how to position myself now. Players weren't blowing by me like they used to.

As the afternoon went on, Samantha switched up the goals for each team. Sometimes we had to defend opposite sides of the diamond, and sometimes we had one goal behind us and one on the left or the right. The drill suited my talents. I had a knack for seeing passes and openings where others didn't. With everyone's attention split among four goals instead of two, there was more room for creative play. I threaded pass after pass through the defense, and was better than anyone at changing direction midway through an attack and charging towards the goal.

Sven and Alejandro and Robbie were on my team. We won the first two games, and even Robbie congratulated me on my play. But the final game was against José, Brock, and Julian's team. I knew it would be tough.

Brock had been glaring at me all day from across the field. You would think, after a lecture from Director Hawk and the threat of dismissal, he would lay off me for a while.

Nope. The brute was just choosing his battles more carefully. He made sure Samantha wasn't looking when he tugged on my shirt, or slide tackled me from behind, or shoved me in the back when I ran past him.

After a particularly hard foul, I spun around and balled my fists at my side. "What did I ever do to you?" I said.

"Nothing," Brock said.

"Then what gives? Why do you keep bothering me?"

"Because you're trash. You're a trash Yank, with a trash country, and trash football. You think you're the most important people in the world, but you know what I think? I think you should all stay home."

"The most important people? Who thinks that? I don't think that. Behind you!" I shouted, causing him to whip around just as a loose ball came our way. I trapped the ball and dribbled around him while he had his back turned. A few players around us chortled at my trick. Brock snarled and chased after me, but Samantha had wandered over, so he was forced to let it go. But the rest of the game he fouled me hard whenever he could get away with it. It made me nervous to turn my back on him, which is just what he wanted.

When it came time to scrimmage, Samantha split the squad into three teams of eight. I was on a team with Javier, Garika, José, Dayo, Sven, and two others. A strong group. The coaches moved all the goals to the center line, and we played 8 v 8 on half the field with keepers and full-size goals.

"Good luck, Iguanas!" Samantha called out as our squads took the field.

"What positions do we play?" José shouted back.

"Organize yourselves," she said, which surprised me, and caused us to mill about in confusion. I drifted towards the center line, but so did Dayo, Javier, Sven, and one of the other players on our team. With eight players, should we play with three forwards, three midfielders, or three defenders? And who should play which position? I hesitated, wondering if I should try to claim the center forward spot, knowing the others would think Dayo was the best. But that was *my* position, too.

"3-3-2!" José called out, taking charge for the group. He was the top midfielder in the squad, a born leader, and no one challenged his authority. "Dayo, you're up front with . . . Sven. Javier, why don't you play right mid, and Leo, you take the left? You're good with both feet," he added weakly.

Oh boy. Not only had José stuck me in midfield, but he had chosen Javier to play on the right side over me. It was a clear acknowledgment of the pecking order among the forwards: Dayo, Sven, Javier and then me.

Unless I wanted to confront José, or challenge Dayo and Sven's ability, I had no choice but to agree. Feeling disappointed and lost, unsure about my basic position, I drifted over to the left side without arguing. I liked José and knew he wasn't trying to be mean.

He just thought Javier and Dayo were better forwards than I was.

The first team we lined up against, a squad from the Gila Monsters, featured a pair of strong forwards: Miguel, the short but compact Nicaraguan I had met at the airport, and who had proven to be a dribbling machine; and Sebastian, the ultra-fast Polish kid who was good enough to challenge Javier and Sven for a spot on the right wing. They also had Sergi, maybe the best midfielder after José, and Conor, an Irish fullback who was really good on the ball.

Playing against the other squads energized us. It was fun to see everyone else in action again, and judge how much they had improved or fallen behind.

Except no one seemed to have fallen behind. While some players stood out above the rest, there were no weak links. Everyone left was super talented. I supposed that applied to me as well, which gave me a tingle of pride, but I was so impressed by the skill on display I didn't really think about my own game. Sebastian was so blindingly fast. Sergi was so clever with the ball, Miguel so hard to take down, Conor so hard to dribble past.

The format was three twenty-minute games with a break in between. We tied the first game, 1-1. Despite playing in left midfield, I held my own, with very few mistakes.

When the next game started, I cringed when I saw Diego

waiting on the other side. The Mexican striker had assumed an almost mythical status. Angry at my timidity, I told myself he was just a twelve-year-old kid like me. But he was so tall and strong on the ball, and had such a presence about him, that if someone had told me he was a professional, I might have believed it.

Garika and our other two center backs put up a valiant effort, but Diego scored two goals, one off a corner kick and one a rocket from ten yards outside the box. Javier stuck one in the goal for us after a nifty one-touch through the keeper's legs—a little bit of luck was involved—but the final score was *Diego Two, Iguanas One*.

Our final opponent of the day featured Mahmoud, a wily Egyptian striker who specialized in free kicks and junk goals. As good as Mahmoud was, their defense was even better, and featured the two best defenders in the camp: Hans and Mateo, the German and Argentinian center backs. To make matters worse, Charlie was their keeper.

Hans and Mateo played side by side in the back, allowing the team to play three midfielders and three forwards. We should have been able to break down their short-handed defense, but Hans and Mateo were all over the place, stalling attempt after attempt.

While I continued to play steady, I had trouble standing out, especially against that defense. But near the end of the game, I made a play that surprised even myself.

Garika started it off by taking an outlet pass from our keeper and sending it downfield to me. So far, we had favored the right side, playing through Sven and Javier. As good as those two were, they had barely gotten off a shot in this game.

The opposing midfielder was close enough to challenge me for Garika's pass. In fact, he was so close that, instead of trapping the ball, I flicked it to one side and ran around him, retrieving the ball on the other side. It was a sweet move that left him flat-footed.

Now I had some open field. With their midfield a distant memory, I found myself bearing down on Mateo, with José running beside me. Dayo and Sven were calling for the ball, but Hans was hovering between them, ready to mark either one. It was four on two, our best opportunity so far.

I dribbled straight at Mateo, not wanting to give the defense time to get set. The stocky, red-headed center back was backpedaling, trying to slow me down but ready to intercept the pass he knew was coming.

Or at least Mateo *thought* he knew it was coming. In fact, I was pretty sure everyone thought I was going to pass, since that's what you do in a four on two situation, especially from the midfield, and against one of the best two defenders in the camp. But something came over me—the lizard inside me reared up and flared its beard—and I didn't do what everyone expected. Instead I called Sven's name and faked a pass across the field, stepping over the ball and selling it with my body language.

Mateo shifted his bodyweight. Just the opening I needed. I kicked the ball ahead, ten yards past him, and sprinted to it. His eyes widened as he realized I was trying to beat him, and he worked desperately to change directions and chase me down.

It was too late. My touch was right on the mark. I surged past Mateo, collected the ball, and found myself on the left edge of the penalty box with an open shot at goal. Hans was closing in, so I wouldn't have time to dribble any closer. I could pass the ball to the middle, where Dayo and Sven were waiting, or take the shot.

I debated passing the ball. I really did. But Hans was such a good defender that he was cutting off the angle. I might have been able to sneak it through, but it wasn't as easy as it looked.

So I took the shot instead.

It was a clean strike with my right foot, and it went exactly where I wanted: streaking towards the top right corner.

Except I had forgotten who was in the goal. Just like the first day, I was sure I had scored, only to watch in disbelief as Charlie's outstretched fingers brushed my shot away at the last moment.

Another incredible save.

The whistle blew, signaling the end of the game.

We had tied 1-1.

"You should have crossed it," Javier said in disgust as we walked off.

"That was a little selfish, Leo," Sven added. "We were both waiting."

But José threw an arm across my back and grinned. "Yeah, but did you see Leo turn Mateo around? He made him look silly. After the way their defense abused us all game, that was almost better than a goal."

We had an early dinner. For the Special that night, the coaches shepherded everyone onto the buses and told us we were going to attend a London Dragons game at their stadium in the city.

I couldn't believe it. An actual, real-life Dragons FC game. The Premier League season had not started yet, so the game was a friendly against Chelsea for charity. I didn't care. It was still real players in a real stadium. Even better, we all had special tickets and would be sitting right behind the players!

It was a dream come true. Carlos was going to flip out.

On the way into the stadium, we were all so full of excitement we could hardly walk straight. But as soon as we emerged from the tunnel and saw that perfect grass under the bright lights, with tens of thousands of people in the stands, and the players jogging out to start the game, a hush overcame us.

"Keep moving!" Director Hawk barked, causing everyone to scuttle forward as if prodded by a hot poker.

We took our seats just as the game started. I sat between Alejandro and Garika. "I can't believe we're here!" Alejandro said, then grabbed me on the arm as he began pointing out his favorite players.

Garika slumped in his seat as if too overcome with awe to sit up straight.

It felt surreal to see faces I had only seen on TV. They looked larger than life but also strangely mortal, as if before this moment, they had only been figments of my imagination, legendary heroes and demigods instead of flesh and blood human beings. When I spotted Christian Pulisic in the midfield, I felt a surge of warmth for my countryman. *American players can make it here, too. They can even star for Top Six teams.*

Soon after the game started, the Dragons' center forward broke free at midfield and raced towards the other goal. The roar of the crowd caused goosebumps to course through me. I could only imagine what it must feel like as a player buoyed by the energy of the home crowd. The forward didn't score, but I knew right then and there, more than ever, that all I wanted in life was to be a professional soccer star. I wanted to play on this field in front of all these fans, test my skills against the best in the world, travel to stadiums in exotic foreign cities, eat and breathe and sleep soccer for the rest of my life.

And yet, I had to admit that watching the players in person, from such a close vantage point, was as humbling as it was exciting. They were so fast and skilled it almost seemed supernatural.

Did that midfielder really just trap the ball so perfectly?

Did that center back really kick the ball that far?

Did that forward really just execute that spin move so smoothly?

Could I ever be that good?

After the game ended in a tie, I walked out of the stadium in a daze, laughing with my friends and crowing about the best plays we had seen, wondering in hushed tones which of us would be out there with the pros one day.

When we returned to the Castle, it was too late to meet Tig and Samantha, but the Dragons game had energized me so much I grabbed my friends and a ball and goofed around on the practice field under the lights, taking corner kicks and pretending we were famous players, dreaming of future glory late into the night.

But our night sessions with Tig and Samantha continued on Tuesday, and lasted throughout the week. We tried to persuade them to teach us some fancy new moves, but they didn't think that was fair to the other kids.

"That's why we suggested this in the first place, Leo," Samantha said. "To make sure everyone has mastered the basic skills."

I attended every session, and missed two more Specials because of it. Garika and Alejandro joined me every night, and Dayo only missed one session. Even José showed up once. Of course, Robbie followed him to the field like a lost puppy, though he looked embarrassed to be there, practicing the basics with the rejects who didn't play for fancy club teams.

I had never worked so hard in my life, but we played hard, too. Some nights we stayed out until midnight. The camaraderie of the sessions drew us together. I began to think of these guys not as my new friends, but as just friends, and I knew we'd stay in touch forever.

There was another benefit. I began to predict my friends' decisions in advance, as well as their positions on the field. It helped us in the scrimmages against the other squads.

On Friday night, thirty minutes after the session was supposed to start, Tig and Samantha still had not arrived. They had never showed up late before. Just as we began to worry something had happened, Samantha walked down to the field in a pair of jeans, a baggy sweatshirt, and no makeup. Her eyes looked red and swollen, as if she had been crying. Although she smiled and began calling out instructions, her smile seemed forced.

"Is Tig coming?" I asked.

"I don't know," Samantha said. Her tone suggested she didn't care whether he showed up or not.

As always, we started the session with penalty kicks. Tig arrived ten minutes later, when we moved on to a one-touch passing drill. He and Samantha didn't even say hello to one another. She took Alejandro and Garika aside to work on defense, while Tig helped Dayo and me with shielding.

Tig was far more subdued than usual, and kept glancing at Samantha out of the corner of his eye. What was going on? This was a terrible development. Not only did I care for them both and want them to be together, but I was convinced the night sessions were key to my survival.

After we finished, I caught up with Tig on his way back to the Castle.

"What's up, Boss?" he said.

I wanted to ask him about Samantha, but I didn't know what to say. "I . . . what do you think I need to improve on?"

"Your skills are getting better," he said. "I can tell you're working hard."

"Thanks. You two have helped a lot."

He winced as if my words had hurt him. "I've noticed you having trouble against the good keepers."

"Especially Charlie."

"He's a beast all right. But here's the thing, Leo. You've been playing checkers so far, and it's time to start playing chess. Your shot isn't the issue. Keep practicing the mechanics, but to beat the top-level keepers, you have to think a step ahead. You're giving everything away."

"You mean I'm easy to read?"

"Yeah, but more importantly, you're too predictable. Charlie isn't Superman. He's just cheating in one direction and out-thinking you. Mix it up every now and then. Don't always go top right. If you're unpredictable, and can score from various angles, you'll make him think a lot harder before trying to guess where you're going."

"Okay," I said, digesting his words. "I'll sleep on that."

I kept walking with him by the light of the moon. When we started climbing the stairs to the Castle, Tig said, "I messed up, Leo."

"What do you mean?"

"Wasn't it obvious something was wrong tonight? Between me and Sam?"

"Yeah. It was."

He shook his head and looked off to the side. "I kissed another girl last night."

"Oh."

"Sam found out about it."

"Why'd you do it?"

"I didn't think we were that serious, but Sam did." He looked off to the side. "Now I wish I hadn't, but it's too late. Sam won't even talk to me. I don't think I should come out here again. At night, I mean. It's too awkward. It's not fair to her."

We had reached the rear entrance to the Castle, and I stared down at my feet. "I understand."

"I'm sorry to disappoint you, Boss. Like I said, you're doing great. Keep up the hard work and you'll be fine."

"Okay."

He patted me on the back. "Thanks for listening."

The Battle With Brock

Saturday morning.

The last day before the World Cup teams would be announced.

During warmups, Samantha jogged around the field with us. I hung back so I could run with her. "Can I ask you something?" I said.

"That depends on what it is."

"Do you think midfield is my best position?"

She considered the question for a long moment. "I think it might be your best position *here*."

"What do you mean?"

"It suits your creativity," she said carefully.

"Center forwards are creative."

"In a different way, absolutely. But I'm not sure . . . ."

When she didn't finish her sentence, I said, "You're not sure if I can beat out the other forwards?"

She pressed her lips together.

"Okay," I said, trying to hide my disappointment. "Fair."

"I don't want to discourage you," she said. "I'm just being truthful. On the other hand, I've noticed—all the coaches have—that you have a knack for the goal. To be honest, Leo, we're not quite sure what to do with you. Hang in there, okay? Just do your best and don't worry. There are more spots open in midfield than up front."

"Okay," I said, still feeling as if someone had stolen my PlayStation.

"I also wanted to tell you there won't be any more night sessions," she said.

I swallowed. "Why not?"

"If you do make the World Cup, I want you to get more rest."

"I can work it in."

She smiled. "We've taught you what you need to know. Though it's always a good idea to keep practicing the basics."

"Is this . . . does this have anything to do with Tig?"

Her smiled faded. "That's between him and me, Leo."

"I didn't mean to interfere. It's just that . . . he told me he was really sorry. I probably wasn't supposed to tell you that."

"That's very sweet of you," she said, with a catch in her voice.

But she didn't say anything else.

Distracted by the conversation with Samantha, I had a rough time concentrating on the drills that morning. Everything seemed to be falling apart. Tig and Samantha had broken up. The night sessions were canceled. Even my own squad leader didn't think I should play center forward.

I didn't *want* to play left midfield. How was I supposed to succeed at a position I didn't even like?

After a water break, Samantha divided us into two groups so we could work on set plays with full size goals. The keepers practiced with the squads most of the day now. Koffi was assigned to our group and impressed us with his saves. He had improved a lot during the summer.

We started out with corner kicks and direct kicks near the penalty box, then moved the ball further out. Halfway through the drill, José sent a free kick from the right side of the field all the way across the box. I had a chance to make a play. I sprinted forward, preparing for a diving header, when someone tripped me from behind, and I landed hard on the ground. The fall knocked the breath out of me, and left my mouth full of grass.

"Hey!" Alejandro shouted, running over to help me up. "Foul!"

I knew who had tripped me even before I turned around and saw Brock with his hands up in mock surrender, a nasty smirk on his face.

"Oops," Brock said.

Everyone stopped playing, wondering what would happen next. Samantha was on the other side of the field with her back to us. Alejandro started forward, his fists balled at his sides, but I put an arm on his chest to hold him back. Not only could I not let my best friend get in trouble because of me, but it was time I dealt with this myself.

I took a step towards Brock and spoke loud enough for everyone to hear. "You think you're better than me?"

"I know I am," he said.

"Then prove it. You and me, one on one."

He laughed. "You serious, Cincinnati? I'll crush you."

"Like I said. Prove it."

"Just name the time and place, loser."

"Nine o'clock tonight, on the practice field behind the Castle. If I win, you agree never to bother me again."

He snorted. "Whatever."

"Promise. Or the game is off, because you're too scared to come, and everyone will know it."

"What's in it for me? You have nothing I want, Yank."

It was true I couldn't think of anything to offer him—until something popped into my mind. "I'll quit and go home, whether I make the World Cup or not."

There was dead silence from the other players.

Brock stared at me. "You're serious? That would be the best gift ever."

"Boys!" Samantha yelled from across the field. "What are you doing? Get back to the drill!"

I looked him in the eye as I backed away. "Nine o'clock."

That night we had another pizza party while we watched a soccer movie, *Escape to Victory*, on a projector screen on the front lawn of the Castle. I expected the movie to be awful, since it was really old and about some prisoners or something during a war, but it was surprisingly good.

Or at least it seemed good when I could manage to pay attention. I was so nervous about the one-on-one game with Brock that I had barely eaten any pizza, and I kept thinking about the ridiculous promise I had made.

What had come over me? Why had I said I would quit?

Would I really do it? Blow my one chance at a professional soccer career and let my family down as well?

On the other hand, only losers failed to pay a bet. If I lost to Brock and didn't quit, the guys would never respect me again. I might never respect myself.

Neither option was acceptable, so there was only one way out of this I could think of.

Make sure I didn't lose.

I arrived at eight-thirty on the practice field behind the Castle to turn on the lights and warm up. I had played there so often it felt like my home field. The dusk air was cool and smelled of pine. A good night for a soccer death match.

Brock arrived while I was juggling. "Your fancy tricks won't help you," he said as he kicked off his sandals and laced up his cleats. Julian and a few other players had arrived with him.

"Leo's gonna bury you," Alejandro called out from behind me. I breathed a sigh of relief when I turned and saw my Costa Rican friend strolling down the hill with Dayo and Garika. I knew Brock would try to cheat, but the presence of my friends would make it harder. In fact, lots of players were starting to arrive, so many I realized the word must have spread through the camp.

As the players gathered around us, José offered to ref the game. Was he here to help me or Brock? I wondered.

"Sure," I said with a shrug.

Brock grumbled that we didn't need a ref, but José promised to be fair, leaving Brock little choice but to agree, unless he wanted to lose face in front of the other players.

We decided on a field twenty yards long and almost as wide. We used the center of the big field, which was already marked, to guide our lines. Julian and Alejandro took off their shoes to make the goal posts three feet apart. All shots had to be on the ground or they didn't count. No goalies. Just me and Brock, one on one.

"The game is to three," Brock said. "I'm not staying here all night."

"Fine," I said.

José walked to the center of the makeshift field with a ball in his hands. The other players lined up around us, Brock's supporters on one side and mine on the other, rooting us on.

I bounced on the balls of my feet, trying to settle my nerves as José prepared for a drop ball at center field. As soon as he let go of the ball, I rushed forward to poke it away. I should have known what was coming. Instead of making a play on the ball, Brock rammed right into me with his shoulder, sending me flying. I scrambled to get up, but it was too late. He collected the ball, took a few dribbles, and passed it right through the goal.

"Hey!" Alejandro shouted. "That was a foul!"

José hesitated, then shook his head. "Fair shoulder challenge."

Brock's followers hooted and clapped and jeered. As much as I hated to admit it, I couldn't fault José for the call. It *was* a fair challenge. I had to deal with Brock's size, and be more careful.

"Leo's ball," José said as he set the ball down inside the center circle at half field.

Brock put his hands up and backed away. "Don't worry, Leo. I'll make this quick."

Man, was I tired of that kid's mouth. When José whistled with two of his fingers, I took the ball and dribbled right at Brock. He seemed surprised by the direct challenge, and came right back at me. Just before we met, I flicked a rainbow into the air, as I'd done a million times before. The ball went over both of our heads and landed on the other side of Brock. A perfect trick. I ran around him before he could react, took a touch, shrugged off his attempt to grab my jersey from behind, and sent the ball through his goal.

"1-1," I said.

After a moment of stunned silence, my supporters exploded with wild cheering.

"Did you see that move?" Alejandro shouted.

"Neymar!" someone else yelled. "It's the new Neymar!"

"Try that again," Brock said as he walked the ball back to the center line. "I dare you."

"Getting embarrassed once in front of everyone isn't enough for you?" I shot back.

Brock snarled and, after the drop, came right at me with the ball. I slide tackled him from behind, and he fell to the ground on top of the ball. He jumped to his feet and yelled for a foul.

"Clean tackle," José said, waving his hands.

"Do you have a death wish?" Brock said to me, right before he scrambled after the loose ball.

In response, I drove my shoulder into him as hard as I could, just as he reached the ball. He was so big and strong he didn't fall down, but the contact made him grunt, and knocked him off the ball. I rolled the ball backwards with the top of my foot, spun, and just managed to avoid his lunging tackle. With no one left to defend me, I took a few dribbles and poked the ball through the two shoes marking the goal.

My side roared again as José whistled with his fingers. "Two to one."

"That was another foul," Brock shouted, waving a hand in disgust.

José shrugged his shoulders.

"So that's how it is?" Brock said, turning back to me. "I'm gonna kill you, Yank."

I looked him in the eye. "Bring it."

But he didn't come right at me this time. Despite his bravado, he knew he couldn't beat me with skill alone. He was an excellent fullback, but I was quicker, and had better touch on the ball. This time, when I approached to challenge him, he turned his back to me and shielded me off as he advanced. Every time I tried to slip around him, he shoved me away with an arm, or used his body to cut me off. He drew closer and closer to the goal, and there was nothing I could do about it. It was maddening. In a game situation, someone would have run over and helped me out, but it was just the two of us. Every time he shoved me away, I knew he was fouling me, but José clearly wasn't going to make a call unless there was blood.

I tried shoving Brock in the back, but he was just too big, and kept backing closer to the goal. When he was two feet away, he grabbed my arm and spun, holding me off as he turned towards the goal. I recovered, but not before he toe-poked the ball between the shoes.

"Two apiece," José said, as Brock's section broke out into cheers. "Next goal wins."

"You can't stop me, Leo," Brock said. "You're too weak."

"Good thing I have the ball," I said, and went right at him. I feinted right and nutmegged him, drawing more aahs from the crowd, but he body-checked me as I tried to go around him, and I lost control of the ball. We fought hard to reach it, both of us committing foul after foul, but José didn't call any-thing until Brock got so frustrated he tripped me from behind.

"Leo's ball," José said, setting the ball down where the foul occurred. "Take it easy, Brock."

"Whatever. He asked for this."

I tried to curve a shot right into the goal before he could set up, but he stuck out a foot and blocked it. Thinking he was going to bully me towards my own goal again, Brock turned his back and advanced. This time I fought harder than before, and managed to poke the ball away. We scrambled after it. Neither of us could get the upper hand, and it turned into a wrestling match more than a soccer challenge. Brock shoved me to the ground over and over, but I bounced up every time, and gave it to him as hard as he gave it to me. He kept trying to shield me and advance on the goal, but each time I found a way to stop him, even if I had to pull him down from behind and draw a foul.

I don't know how long we fought for that last goal. It seemed like hours. Both of us heaved with exertion, bleeding in half a dozen places from hard falls. I could see the frustra-tion in Brock's eyes, and it gave me the strength to continue.

"Just give up, Yank," he said, holding his hips and breath-ing hard as José set the ball down for me near the center line after yet another hard push. "You're never getting past me."

"Is that why I have two goals?"

He sneered. "You're not getting a third."

While I was exhausted, my night sessions had paid off, and I could tell Brock was even more spent. As soon as José blew the whistle, I didn't bother trying to dribble. Instead I kicked the ball past Brock, to the left of his goal. He hesitated, wondering if he should guard the goal mouth, then sprinted for the ball. I had caught him off guard, but he was closer to the ball.

The momentum of the ball had slowed to a lazy roll. We were going to arrive at the same time. I knew he wouldn't bother with a play on the ball, and try to foul me again. Anticipating this, I shoved my shoulder hard into his before we reached the ball, a fair charge that caused us both to stumble.

The ball stopped rolling a few feet from the shoe marking the left side of his goal. Realizing I was a step closer to the ball, Brock lunged at me, not bothering with a fair tackle, trying to bring me down any way he could.

I tried to sidestep him but he clipped me hard in the hip, causing me to grunt in pain, leaving us both off-balance.

No whistle.

José was letting this play out.

We were tangled up a few yards from the mouth of the goal, pushing and grabbing each other, breathing hard and heavy, trying to break free and reach the ball perched like a golden egg in the center of an eagle's nest.

Brock elbowed me in the chest. It felt like a hammer blow. I took a step back but recovered enough to wrap an arm around his waist and pull him towards me, trying to surge ahead. Just as I gained a step, he grabbed my shirt and jerked hard, stopping my momentum.

Still no whistle. José seemed to sense this was no longer a soccer game. This was war. We had reached the final stage of the battle, both giving it all we had, and whoever ended up on top of this final play would be the victor.

Brock's tug on my shirt had allowed him to gain a step. I tried to pull him back but he hunched his shoulders and plowed forward. I yanked harder but it was like trying to rein in an ox with my bare hands.

With me hanging on his back, Brock moved forward inch by inch. I tried to slip around him but he stuck his arms out in perfect shielding position and held me back.

The ball was only a foot away from his goal but I was about to lose the battle. If he got the ball back, I didn't think I'd have the strength to stop him from scoring.

As my enemy howled in victory and reared back to kick the ball away, I released his shirt and threw my body forward, dropping beneath his arms in a desperate slide tackle, stretching as far as I could to reach the ball. Brock realized what I was doing and fell on top of me to stop the lunge, sticking out his own leg to try to reach the ball.

He landed on me so hard it rattled my teeth and knocked the wind out of me. I ignored the pain and tried to stretch my leg as if it were made of elastic, reaching as far as I possibly could, stretching and stretching, willing my foot to extend, giving it every last ounce of my strength and mental focus. The end of my toe touched the ball a millisecond before Brock's foot arrived, and I managed to nudge the ball forward.

Gasping for air, a little dizzy from the fall, I looked up just in time to watch the ball trickle between the shoes marking his goal.

"Three to two," José said. "Leo wins."

The supporters on my side of the field threw up their hands and roared. For a moment, Brock seemed frozen, unable to believe he had lost. I decided to help him remember. Although I hadn't regained my wind and couldn't speak, I pushed him off me and rolled on my back on the ground. When he turned towards me, eyes blazing with fury, I held up my hands in the air, three fingers raised on one hand, and two on the other.

A Surprise Announcement

No one dared miss Sunday breakfast. The cafeteria had the best buffet on Sundays, piled high with eggs, sausages, pancakes, and waffles, plus all the toppings you could ever want. I'm talking fresh strawberries, whipped cream, chocolate sauce, sprinkles, the works.

My friends had gathered around me at a long table, reliving the one-on-one match with Brock the night before, talking about my rainbow and all the punishment I had received. I was bruised all over and had a cut below my left eye. All over the cafeteria, I saw players looking at me with new respect. Brock and his cronies were huddled on the opposite side of the room. After our battle, Brock had stalked off the field without a word to me. I wondered if he would keep his promise to leave me alone, or take revenge in some way.

Halfway through the meal, Director Hawk shocked us all by standing up at the coaches' table and calling for our attention. He was holding a clipboard in his left hand and dressed in a Dragons tracksuit as always. We all stopped talking and swallowed whatever food we had in our mouths, afraid to chew loudly in his presence.

"I'm told everyone is here this morning," he said. "That's good, because I have a special announcement to make. I know you're all eager to learn if you've made the World Cup, and we've decided not to make you wait until the evening."

Even the presence of Director Hawk couldn't stop the titter of excitement that spread through the cafeteria. The news caused my stomach to clench in anticipation.

"Before I announce the final squads, let me also say there will be no more Specials. Practice will continue during the day, and the World Cup games will take place at night. As for the cup itself, four teams have been selected, one from each Squad. Those who didn't make the World Cup will not have a chance to join the Academy, but we'd like all of you to stay at the Castle to continue practicing, cheer for your squads, and be available as substitutes, should anyone get injured."

This was great news. No matter who made the Iguanas World Cup team, I wouldn't have to say goodbye to any of my friends today.

"For the first round of the tournament," Director Hawk continued, "the teams will all play each other one time, in a round robin. After that, we'll seed all four teams for the semifinals. The first-place team will play the fourth-place team, and the second will play the third. The two winners will face off in the finals in the Dragons FC stadium in London."

Wait, did I hear that right? The championship will take place in the actual London Dragons stadium?

"Yes, you heard that right. The final game will take place under the lights in the actual London Dragons stadium. Sometimes the first team players like to watch the young talent, so you might spot a few familiar faces in the crowd."

Goosebumps rose along my arms at this announcement. London Dragons players watching the final game? I thought I might faint from excitement. The news caused applause to resound through the cafeteria.

When the noise died down, Director Hawk said, "The final eleven players selected to join the Academy will come from all four squads. You do not have to win the World Cup to advance. But your performance in the games will be the deciding factor in our decision. And we like winners. Keep that in mind, lads—and give it your very best. Now, are we ready to hear the team rosters?"

After another round of cheers, Director Hawk lifted his clipboard to read the names. The room grew as quiet as a principal's office. I leaned forward in my chair, hands clenched at my sides, as he read the names.

First up was the Gilas, with all the players I had watched excel during the summer: Miguel, Sebastian, Conor, and Sergi.

Same with the Komodos and Monitors. The stars had advanced: Diego, Hans, Mateo, Simon, and all the others. Charlie was assigned as the goalkeeper for the Komodos World Cup team, along with Diego at forward, which caused a shudder to roll through me. Diego and Charlie on the same team?

"For the Iguanas," Director Hawk said, causing my heart to beat faster, "we have José, Sven, Dayo, Robbie, Garika, Alejandro, Brock, Julian, Koffi in the goal, Javier—"

The director paused to take a drink of water, which almost caused me to scream in frustration. I had counted on my fingers as he read the names. Nine Iguanas and a goalie had been selected so far. That left only one place on the team. Why had he paused? Was he really that thirsty? Maybe they still had not decided—

"And Leo," the director said, causing me to slump in my chair, barely able to believe he had called my name, relieved and stunned and excited all at the same time. Alejandro punched me in the side to congratulate me.

"Those are your teams, lads," Director Hawk continued. "Good luck in the Cup."

I spent the rest of the day hanging out with my friends and dreaming about playing at Dragon Stadium in the finals.

The remaining forty-eight players all had a legitimate shot to make the Academy. Now we just had to prove ourselves among the absolute cream of the crop. On the Iguanas, only José seemed to be a shoe-in for the final eleven, but even he would be challenged by all the talented midfielders at the camp.

Though ecstatic I had made the World Cup team, I was left wondering, once again, where I fit in. Part of it depended on where Samantha decided to play me. I had a feeling she would slot me in at left midfield, which meant I would be competing against, among others, Sergi. The Spanish player was considered the second best midfielder after José, and would be nearly impossible to beat out, especially since it wasn't even my position. Or maybe Samantha would play me at winger. That would be better than midfield.

Enough, Leo. Stop worrying and go play the game. You never used to worry like this.

Yeah, but I've never had so much at stake.

Really? Is making the team that important?

Nah. It's just the rest of my life and my family's future.

Another issue was Brock. How was I supposed to play on the same team with someone who hated me?

I played video games late into the night with my friends.

Although I needed a good night's sleep more than ever, my mind wouldn't stop racing in bed, and it took me forever to fall asleep.

First thing the next morning, Samantha gathered all the Iguanas together, congratulated those of us who had made the World Cup team, and told us the schedule for the week. The first game was that night, against the Komodos. Oh boy. That meant we'd be facing Diego right off the bat.

Game Two was on Tuesday, and Game Three on Wednesday. The semifinals began on Friday. The final game, if we made it that far, would be Sunday at nine p.m.—under the lights at Dragon Stadium.

As that sank in, Samantha told us we still had to practice on game days, as the director had said, though we wouldn't go that hard. Now that she had our final eleven, we would be working on positioning, set pieces, and coming together as a team.

"So," she said, "I'm going to line you up in your positions right now, so we can work on bringing the ball up from the back. I've decided to play a 4-3-3. Koffi, you're our center forward. Just kidding," she said, as Koffi jumped to his feet with a look of confusion. The team laughed, and she flung a wrist towards the goal. "You know where to go. Garika and Brock, you're our center backs, and I want Garika on the right. Julian, you're on the right too, but you'll need to be strong pushing up. Alejandro, you're on the left with Brock."

Interesting choice of formation, I thought. Julian would be a strong right back, since he was an excellent two-way player, but Alejandro might struggle pushing forward on the wing.

"Dayo, you're our center striker, with Sven on the right and Javier on the left."

I worked hard not to show my disappointment. *There goes my shot at playing forward.* Now it was official: I would have to prove myself in midfield.

"José at center mid," Samantha continued. "Robbie on the right, Leo on the left." She clapped her hands to shoo us away. "Let's get started, Iguanas! I want to win that cup!"

The rest of the day was a blur. I couldn't think about anything except the game that night against the Komodos. Despite all the small-sided scrimmages and exciting drills over the summer, I realized how much I missed the excitement of a full-length game with referees.

All of the teams had some great players, but the Komodos might have had the two best at their positions in the whole camp: Diego and Charlie. They also had Simon, a Canadian defender who always managed to be in the right place at the right time, and Fabio, an Italian midfielder who I didn't know very well, but who had steadily improved over the summer. No one had picked him to advance in the beginning, and he wasn't the most athletic player, but like José, he never seemed to lose the ball or make a wrong decision.

Samantha wrapped up the easy practice at two p.m. We returned to our rooms to relax for the rest of the afternoon. After an early dinner, we had some time to ourselves before heading out to stretch beneath the lights.

As we took the field, I bounced on my toes, ready and eager. Director Hawk was watching from the bleachers with a clipboard in his hands. Oh boy. I glanced behind me. Alejandro gave me a thumbs up, and Garika shook a fist in the air, but Brock stared right through me, pretending I wasn't there. I had to watch out. I wouldn't put it past him to try something nasty on me during the game.

The Komodos won the coin toss. Diego stood with his foot on the ball, tall and imperious like a war general, as the ref blew the whistle.

We were on.

Game time!

Everyone played tight for a few minutes, working through their nerves. But then Diego set the tone early. After Javier launched a shot from the right wing that had little chance of going in, Charlie caught the ball and immediately punted it past half field. I had never seen a kid my age kick the ball that far. It surprised our defense, too. Garika liked to play high on the field because he was so fast. But Diego knew exactly how far Charlie could kick, and had already started running. He took one touch on the ball and blew by Garika. Brock ran over to intercept him, but he was too late. Diego raced downfield and fired a bullet from the edge of the penalty box. Koffi had no chance to save it, but lucky for us, the shot pinged off the crossbar. Alejandro slid to kick it out of bounds.

Diego threw his hands in the air, furious with himself. He knew he had wasted a golden opportunity. After that, the game evened out for a while. Fabio was even better than expected in midfield. Watching him and José compete was like watching two chess masters at work.

Robbie was his usual solid self. He worked the ball to Sven time and again on the wing, and in turn, Sven excelled at getting open to cross the ball. But neither Dayo nor Javier could manage to get past Simon, the Komodo center back. He was strong in the air, and always managed to stick a foot in just in time to poke the ball away.

I spent most of the first half running up and down the field without touching the ball. Growing tired of waiting, I decided to overlap Javier, and he passed it to me on the left wing. Charlie intercepted my cross and promptly threw it downfield like a baseball. Instead of racing back after my cross, I lingered too long near the corner.

"Get back, Leo!" José screamed.

I sprinted as hard as I could, but it was too late. Their right midfielder—the player I was supposed to mark—surged downfield with no one around him. Diego swung in towards the right side to support him, and Fabio was on the right wing. After a quick series of passes, Diego flicked the ball past Brock to Fabio, who rocketed the ball into the top right corner of our goal.

Brock glared at me as I ran back to apologize, and even Alejandro wasn't happy. I was used to playing forward, where it didn't matter that much if I sprinted back to help on every play. Feeling awful, I realized I couldn't afford to take a single play off on defense, not at this level.

After that, I made a few nice passes to Javier and Dayo, but they couldn't break down the Komodo defense. Simon was not as fast as either one of them, but he was very crafty. He let them shoot from outside, because he had Charlie lurking behind him like a giant broom.

Just before halftime, José and Robbie and I knocked the ball around in midfield, looking for an opening. Dayo had crept towards us, calling for the ball, and it gave me an idea. There was a play we had practiced in the night sessions which I thought might work. Calling for the ball from José, I made eye contact with Dayo right before I received the ball. I thought he might be on the same page, and hoped he would remember the play we had practiced.

Dayo ran a few steps towards me, separating himself from Simon, who was right on his back. I hit a sharp pass to Dayo's feet and immediately took off running upfield. He hit it right back to me, then turned and curled around Simon. I passed the ball as soon as I received it, another one-touch, putting it behind the defense and to the left, in between Simon and the right fullback, where I hoped Dayo was headed.

And I was right. The pass was on the money, waiting for Dayo as he split the gap between the defenders. He didn't have a good angle on goal, but Javier had run inside to support him. Dayo slipped the ball to our French winger, who one-touched it across the goal to Sven, who blasted it by Charlie.

Goal!

Not even the Australian keeper had a chance against Sven's wicked right foot from point-blank range. The referee blew the half time whistle, and we celebrated like mad men, making a pile on top of Sven.

"Okay, okay," Samantha said with a smile as we huddled around her. "Great way to end the half."

"Sorry about the goal," I blurted out. "I didn't get back."

"That's true," Samantha said. "You should learn from that. But you made up for it by starting off the goal with Dayo. Great work up there."

I beamed with the praise, and Alejandro slapped me on the back. After Samantha finished her speech, Robbie took me aside and said, "You're playing well, but they're going to overload the right. Be ready to stay back and help."

"How do you know?"

"Garika is our only defender fast enough to mark Diego. They'll try to avoid him and pressure Brock and Alejandro."

"Okay," I said. "Thanks."

The second half started, and Robbie's warning proved true. The Komodos went right at Brock and Alejandro on the first play, pressing hard on our left side. Diego collected a pass near the penalty box with only Brock between him and the goal. The Mexican striker cut left and then flicked the ball to his right, just past Brock's outstretched leg. Diego reared back for a shot at goal, but when he tried to kick the ball, he found that it had disappeared. I had been sprinting towards the play and slid to kick the ball from behind, just managing to knock it past the goal line.

As Koffi pumped a fist in the air and yelled my name, thrilled Diego was cut off, I groaned and rolled over, knowing I would have a strawberry after that one. A hand was waiting to pull me up, and to my surprise, it wasn't Alejandro.

"Thanks," I said, as Brock yanked me to my feet as if I were a feather.

"Go!" he barked, as the Komodos lined up for a corner kick. "Watch the near post."

It wasn't a warm and fuzzy response, but I nodded, followed his order, and got into position by the goal. Diego's header off the corner kick sailed just wide, and again he berated himself at the near miss.

"You were right," I said to Robbie as we ran back for the goal kick.

"They'll keep it up," he said. "Be ready."

I spent the rest of the half mostly on defense, helping Brock and Alejandro try to contain Diego and their other forwards. The night sessions saved me once again. If I had not learned the basics of defense from Tig and Samantha, or strengthened my stamina by playing every night, I could not have helped as much as I did. Time and again I intercepted a pass or saved a goal at the last minute by racing back to break up a play.

José played as brilliantly as usual and created a number of chances for our forwards. But we couldn't slip another goal by Charlie. He batted away shot after shot with hands that seemed as big as baseball gloves. The game went back and forth for a long time, until Diego broke through after Charlie sent another punt sailing over the half field line. Instead of trapping the ball, Diego headed the ball backwards, over Garika's head. Diego spun around him and chased it down, arriving a step before our defense. After shielding Garika off the ball, Diego kicked it ahead again, and outpaced Julian in a sprint to the ball. Koffi raced out to head him off, but Diego chipped it over him, a perfect ball that dropped on the goal line and bounced into the goal. It was a display of individual brilliance that I could only shake my head at and admire.

We tried to press the attack during the last few minutes, but they packed in their defense and held us off. The final whistle blew.

Komodos 2, Iguanas 1.

As we gathered in a circle after the game, Samantha told us we had played well and to keep our heads up. "There's a lot to work on in practice tomorrow. That was just one game. Let's focus on the next one now. Get some rest, Iguanas. I'm proud of you."

After she left, Julian walked over to me and said, in front of the whole group, "It would have been a tie game if you'd gotten back for that first goal."

Embarrassed, my eyes slipped downward as someone tossed a ball at Julian and hit him in the chest, doubling him over. "Hey!" Julian said. "What the—"

Julian cut off when he raised up and saw who had thrown the ball. I thought it would be Alejandro or Garika, but I was shocked to see Brock standing on the edge of the circle of players with his bag slung over his shoulder, pointing a finger at his best friend.

"Shut up, Julian," Brock said. "Were you watching the game? If it wasn't for Leo, the score would have been four to zero."

ENTRY #19

All Hope Seems Lost

No one was more surprised than I was by Brock's outburst. The next day at practice, he still didn't say a word to me, but he didn't glare at me or try to take me down, either. While we might never be friends, I got the feeling he respected me now, and things between us were okay.

Our squad spent the day talking about what we did right during the first game, as well as how to improve. Samantha wanted to see more ball movement and creativity in the offense. *Then let me play forward*, I wanted to scream.

Before I knew it, the day had slipped by, and our team was under the lights again, warming up to play the Monitors. This game would be just as challenging as the first one. The Monitors had Mateo and Hans as center backs. That wasn't even fair. They would be incredibly tough to score on, and I knew Mateo remembered the move I had put on him the last time we had met. He would be looking for revenge.

The Monitors also had Mahmoud, the clever Egyptian striker who always found a way to score. Every time a ball slipped out of a goalie's hands, or ricocheted off a post, he seemed to be in the right place at the right time to poke the ball into the net.

"We need to win this game," José said as he gathered the team before kickoff. "We don't want two losses in the round robin. We'll have a terrible seed for the semifinals."

"Their center backs are top notch," Robbie added, "but their keeper is the weakest of all four teams. Don't be afraid to shoot if you're open."

We all stuck our hands into the huddle and shouted, "Iguanas!"

José, our captain, won the coin toss.

The whistle blew.

Time to play!

Dayo passed the first ball to Javier, who kicked it back to me. I slipped it across to José, and he chipped it over the defense to Sven. Before he could cross it, Hans ran him down with a slide tackle that knocked our Danish winger off his feet. Sven was a stout kid, but Hans was the largest player at the camp, and it took Sven a few moments to recover.

It was the same story every time we advanced. Hans and Mateo gobbled up every ball in sight. Unable to dribble close to the goal, Javier, Sven, José, and even Robbie tried a few long-range shots with no success. I didn't trust my leg strength enough to try one myself. I stubbornly kept trying to work the ball closer.

Our defense held up against their offense until Mahmoud took a free kick from thirty yards out. The curving shot bounced off the side post, inches from Koffi's fingers, and caromed high in the air. Players from both teams headed the ball back and forth like a herd of seals, until somehow, the ball landed at Mamhoud's feet again. He took a wild shot that bounced off Garika's leg—nothing Garika could do about it—and landed in the side netting.

1-0 Monitors.

Another lucky break for Mahmoud.

The score remained the same at halftime. As we drank water on the bench, Samantha went around the team, offering encouragement and advice. "Leo, you need to involve yourself more in the game."

She was right. I had barely touched the ball that half.

"You're getting back on defense, which is excellent. But you're doing a lot of running, sometimes for no reason. You have to learn to pick your battles, okay?"

"Okay," I said, though I didn't really know how to improve. Great midfielders had a knack for understanding the flow of the game. When to press forward and when to pull back. I was still learning the position, and felt more like a headless chicken running blindly around the field.

Brock took a long drink of water and scowled at the forwards. "You're letting Hans and Mateo intimidate you. Push them back when they get physical."

He was right, too. After the hard tackle on Sven, I had noticed our forwards backing off from challenges on Hans and Mateo. That was no way to win a game.

Soon after the second half started, we earned a corner kick. Brock waved his hand and asked Samantha if he could push forward. She agreed, and he went crashing into the penalty box, bumping players left and right, as Javier crossed the ball. Brock gave Hans a heavy shoulder from behind that knocked him off his feet, resulting in a foul and a free kick for the Monitors.

As Brock ran back to his position, I saw a grim smile on his lips, and I knew he had charged in there to help protect our forwards and set a new tone. I was surprised, since Hans and Brock were friends, but I was learning that Brock was extremely competitive. And it didn't hurt to have someone physical on our team who could stand up to the bruisers on the other side.

During the game, I noticed Tig in the bleachers, watching Samantha as much as the game. Seeing him there gave me a burst of energy. I tried to insert myself more, calling for the ball and pushing forward. I managed a sweet cross to Sven, and a nice through ball to Dayo, but neither resulted in a goal.

Late in the half, Mahmoud was dribbling in the penalty box, weaving back and forth like his usual slippery self. He beat Julian off the dribble, forcing Alejandro to race all the way across the box for a slide tackle. Mahmoud sprang to the side at the last second, but Alejandro caught his left foot and tripped him, drawing a penalty kick.

"C'mon Koffi!" I yelled, as our keeper danced back and forth in the goal, ready for the shot.

Mahmoud ran on to the ball, then leaned left so convincingly that Koffi dove to that side in anticipation. Mahmoud paused for a split second before kicking the ball, slipping an easy shot into the right-side netting.

That was the last goal of the game. Just like the Komodos, knowing they had a victory in sight, the Monitors pulled back the midfield on defense, making it hard to score. It was so frustrating. I wanted to take Hans or Mateo off the dribble and make something happen, but I didn't want to make the wrong play, or look selfish in front of my teammates.

When the final whistle blew, we left the field with our heads down. Samantha did her best to encourage us, and told us it didn't matter if we lost all three games in the first round, because we still would advance. That might be true, but it would mean we'd have to play the Komodos or the Monitors in the semifinals. Diego's Komodos had just beaten the Gilas 3-1, and the Monitors had slipped past the Gilas 1-0 the day before.

"Get a good night's rest, Iguanas," Samantha said. "I have a couple of tweaks to the lineup in mind that I think will help us. I'll let you know what they are tomorrow."

After that cryptic remark, Samantha walked across the field to join one of her friends. On the way, I noticed her staring at Tig in the bleachers when he was talking to one of the other coaches. When Tig turned in Samantha's direction, she looked quickly away, and her shoulders tightened.

After she left the huddle, everyone began to bicker and point fingers. Alejandro had his head in his hands, distraught about the penalty kick. "It's not your fault," I said. "You ran over to help out."

"I should have been more careful," he said.

I couldn't stand all the arguing, and wasn't happy with my own play, so I grabbed my bag and left. On my way to the Castle, Tig caught up with me. He was holding a phone and had some earbuds in, bobbing his head to the music.

"Hey, Boss."

"Hey."

"Tough game, eh?"

"We're 0 and 2 now. I couldn't do anything right."

He gave me a long look, then took his earbuds out and stuck them in his pocket, along with his phone. There was a ball on the ground nearby. He walked over, scooped it into the air with his foot, and passed it to me. "Incoming!"

I had to drop my bag to catch the ball in the air, but I

trapped it on my thigh and sent it back to him. We juggled together for a while, doing a few tricks, before I dropped one of his passes and got angry at myself. "Like I said. I can't do anything right."

"Hey Leo?" he said, lifting the ball into the air again, balancing it between his shoulder blades, and flicking it to me.

"Yeah?" I said, struggling to follow along.

"Where's that kid I met on the plane?"

"What do you mean?"

"The one who loved the game? The one who played for *fun?*"

I stopped juggling and put a foot on the ball. "It's hard to have fun when there's so much at stake."

"Oh boy," he said, pressing his hands to his forehead. "Who is this guy? What did they do to you? If you're not having fun, you'll never unlock your potential. You know why most kids stop playing sports, Leo? Not because they're not winning. That doesn't even make the top ten. It's because they're not *having fun*. They get older and they're afraid to make mistakes, or disappoint their parents, or get cut from the select team."

I lowered my eyes, toeing the ball back and forth on the ground.

"Chin up, Boss. You have to work hard and play your best, that's true. There aren't any shortcuts, not in soccer and not in life. You have the skills now, though. Unleash yourself. Have fun again. When I first saw you play, that's what made you stand out from the other players. This last game, you were playing so uptight you looked like a robot. If you want a shot at the Academy, a real shot, you've got to be yourself and take some chances. Play for the love of the game."

"She won't even play me at forward," I said in a small voice.

"And who's fault is that?" he said, backing away as he put his ear buds back in.

Iguanas Shed Their Skins
At Least Once a Year

After the game with the Monitors, I returned to my room and found Robbie hunched over his phone on his bed.

"What are you watching?" I asked, happy to see him wasting time on a device for once. "A movie?"

"Huh?" he said, looking up. "A movie? Uh, no, Leo. One of my coaches flew in for the World Cup. He taped our first two games and I'm watching them, trying to see how I can improve."

When he returned to his phone, I stared at him for a few moments, until he sent me away with an annoyed wave. I lay on my bed but wasn't tired enough to fall asleep. I supposed I could ask Robbie to send me the video of the game so I could watch it myself.

All of a sudden, I realized how ridiculous that thought was. Tig was right.

What had happened to me?

I decided to relax with a video game, then changed my mind. Instead I took my ball, went to the practice field behind the Castle, turned on the lights, and practiced a new set of tricks. I didn't get mad at myself but just had fun, trying the hardest tricks I could think of, staying on the field late into the night as I thought about everything Tig had said.

The next morning, I felt more myself than I had in a long time. All the pressure to win was still there—I didn't think it would ever go away—but it was no longer the most important reason for playing the game. Somehow, overnight, Tig's speech had sunk in, and I realized that, while I could have all the training in the world—and I had worked very hard to acquire my new skills—in order to succeed, I had to be myself, too.

As Samantha led the morning stretches, she told us she was going to make a lineup change. I perked up at once.

"We're going to play a 3-4-3," she said. "Garika, you'll be in the middle back there, and Julian, you're going to push up to midfield. You and Leo are working really hard, and you two will be great on the wings. I think it will help our attack. Okay?" she said, looking at Julian and then at me.

"Sure," I said, unable to hide my disappointment, but also remembering what else Tig had said.

And who's fault is that?

Nine o'clock arrived before I knew it.

As we took the field against the Gila Monsters, our last game in the round robin, I forgot about all the pressure, and the coaches watching from the stands, and the bright lights overhead. I pretended I was back in Ohio, on a lumpy field at the park on a cool Saturday morning, barely able to wait until the ref blew the whistle. Samantha had stuck me in midfield again, way out on the left wing, but that was okay, because I was going to play my game the way I knew how to play it.

The Gilas had some excellent players, and a very balanced squad. Up front, they had Sebastian, the fastest player in the whole camp, and Miguel, the Nicaraguan striker who played low to the ground and was difficult to knock off the ball. A tall, quiet, Irish kid named Conor anchored their defense. We had played together on the first day of the camp.

Right before the game started, I noticed that for some reason, Sergi, their best player and left midfielder, was playing on the right side for this game, lined up against me.

Is it because their coach thinks he can take advantage of me? I wondered. *Do they consider me a weak link?*

Having two central midfielders, along with Julian and me on the outside, allowed me the freedom to push forward. I wasn't in the middle where I preferred, but as long as I got back on defense, I could make runs down the wing.

Soon after the game started, José sent the ball my way, but his pass did not have enough pace. Sergi flew in to intercept it. We made contact on the ball at the same time. I pushed a little harder than he did, and managed to come up with the ball. As he tried to steal it away, I gave him a quick shoulder fake, throwing him off balance, then dribbled to the right and snapped a pass up the field to Javier.

A good start to my duel with Sergi.

Right from the start, their two best forwards, Miguel and Sebastian, really tested our defense. Miguel kept trying to take Garika one on one, but so far the Zimbabwean had kept him at bay. On the wing, Alejandro was much slower than Sebastian, but my friend survived by playing off him, giving me time to get back and help. I ran myself ragged in the first half supporting Alejandro, trying to contain Sergi in the middle, and pushing forward alongside Javier whenever I could. I was playing well, but in danger of tiring out before the half ended.

Knowing I was gassed, Sergi tried to beat me off the dribble in midfield. I read his move and poked the ball away. It ended up beside us, with no one else nearby. Somehow I managed to beat him to it, then shielded him off as I held onto the ball.

"Leo!" Javier called. "Down the wing!"

I would have loved to play the ball on the wing to Javier, except I was facing my own goal, and Sergi was right on top of me. I had just run up from the back again, and was too exhausted to try a move. Using my arms to shield Sergi, I flicked my head to the right and saw Javier sprinting downfield, ahead of his defender.

I had to try to get it to him. Still pressing my back against Sergi, I did a half-turn to the right, holding him off when he tried to stick a leg in. Before the summer, I would never have been able to shield a player like Sergi that well. I pushed the ball out a foot from my body, whipped my leg around, and sent the ball sailing down the wing. It wasn't the prettiest pass, but it landed ahead of Javier. He managed to reach it just before it went out of bounds, rolled the ball back with the bottom of his foot, spun, and crossed the ball to Sven. The Dane leaped high, made great contact with the front of his head . . . and put the ball just over the goal.

"Nice pass," Javier said, as he ran back into position. "Way to find me."

I could only nod, too tired to respond. Three games in three days, on top of light practices, had taken their toll. When the halftime whistle blew, with the game tied 0-0, I trudged to the sideline, thighs aching, in desperate need of some water.

"Great job, Leo!" Samantha said, thumping me on the back. "I think they put Sergi on your side for a reason, but you got the better of him. Keep it up!"

"I'll try," I said, thinking, *if I can last until the end of the game.*

Although I felt better after the short rest, when the second half started, I knew I had to change my strategy and pick my battles. I couldn't play all over the field again. I decided to cheat back on defense and guard the midfield, rather than try to push forward every time. It meant I wouldn't have as many chances to score or provide an assist, but I would just have to make those chances count.

Both teams went back and forth in the second half. Miguel missed a volley at a wide-open goal, Sergi almost headed the ball in on a corner kick, and Sebastian finally beat Alejandro down the wing, only to watch in frustration as Koffi dove to save the shot, brushing it aside with inches to spare.

Our forwards missed just as many opportunities. Javier and Sven sent cross after cross into the middle, but Conor kept rising over Dayo to head the ball away. Dayo had the advantage on the ground, but he failed to convert on two break-aways. He struck the ball wide on one attempt, and their goalie saved the other. Robbie had the best shot of the game so far, a screamer from thirty yards out that clanged off the crossbar, causing him to fall to his knees and clutch his hair.

As the end of the game drew near, still in a deadlock, everyone looked as exhausted as I felt. I knew the coaches had scheduled the games so close in order to test our physical and mental endurance.

"Three minutes!" Samantha called out as she checked her watch on the sideline.

No one wanted to go to overtime, so both teams made one last push. I don't know where Sergi got the energy, but he started playing like an anime demon, racing all over the midfield. In fact, I thought he was playing selfishly, trying to put the team on his shoulders and win the game by himself. Either because of this, or because he still thought he could get the better of me, he tried to beat me one on one again. It was silly. He had an easy pass to his left. But whatever his reason, he came straight at me well into our half of the field. If he beat me, our defense would be exposed behind me, and the Gilas would have a late chance to score.

Sergi stepped over the ball once, twice, dancing to get me to commit. I faked a rush forward, causing him to flick the ball to the right, trying to push it around me. But I dropped back and stole the ball right out from under him. Before he could recover, I pushed it through his legs, nutmegging him with a pass to José. I ran around Sergi like he was standing still, and José gave it back to me as I surged forward.

I wasn't sure if there was enough time for a final attempt, but I pushed that thought away and willed my tired legs forward one more time. Side by side, José and I raced downfield, passing it back and forth between us, knowing the clock was running out. Sven called for the ball frantically on the wing. I faked a pass to him but gave it back to José instead, confusing their defense. For this last run, I was trusting only myself and José. I think he had the same idea, because instead of pushing the ball to Javier or Dayo, he gave me another return pass. We came charging out of the midfield, putting heavy pressure on their defense.

Conor stepped up to defend me. This time, instead of

passing to José as everyone expected, I stepped over the ball in his direction and took it back to my right.

The move took Conor by surprise. He lunged towards José, leaving open space in front of me. I took two dribbles and was right at the edge of the penalty box. Their center back streaked in to help defend.

All of my forwards were calling for the ball. The box was filling up quickly, and their center back had almost reached me. I had a split second to decide.

Instead of taking the shot, or passing to one of the forwards, I slipped another pass to José on my left, right in front of the goal. I had caught a glimpse of him in the corner of my eye, darting forward. We had followed each other all the way downfield, and I decided to give it back to him for the final attempt.

My pass slipped right by their center back and rolled just in front of José, catching him in stride eight yards from the goal mouth. He didn't hesitate, and the goalie never had a chance.

Bottom left corner.

Goal!

The ref blew the whistle. My team went wild, running towards José to congratulate him, but he raced around in a circle to evade them, and came up behind me to give me a bear hug. Instead of winning the final game of the round robin, you would have thought we'd won the real World Cup.

Samantha ran onto the field, her fist pumping in the air, just as excited as her players. But as everyone raced to pile on top of me and José, I saw Samantha wobble and then fall over, crumpling to the ground as if someone had pulled a rug out from underneath her.

She screamed in pain, and the last thing I saw before my friends smothered me was Samantha clutching the brace on her left knee, her face twisted in agony.

ENTRY #21

Iguanas Versus Monitors

As soon as Samantha went down, I threw José off of me, dodged Alejandro and the others, and raced to help our coach. I was fast, but someone else was even faster, a tall figure who darted off the sidelines and sprinted towards Samantha. I realized it was Tig as he knelt beside her, shouting for help and holding her hand as she writhed in pain on the ground. The rest of the players ran over to surround us, but Tig kept everyone back until the camp medic arrived. I could only watch, stunned and helpless, as the medic gently probed her leg and asked questions, then called for a stretcher to carry her off the field. A lump formed in my throat as they left with her in a van.

"It's that knee again," Tig said as he watched the van disappear down the long drive. There was a catch in his voice, and he turned away. "She's not supposed to be running like that. She must have come down on it wrong when she went to celebrate."

"How serious is it?"

"I don't know, Boss. I just don't know."

As he began to walk away, I said, "Where are you going?"

"To the clinic. I'm not sure . . . she may not want to see me, but I want to be there."

"Can I go with you?"

He hesitated. "It's late, and I'm not sure if the coaches—"

"I don't care."

He pressed his lips together and waved me over as he broke into a jog. "C'mon," he said.

Tig found one of the Dragon FC chauffeurs in the stands and begged him to drive us to the hospital. After he agreed, Alejandro and Garika noticed us running towards the vans and asked us to take them as well. The word spread quickly, and before the van could leave, the rest of the Iguanas swarmed the vehicle. The driver took a look around, saw how many players there were, and decided to take a bus instead. All twenty-five of us piled on board, plus Tig and the driver.

The local emergency clinic was only a few miles away. We overran the waiting room and spilled into the hallway. Our excitement from the win was still fresh, and we relived the game as we waited, especially José's goal. But I couldn't stop thinking about Samantha's injury and what the doctor would say. What if something really bad had happened? What if Samantha would never walk again?

An hour later, the double doors to the inside of the clinic swung open, and Samantha walked into the waiting room on crutches, her left knee wrapped in a bandage and supported by an even larger brace than before. Coach Tanner was right beside her. At first, Samantha's eyes were downcast, but when she saw the entire squad gathered in the waiting room, the corners of her mouth lifted. "What's everyone doing here?" she said. "You should be at the Castle resting!"

In response, we all started to clap, hoot, and chant her

name. The receptionist, startled by all the commotion, made us quiet down. Samantha glanced at Tig, who was leaning against a wall with his arms crossed, his eyes filled with concern.

"I can't believe you all came," Samantha said, taking her eyes off of Tig as she wiped away a tear. "Thank you. I tweaked my knee again, but—" she shrugged and flashed a sad smile. "My playing days are over anyway. I have to rest tomorrow, but you better believe I'll be on the sidelines for the semifinals. And what a win today, you guys. What a win! Let's go Iguanas!!!"

We all began cheering again, louder than before. This time, when the receptionist tried to quiet us down, we completely ignored her.

On Thursday, Coach Tanner stood in for Samantha at practice. The semifinals did not take place until the following evening. Our victory over the Gilas had secured us the #3 seed, and our opponent in the semifinals would be the Monitors, the #2 seed—the team with Hans and Mateo at center back, and Mahmoud at striker. Things could have been worse. We could have been the fourth place seed and had to play the Komodos, Diego and Charlie's squad. But beating the Monitors was going to be a very tall order, so we practiced hard that day, and tried to think of ways to break down their airtight defense.

After practice, I told the guys I was going to kick the ball around later that night, on the field behind the Castle. I did not expect anyone other than Alejandro, Garika, and Dayo to join me.

To my surprise, when I showed up on the field at nine o'clock, the lights were already on, and most of the Iguanas had arrived. I was even more surprised when Brock and Julian showed up five minutes later. The entire starting eleven had come.

"Hey," Brock said in a gruff voice as he walked over to where we were taking penalty kicks on Koffi. "Got room for two more?"

"Sure," I said, passing him a ball. "Just don't hurt anyone."

Julian did not look happy to be there, but Brock cracked a grin at my remark. "You keep playing like you have, Yank, and you'll stay on my good side."

We kept the session light, just roasting each other and taking shots and doing tricks under the lights. It was good for team chemistry. Even Julian relaxed after a while. Later on, when Robbie said he needed to get some rest, some of the guys started laughing. Sven asked if Robbie's coach was going to tuck him in.

Robbie turned bright red at the comment. By now, everyone knew his club coach had flown over to tape the World Cup games, and teased him mercilessly about it.

"Listen," I said. "My roomie's a great player, he just needs his beauty sleep."

Javier sneered and ran a hand through his green hair. "You Americans could all have some beauty sleep. I have never seen such poor taste in style. Your, how do you say, your haircuts are all the very same."

José started laughing so hard he started to cry. "This," he sputtered, trying to calm down enough to speak. "This from the guy with green hair?"

"And hey, Frenchie," Alejandro said. "I'm an American also. So is José."

Javier bowed. "Thank you for proving my point."

Alejandro tackled him, starting a playful wrestling match among the players. Robbie shouted for us to quit, worried someone would get injured. For once, I agreed with him, and whistled loud with my fingers.

"Before everyone leaves," I said, "I want to say something. We all know the Monitors are really tough."

My comment quieted the group, and I saw a few eyes, including Brock's, spark with anger. Good. I wanted them to be fired up.

"But there's one very important reason we're going to beat them," I continued. "We're going to win because we're going to play this game for Samantha. She got us here, and she's hurt, and we can't let her down. Who's with me on that?"

"For Samantha," José agreed, holding his arm straight out, palm down.

"Samantha," Koffi said, putting his hand on top of José's. One by one, every member of the Iguanas crowded in and stuck their hands together. We shouted our coach's name in unison and broke the huddle.

"Oh, and guys," I said before we parted ways. "There's one more thing we need to do."

I told them what I had in mind. With no hesitation, every single player agreed.

Samantha didn't return to practice on Friday. Despite what she had said, I worried she wouldn't make the game. But later that night, as we were warming up on Field Two before the semifinal game against the Monitors, Garika pointed towards the parking lot and shouted, "It's Coach!"

We all turned to see her stepping out of one of the Dragon FC vans that had pulled up next to the field. The driver, a young woman I didn't know, tried to help Samantha walk, but she waved her off. Samantha hopped on one foot as she pulled her crutches out of the car and used them to limp towards the field. We all ran over to meet her, and a smile creased her face. "You didn't think I'd miss the game, did you?"

When Dayo offered to help her walk, she shooed him away. We gathered around her like chicks following a mother hen as she made her way slowly to the sidelines and eased onto the Iguanas bench. Coach Tanner handed her the clipboard with a solemn bow. "Glad to see you back, Coach. Your team needs you."

"Thanks for filling in," she said, waving everyone in close. "And thank you all for your support. But let's not make this about me. This is your time to shine. We're going to beat these guys. To do that, I've decided to make another couple of changes."

I perked up, certain she was going to elevate me to forward after my performance in the last game.

"We're going to play with three midfielders this time," she said. "Leo, I want you on the right, and Robbie, I'm moving you to the left."

Neither Robbie nor I were left-footed. In fact, I had a stronger left foot than he did, so by moving me to the right side, Samantha was favoring me as an attacking player. I didn't care about that, because I didn't want to play midfield at all. "Okay," I said, doing my best to hide my disappointment with her decision.

"Left mid?" Robbie said, somewhat incredulous.

"Yes, Robbie," Samantha said. "That's what I said."

"But I'm better in the center. Or at least on the right. I've never played on the left."

"Robbie," Samantha said evenly, "I'm making the best decisions I can for the team. Okay?"

He lowered his eyes and nodded.

"*Okay?*" she repeated.

He looked up. "Yes, Coach."

"Thank you. You'll do great over there. I'm going to do something different on defense, too. Mahmoud is their biggest scoring threat by a long shot. Julian, I want you to play right in front of Garika—but your main duty is marking Mahmoud. I want you to follow him around the entire game. Pretend you're stuck to him with glue. Okay?"

Julian, to his credit, didn't hesitate. "Got it."

"If you stay on Mahmoud, and we can slow him down, I think they'll have a hard time scoring. Garika, be sure to talk to Julian, okay?"

"I will," Garika said.

We broke the huddle with a resounding "Iguanas!" cheer and took the field. The stands were even more packed than last time, as were the stands on the next field over, where the Komodos were playing the Gilas. Even though I was stuck in midfield, I felt worse for Robbie. Knowing my roommate, he was probably stressing about how his demotion would keep him out of the Academy, and disappoint his coaches back home, and affect his choice of college, and change the course of his entire life.

"Hey," I said, slapping him on the back as I passed him. "Good luck out there. Let's own the midfield."

He mumbled a response too low for me to hear.

As I jogged into position, bouncing up and down to get my blood flowing, I wondered why Samantha kept refusing to play me at forward. I respected her opinion and knew she was acting in the best interest of the team. But when she had told me that my best chance at making the Academy was in the midfield, and not as a forward, I just didn't believe that in my heart. It was true I was a step slower than our forwards on a breakaway, and I wasn't very good at headers, and I wasn't as physically strong as Dayo or Manuel, not to mention Diego. But over the course of the summer, during the games and scrimmages, I had as many goals and assists as anyone on our squad.

So why wouldn't she move me up?

Put it aside, Leo. Focus on the team and win the game.

The whistle blew. The pace of the game was fast right from the start, as if the stakes had elevated the level of play and the intensity of the competitors. We Iguanas were especially energized because we knew we were the underdogs, at least to everyone watching, and that gave us something to prove.

José worked the ball over to Robbie, to give him a feel for the left side. Robbie took a few dribbles and passed it to Javier on the left wing. The Monitor fullback blocked Javier's cross attempt, then kicked it downfield. The ball fell right to Mahmoud, who looked surprised to find Julian lurking right behind him when he tried to turn. Julian stripped the ball and knocked it over to Alejandro, who worked it back up the field again.

Dayo's first touch on the ball ended with Mateo shouldering him away and calmly taking possession. On our next trip downfield, Hans slid into Sven, sending both the ball and our Danish winger sailing out of bounds. The referee called a foul, but as usual, the Monitor defense was setting the tone for the game.

And that tone was that they owned us.

Samantha called on me to take the free kick from the right side of the field, just outside the penalty box. That surprised me. She had never called on me before. I surveyed the scene, trying to decide what to do. Should I try to score? Connect with Javier on the far side of the goal? I noticed Brock running in from the back and decided to use him. Even if the attempt failed, he wouldn't let Hans or Mateo push him around.

My free kick was a good one. It sailed over the defense, right towards Brock's fat head. He rose high to meet the ball. Hans was marking him and jumped right beside him. Brock arrived a shade sooner, and I could see his hands working hard, grabbing onto Hans to keep him at bay. I held my breath as Brock made great contact on the ball, but his header sailed just out of bounds.

"Good job, guys!" Samantha yelled from the bench.

"Keep it up," Brock added as he ran by me.

"You too," I said. "The defense doesn't like you in there. It makes them nervous."

He bared a wolfish smile and ran back into position. The game slogged back and forth after that. Samantha's decision to mark Mahmoud with Julian turned out to be a wise one. As she predicted, their offense had trouble penetrating our defense with Mahmoud so closely guarded. He broke free from

Julian once or twice but either Garika, Brock, or Alejandro was always there to meet him. Mahmoud's strength lay in finding garbage goals, but with someone always by his side, it made his job much harder.

The problem was, pinning Julian to Mahmoud meant we had one less player up front, against the awesome defense of the Monitors. José, Robbie, and I had success controlling the midfield, but Hans and Mateo shut down everything within spitting distance of the penalty box. They were both so tall that Sven's crosses were not effective. Javier couldn't dribble around them, and Dayo couldn't seem to break free.

How were we going to score?

"You and me again," José said to me as we stood side by side, catching our breath when the ball was out of bounds. "Let's break them down."

"Okay," I said, as Alejandro threw the ball in to me. I kicked it to José and ran downfield, past the player marking me. José hit me in stride with a perfect one-touch pass.

"Back to me!" he said.

I gave him another pass which he collected near the center of the field. One of their midfielders challenged the ball. José evaded him and dribbled further downfield. After faking a cross to Robbie, José again sent the ball back to me. A defender closed in to intercept the pass. It was going to be close. I lunged forward and flicked the ball away just in time, hopping over the sliding defender and collecting the ball thirty yards out from their goal.

Now Hans was closing in. Beside him, Mateo had pushed up so that our strikers couldn't get behind him without being offside. Should I take Hans one on one, try to chip the ball to one of our forwards, or risk another pass to José?

"Leo!" José shouted, racing in beside me. "Let's go!"

My instinct was to chip the ball to Dayo, just over the head of the defense. But I felt guilty not giving it back to José. We had scored together on Wednesday, and he wanted to try again.

Hans was approaching quickly, a steam train bearing down on me. I glanced at Dayo and then gave José a sharp pass on the ground, right at his feet. He trapped it, but Mateo came out of nowhere and flattened him with a slide tackle.

"Fair charge!" the ref called out.

José looked shaken by the play. I helped him to his feet as Mateo sent the ball downfield. "Not today," the Argentinian said, wagging a finger at me. "Not on us."

"We'll see," I snapped, running back to help on defense.

For the rest of the half, neither team managed a single shot attempt. During the break, we gathered around Samantha, hoping she had a good strategy.

"Their defense is not going to make mistakes," she said, which did not raise my hopes. "You're all playing great, so keep it up, but you're going to have to take some chances, Iguanas. Try something different."

"What do you mean?" Robbie asked, as if she had just spoken in a foreign language.

"Don't go down the wing every time. Switch the field more. José and Leo, that was a nice run towards the end. Julian, you're doing a wonderful job on Mahmoud. So is our entire defense, for that matter. C'mon, Iguanas. Stay strong and figure out this puzzle. They're good, but they're not invincible."

As soon as the half started, I did my best to switch up our tactics. After receiving a pass from José, instead of sending the ball down the wing to Sven, or chipping a ball over the top, I tried to split their center backs with a pass on the ground. Dayo made eye contact right before I passed the ball, and seemed to understand what I wanted, because he ran forward to collect the pass. As Hans closed on him, Dayo flicked the ball with the back of his foot to Javier, who was streaking in behind him. Javier slipped past Mateo and managed a shot on goal. The goalie saved it, but at least we had a chance. Knowing they could penetrate the Monitors defense seemed to energize our forwards.

On the other end, Mahmoud slipped free of Julian with a nifty spin move. He tried a tricky shot on the ground, but Koffi had improved in that arena. He laid out his long body and got a toe on the shot, deflecting it out of bounds.

That was the only real chance the Monitors had for some time. Our back line played incredible defense. The Monitors' front line couldn't breathe. If only we could get a goal, I felt sure we could hold them off and win.

José controlled the flow of the game in midfield, but beating people off the dribble wasn't his superpower. He wasn't the guy to make a spectacular play and win the game. Javier could make that kind of impact, but Mateo had shut down his dribbling attempts over and over. The Argentinian center back was just too solid.

Back and forth it went. Neither team made a serious threat. Time was running out, and we didn't want the game to end with penalty kicks, because that would come down to luck. Anyone could win a shootout.

"Come on Iguanas!" Samantha shouted. "Five minutes to go. Push hard!"

José trapped a ball near the half line and surveyed the field. Julian sprinted away from Mahmoud and surged forward, trying to add a player to our offense and make something happen. José passed him the ball and called for everyone to push up.

Julian sent the ball to Robbie, who faked a pass to Javier and then chipped it to me, all the way across the field. I completed a quick pass to Sven, who one-touched the ball to Dayo. Hans was closing fast. In a surprising show of strength, Dayo lowered his center of gravity and shielded the German center back long enough to flick the ball to Julian, who was still running forward, overloading their defense. Julian took the ball and pushed deep into the box. Before he could shoot, Mateo raced over and slide tackled him, breaking up the play, but the ball went across the goal line.

Corner kick.

"Javier, you take this one!" Samantha said.

This was only our second corner kick of the game. The crowd was buzzing, sensing an opportunity. Julian and Brock tried to move forward, but Samantha held them back, fearing a late counterattack. Not having Brock in the middle would hurt our chances at winning a header.

Javier raised his arm to signal he was about to kick the ball. We all scrambled for position in the box. I ran past José, swerved around Dayo, and bumped into Hans. It felt as if I had struck a brick wall. A little dazed, I spun as I heard Javier thump the ball from the corner.

It was chaos in the box. Everyone was shouting and grunting, struggling for position. Jerseys brushed against my chest and back. I could smell the sweat from all the players crowded together.

Javier's cross was excellent, a curving bullet that would be extremely hard to control. Sven, our best header after Brock, rose up to challenge their goalie. The ball kept curving, out of easy reach, and their goalie was forced to punch the ball away.

I was standing near the back of the penalty box. The ball was headed right for me. Defenders clogged the box, including one right in front of me. I couldn't even tell who it was. The ball landed at my feet, and, knowing I was under heavy pressure, I tried a very difficult first touch, taking the ball straight out of the air and pushing it a few feet away with the top of my foot. It worked. The nearest defender lunged for the ball and missed.

I took another touch forward as a second Monitor closed in. It was Hans. All around me, players were shouting: my teammates calling for the ball, and Monitors clamoring for someone to stop me. On the periphery of my vision, on both sides, I spotted the green jerseys of my teammates, their hands waving in the air.

But I never considered passing. It was too risky. The box was jam-packed with players. Instead, as Hans closed in, I acted on pure instinct, stepping over the ball and making a behind-the-leg pass to myself, a few feet to the right.

The move caught Hans by surprise. I streaked by him, barely avoiding his outstretched leg. Another Monitor took his place between me and the goal. This time it was Mateo. Again, I didn't even think about my next move. There was no time. Mateo was all over me. I stutter-stepped, causing him to hesitate, then rolled it to the left with the bottom of my foot. When he lurched to that side, I rolled it back the other way. Trying to compensate, he stuck his left leg out, opening his stance too wide. I poked the ball through his legs and spun around him on the right side.

Somehow the move worked. I felt Mateo grab my jersey in desperation, but I pushed through and broke free.

Two more Monitors were closing in, one from each side. I had a shot on goal from ten yards away, but I was too far to the right, with a poor angle. I wanted to dribble to get into better position but didn't have time. Instead I took the shot, knowing my attempt had little chance of success.

But the box was so crowded with players my shot deflected off the leg of a defender, altering the trajectory just enough to cause the ball to slip past the keeper's hands and sail into the back netting.

Number Tens and
Sunset Sweets

After I scored, the Monitors goalie slammed his hand against the goal post. Hans slumped to the ground with his head in his hands, and Mateo stared at me in disbelief.

My teammates, and the crowd watching the game, went bananas.

Someone tackled me from behind, and the rest of the team piled on. Before they could smother me, Brock threw everyone off and lifted me in the air with one arm, roaring my name at the top of his lungs.

"Way to go, Iguanas!" Samantha shouted. "Now everyone get back! The game isn't over!"

We celebrated until the referee blew the whistle and gave us a warning. I didn't throw a bomb on Mateo as I ran past him, because I couldn't think of anything good enough, but I did give him a long, cheeky wink as payback for his earlier comment. He turned away, seething, and shouted for his forwards to kick the ball off.

The Monitors moved the ball downfield as quickly as they could. Mahmoud received the ball in the middle and beat Julian off the dribble, but Garika was right behind him to fill in the gap. He kicked the ball back up the field, squashing that attempt.

They didn't get another chance.

Within seconds, the final whistle blew. I sank to the ground, barely able to believe what had happened.

We had proven everyone wrong and beaten the Monitors.

Our next game would be under the lights at Dragon Stadium.

After we finished celebrating, Samantha gathered us on the field and made us promise not to stay up all night. Though we had won an important game, we still had one more to go to achieve our goal. It wasn't just the World Cup on the line. Our performance on the field would play a key role in deciding who the coaches picked to join the Academy.

By the time I returned to my room, it was eleven-thirty. Robbie said a quick goodnight, put his headphones on as he climbed into bed, and turned his back to me. I knew he felt let down, maybe even betrayed, but I didn't know what to say.

I tried my best to wind down, but the final minutes of the game kept replaying in my head. I texted Carlos to tell him about the victory, but he must have been at dinner or with a friend because he never responded.

Our opponent for the finals was the Komodos, which meant Diego and Charlie. In the other semifinal game, they had beaten the Gilas 4-0. Ouch. That was a strong statement.

As I lay in bed, trying to coax my spinning brain to shut down, I couldn't stop thinking about how good Diego was, and how if I wanted to make the Academy as a center forward, I would have to outplay him in the final game.

That was the stuff of which nightmares were made.

The next morning, as I arrived at the practice field, I was happy to see Samantha standing with her crutches near midfield, talking to Coach Tanner. Robbie and José had already arrived and were passing the ball back and forth. I juggled on my own as the rest of the players drifted in. Before the stretching started, I approached Samantha when Coach Tanner stepped away to take a call on his cell phone.

"How are you?" I asked. "Are you coaching today?"

"I'm fine," she said. "You're sweet for asking. I'm going to start the morning off, then hand the reins to Coach Tanner. I can't stand all day on these crutches."

"I'm just happy you're here," I said. "Hey, I was wondering if you had plans tonight? All of us, I mean all the Iguanas, have something for you. A little gift for being our coach."

Her face softened. "You didn't need to do that." She raised one of the crutches with a rueful grin. "And no, I'm not going anywhere tonight."

"Good. I mean, not good that you're stuck on crutches . . . we thought it would be nice to give you the gift before the night session. We're still doing those, you know. The whole team came to the last one."

"I thought I noticed some great chemistry out there. What time do you want me?"

"Nine o'clock?"

"I can make that. Listen, Leo, I'm glad you came over, because there's something I wanted to discuss with you. It's about your position for the World Cup final."

"Okay," I said, wary of getting my hopes up again.

"You've been playing amazing, as I'm sure you know. I don't think I can keep you out of the attack any longer."

I blinked. "You can't?"

"Do you know what position a number ten is, Leo?"

I almost laughed at her question. *Do I know what a number ten is?*

Do baseball pitchers know what a curveball is? Do basketball players know how to shoot a three pointer?

Number ten was more than a number. It was a badge of honor, a status symbol, a mythology. Wearing number ten on the back of your jersey commanded instant respect. It was the soccer equivalent of the quarterback. Messi was a number ten. So was Pele, Maradona, Neymar, Benzema, Ronaldinho, all the greats who ever lived.

"It means you're the best player on the team," I said.

She smiled. "Sometimes, yes. But do you know what it *means*? What the position is?"

I opened my mouth and then closed it, realizing that as many players as I knew who wore the jersey, I did not, in fact, know exactly what it meant. "Scorer?" I said weakly.

"That's part of it. Traditionally, as you probably know, jersey numbers in soccer were assigned based on positions. Goalkeepers wore number one. Forwards were tens and elevens. But modern football has evolved since the early days. Nowadays, the center striker wears number nine, while the best playmaker on the team, the most creative offensive player on the pitch, is usually assigned the ten. It's not always that simple. Sometimes, yes, the team just gives the number ten to the best player, no matter where they play. Take Messi, for instance. He isn't good at winning headers, he isn't that physical, and he isn't the fastest player on the pitch. Sound familiar?" she said, giving me a knowing look.

I hung my head. "Yeah."

"Chin up, Leo. Messi is also the best dribbler in the game, has the quickest feet, and is the most likely to produce a magical pass right in the heart of the defense. The attack *has* to go through him. And that also reminds me of you."

I could barely find my voice, I was so stunned by the compliment. "It does?"

"Messi is more of a false nine, but you don't need to worry about all that terminology. Like I said, modern football is complicated. But the rule of thumb is to use your players in the place that maximizes their talents. I have to say I was wrong about you. I knew you were good, but I didn't think you would turn out to be one of our best players. You make things happen, Leo. You play the game with passion and creativity and you're our top playmaker."

"Thanks," I said in a near-whisper.

"You don't need to thank me. I call it how it is. You worked hard for this. Now listen, these days, a traditional number ten plays right behind the forwards. That's where I'd like to use you. We'll talk more about our strategy during practice, and discuss everyone's role, but I wanted to run it by you first."

"Why?" I blurted out.

She laughed, and then her expression turned serious. "Because it's very late in the evaluation process, and the other coaches haven't seen you as a ten. Playing you there might surprise the other team, but I have to be honest and tell you it could hurt your chances at selection, especially if you don't have a good game."

"I don't care. I want to play up top."

She smiled. "So you're okay with it?"

I started jogging backwards, grinning ear to ear. "Never better."

Just before nine o'clock that night, I stood outside a side entrance to the Castle that was adjacent to a sloping walkway leading to the practice field we used for night school. Alejandro and Garika had joined me. We intercepted Samantha as one of her friends pushed her in a wheelchair through a handicap accessible door. Samantha had her crutches on her lap. She had told us she would arrive this way.

From her vantage point, Samantha still couldn't see the field.

"Hi guys," she said. "It's just the three of you?"

"Everyone else is down below," I said. "But we're going to have to blindfold you."

"Oh, the mystery! Okay. Sure. I'm game."

I tied a long sleeve Dragons FC T-shirt around her forehead. It draped her face and concealed her eyes. Her friend pushed the wheelchair down the long, paved walkway to the field. She stopped the chair at the edge of the grass, where the rest of the Iguanas were standing in a tight-packed group. Alejandro, Garika, and I walked over to join them.

"You can take the blindfold off," I said.

As Samantha removed the T-shirt from her forehead, we all clapped and chanted her name. "Thank you, guys," she said. "But why are we down here? Do you have a new trick to show me? A team juggling act?"

I stepped forward. "We wanted to find a way to show our appreciation. We don't have a lot of money, but we put our funds together and bought you a coconut cake with vanilla frosting."

"You did what? I . . . I don't know what to say. But how did you know that was my favorite?"

"Because," I said with a flourish, signaling for the Iguanas to move aside, "this guy told us."

Samantha's friend had positioned the wheelchair so close to the team, and we had bunched so tightly together, that Samantha couldn't see the field directly behind us. But once we stepped aside, I could tell by her widened eyes she had noticed the candlelit table and two folding chairs set up on the field. A white sheet draped the table, and a plastic stand in the middle supported the cake. The table was set with two saucers, forks, knives, napkins, and cups of milk we had taken from the break room with permission from Coach Tanner. All the Iguanas had put our summer money together and bought her a cake from a bakery on the local high street.

But the biggest surprise of all, and one which we weren't even sure Samantha would appreciate, was the person sitting in one of the chairs, waiting nervously to join her for dessert by candlelight.

Tig rose and walked over to the wheelchair. "I didn't think you'd want me here, but the guys begged me. So you can tell me to get lost if you want. I wouldn't blame you if you did. But either way, I wanted to say, right here in front of everyone, that I am truly, deeply sorry. I screwed up and don't deserve you. But there's nothing more I'd love than to have a piece of cake with you tonight, and just . . . just talk."

Samantha didn't speak for a long moment. She glanced at the team, and then at Tig, and her mouth started to tremble. She swallowed a few times and said, "You can stay." This caused us all to start cheering again. Both Samantha and Tig blushed, and he held her crutches as she eased out of her chair.

"C'mon guys," I said. "We need to rest up for the game tomorrow."

"No way," Samantha said. "I insist you all have a piece of cake with us first."

"Sorry, Coach," I said. "You told us we had to eat right and get a good night's sleep. We're just following your own orders."

The team walked off the field over her objections, leaving the two of them to work things out under the stars. As I passed by Samantha, she took me by the arm and leaned in close to my ear. "Was this your idea?"

"Kind of," I admitted.

"Thank you," she whispered, then squeezed my arm and let me go.

I went to bed that night feeling good about myself. I didn't know if Tig and Samantha would get back together, but at least they were talking. Samantha had finally moved me to the attack, and paid me a huge compliment. Now I just had to prove myself in front of the other coaches in the World Cup final.

Easier said than done—especially if I had to score on Charlie and outduel Diego.

Before I turned out the light, I took a long look at the picture of my family, and then wondered how Messi—my pet lizard, not the real player—would sleep before a big opportunity like this.

Like someone without a care in the world, I thought with a smile, conjuring up a mental image of Messi strutting around his cage like an emperor, waiting for me to toss a cricket inside.

That's exactly how he would sleep.

The King of the Lizards

Sunday night arrived before I knew it.

Just like the real London Dragons would have done, both the Iguanas and the Komodos took a team bus to the stadium. As we drove through the heart of London, the pedestrians on the street cheered when they saw us, and for a moment, as I stared out the window, I pretended we were professional soccer players, on our way to meet Liverpool or Manchester United for a Premier League clash.

When we arrived at the stadium, I was a ball of nervous energy. I couldn't stop grinning as we sat on red leather benches and listened to Samantha's speech in the London Dragons locker room. I had trouble paying attention because I couldn't stop ogling the names on the mahogany lockers set into the walls.

Soon I was running onto the field through the same tunnel the professional players used, and which I had seen on TV. On the other side of the tunnel, we all stopped in our tracks when we emerged, dumbstruck by how gigantic the stadium appeared from ground level, the lights that seemed as bright as day, and how smooth and green the grass was beneath our feet. I had never seen anything so magnificent in my life.

While the crowd filled only a portion of the bottom section of the stands, that was still enough people to make my knees weak. There had to be a few thousand faces up there. Who were they all? I remembered what Director Hawk had said when I spotted a group of guys sitting in the first two rows at half field. They were young, athletic, and wearing casual clothing that looked expensive. My jaw slowly dropped as I recognized some of the first team London Dragon players. I turned and spotted Director Hawk a few rows over, all the camp coaches, and even Philip Niles, the scout who had recruited me. Tig was there too, with a group of his friends who were probably all players on the Dragons U-21 team.

Now my stomach was flipping and churning like a washing machine.

"Don't worry about all that," Samantha said, as she entered the field behind us on her crutches. "Just play your game and ignore the fans."

Easy for her to say, I thought. *She's played in Serie A. I've only played in the Middleton YMCA League.*

I thought about my pet lizard again, and how Messi wouldn't care if the entire world was watching. He would just do his thing and not feel self-conscious about it. I grinned, channeling my inner lizard, feeling better already.

The digital scoreboard was lit up. I saw three referees stretching on the sidelines. After the warmups, Samantha told us to line up in front of our bench. The announcer called us out one by one, announcing our names, our numbers, and the countries we represented. The Komodos went first, and when Diego ran onto the field, so tall and sure of himself, I gritted my teeth and made a promise not to be intimidated.

Since Samantha wanted to use me at the ten, she had decided to move Julian to left midfield. It was risky not to mark

Diego in the same way we had marked Mahmoud, but Samantha said their midfield was too good to double-team anyone. She also thought we had to score goals to win this game, and needed more offensive firepower.

Diego is going to score, she had said, *regardless of whether we mark him with Julian. Let's control the midfield, contain Diego the best we can, and score more goals than they do.*

When my name was called, and the crowd cheered, a tingle of pride shot through me. I ran out to join my teammates, standing between Alejandro and Garika, linking arms with my friends. After the announcer had finished, we all gathered in a huddle, shouted "Iguanas!" and took our positions on the field.

I pumped my legs to get the blood flowing and calm my nerves. The anticipation was killing me, standing there under the lights with all those people watching. We were facing off against the Komodos, the king of the lizards both in nature and at our summer camp.

At last the whistle blew.

Let the battle begin!

I was so nervous I botched the first ball I touched. My pass to Robbie on the right went wide and landed at the feet of Fabio, their ace defensive midfielder. Robbie threw up his hands in frustration, making me feel even worse.

"It's okay, Iguanas," Samantha said. "Take it easy."

Her voice calmed me. I glanced up at the stands where Tig was sitting. He pointed his finger right at me, then gave me a thumbs up.

The Komodos pushed deep into our territory. Fabio sent

the ball to the right winger, who crossed it to Diego. As tall as Brock was, and as high as Garika could jump, neither had a chance against the Mexican striker. He was half a foot taller than both of them. I held my breath as Diego leaped into the air like a jaguar, awed by his power and grace. His header went just wide. I glanced at the bench and saw Samantha leaning on her crutches and lifting her head to the sky in relief.

Our first chance came when José stripped the ball from their right midfielder. José turned and fired a pass to Julian, who one-touched the ball to me in the center. Simon, their best defender, came right at me. I stepped over the ball, but he didn't bite on the fake. I debated trying to take him on, then flicked the ball to Dayo in the middle. I ran alongside him, calling for the ball, but Dayo rolled the ball with the bottom of his foot back to José, who came streaking in from midfield. It was a clever pass, and José took a shot in stride. The ball screamed towards the top right corner. I thought for sure it was a goal until I remembered who the keeper was.

Like a giant magnet sucking in a paper clip, Charlie reached to his right and caught the ball with both hands. In one continuous motion, he took a step and slung the ball to Fabio in midfield. Now José was out of position, and the Komodos had a breakaway.

Fabio kicked the ball ahead to the right winger. This time, instead of looking for a cross, Diego curled in to collect a pass on the ground, five yards outside the penalty box. Alejandro came sliding in, but Diego took a step to the side, evading him, and unleashed a missile that curved into the top right corner, just above Koffi's outstretched hand.

Their first goal, less than five minutes into the game.

Uh-oh.

I looked over at Samantha, wondering if she would make a change and have Julian mark Diego. She put her hands out, palms down, conveying a clear message.

Calm down, Iguanas. Stay the course.

José gathered me and the midfielders together before kickoff. "That goal was too easy," he said. "We can't let them move the ball like that. Diego's their finisher, but Fabio is their playmaker. I'm going to stay with him. Leo, that means more pressure on you in the center. We need you."

I nodded. "Okay."

Dayo kicked the ball off to Javier, who sent it back to me. I darted into a patch of open space and sent the ball over to Robbie. We knocked it around for a while in midfield, and I was very active, running to the ball and calling for it. For the first time since I had arrived at the summer camp, I felt like I was playing *my* game. I was controlling the pace of the attack and had the option to dribble or pass as I wanted. I had to admit the position felt even more right than center forward, where I would be stuck waiting for a pass, and then have to outrun the defense. While that worked fine back home, it didn't work so well here.

Behind me, José was a blur in midfield. Every time the Komodos got the ball, he stuck to Fabio as closely as Julian had marked Mahmoud. José intercepted pass after pass, or forced Fabio to turn and move the ball backwards instead of pressing up the field to Diego.

The Komodos finally managed to work the ball to the left wing. I held my breath as the cross went in. The ball sailed over Diego's head this time. Alejandro trapped it, took a dribble, looked up, and chipped the ball far over the midfield to Javier.

It was a monster pass, and caught everyone by surprise. The wingback closed on Javier, but he kicked the ball forward and won the foot race to the ball. Sensing an opportunity, I raced downfield. Sven and Dayo went with me, pushing hard to keep up.

Our French winger did what I hoped and passed it back to me on the ground. I was just outside the penalty box with plenty of options. Simon was closing fast, so I made a one-touch pass to Dayo, just ahead on my right. He debated taking a shot, but the space was too tight. He pulled it back and passed to me again.

Out of the corner of my eye, I saw Javier streaking towards the goal from the left wing. I faked a pass to Sven, pulled the ball back, and flicked a nifty little pass over the defense. Javier was a step ahead of his defender. I don't think anyone had expected me to lift the ball over the top instead of playing it on the ground. I held my breath as Javier dove, his green hair flying, and headed the ball at Charlie's feet from six feet away. Expecting a higher ball, Charlie tried to recover and fall to the ground, but the ball slipped by his leg and bounced into the goal.

For a moment, both teams paused, unsure if Javier was onside. The lead referee turned to the linesman, who gave a small nod, and kept his flag down.

Goal!

Javier pumped his fist and yelled something in French.

We all swarmed him to celebrate, and he threw an arm around my shoulders. "Amazing pass, Leo."

"You made the run," I said. "I just delivered."

For the rest of the half, José stuck to Fabio like sap on dry fingers. With their playmaker smothered, the Komodos couldn't seem to mount an effective attack, and their frustration began to show. Fabio pushed José hard at one point, earning a yellow card, and on the next play, after the ball sailed out of bounds, Diego threw his hands in the air and pointed emphatically at his feet with both hands. *Get me the ball*, his gesture said.

I worked hard to press our attack. Julian, Robbie, and I ran their team ragged with crisp passes and short runs. José helped out whenever he could, though he wouldn't push too far forward for fear of losing Fabio.

The pace of the game and the long week took its toll. My legs started to feel heavy, and I saw Robbie with his hands on his knees, breathing hard, every time the ball went out of bounds. If we could just make it to half time with the game tied, we could regroup.

Diego had other ideas. Our next trip downfield, Sven crossed a ball that hung too long in the air, allowing Charlie to run out and grab it. Without stopping, the Australian keeper took a few quick steps, bringing him to the edge of the box, and punted the ball well past half field, over the heads of the midfielders.

It was going to be a footrace between Diego and our defense.

C'mon, I urged, as Garika sprinted for the ball. At first, I thought he was going to beat Diego, but with a burst of speed, the Mexican striker overtook him, just managing to poke the ball forward with his long right leg before Garika arrived.

Diego kicked the ball ahead again and left Garika in the dust. The only chance now was Brock streaking in from the side. Diego took another dribble, and Brock threw his body to the ground, trying to slide tackle him from behind. He didn't really have a play on the ball, and I winced, thinking Brock would get a red card if he took Diego down.

But his slide tackle fell short, leaving Diego alone in front of the goal. Koffi raced out, trying to cut off the angle, but Diego was too good. As smooth as shaved ice, he sidestepped Koffi's lunge, and made an easy pass into the goal.

The half time whistle blew.

Just like that, we were down 2-1.

We hung our heads as we walked off the field, but Samantha berated us as we gathered around her, breathing hard and sucking down Gatorade in huge gulps.

"Don't get down on yourselves, Iguanas. You hung with them for the entire half, right until the last second. You let your guard down and they made you pay. What does that tell you?"

After a moment, José said, "Not to let our guard down. Ever."

"That's right. What else?"

"That we can beat them," I added.

"Bingo," Samantha said. "We're winning the midfield battle, and we've had some great chances."

When she hesitated, we all knew what was on her mind.

How do we stop their best player?

"Do you want me to drop back?" Robbie said. "Try to smother Diego?"

Samantha pursed her lips as she considered the question. Finally she shook her head. "It's too risky. We're down a goal already. We have to have chances to score. José, I love what you're doing on Fabio. I think that's the right idea. Brock and Alejandro, why don't you drop a little deeper than usual? Forget the offside trap. Be ready to back up Garika the second Diego touches the ball."

We retook the field. Whether or not we managed to corral Diego, we had to score at least two more times to win the game. Was that even possible with Charlie lurking in the goal?

Stop putting him on a pedestal, Leo. I summoned a mental image of the Australian keeper lying on the ground, and my pet lizard walking across him with his back arched and his beard flared. The image made me laugh out loud, causing Alejandro to ask me what was so funny.

"Nothing," I said, as we walked onto the field.

Alejandro fist bumped me. "Let's do this, Leo. Do something amazing and put one in the goal."

The crowd cheered as the ref blew the whistle. I realized I only had forty-five minutes left in this magical summer, and decided to make the most of it.

As soon as I got the ball, I headed up the field with a vengeance. I spun with the ball around the first Komodo who challenged me, drawing a gasp from the crowd. Two more closed in, and I kicked the ball behind my legs to Julian, a trick pass that again excited the fans.

"Leo," Samantha warned. "Not too fancy."

Julian's pass to Sven sailed wide and out of bounds. I laid off the tricks, but continued to press the attack. I wasn't going to sit back and toy with the ball this half. We had to score at least twice.

On the next run down the field, the Komodos pressed high to trap us offside, but Dayo slipped a tricky pass through the defense. I was the closest Iguana to the ball, and sprinted after it. If I could beat Simon in a foot race, I would be alone with the goalie. I gave it everything I had, but Simon arrived a step before me, shouldered me to the side, and knocked the ball away.

I turned to see Samantha putting her hands over her face. I knew I had missed a golden opportunity. I had to be stronger.

The next time I received the ball, I tried to make up for it. José and Julian made a run through the midfield that put us deep into Komodo territory. José passed the ball to me, and I gave Fabio a shoulder fake that stopped him cold. I surged past him and into the box, beat another Komodo off the dribble, went to take a shot—and the next thing I knew, I was lying on my stomach, with my face pressed into the grass.

Someone had tripped me from behind. Hard.

My teammates helped me to my feet. I was shaken up, with grass stains on my jersey and a sore jaw, but when I turned around, I saw the referee point to the penalty spot and pull out a yellow card for Simon, the player who had tripped me.

"That should be a red!" Brock screamed, running up from the back.

"Brock!" Samantha called out. "Keep your cool. Different rules tonight."

Not wanting to earn a yellow card himself, Brock backed away, fuming. I didn't care about the card on Simon—we had a penalty kick!

"Leo," Samantha said. "You take this."

Though surprised by her choice, my penalty kicks had

gotten much stronger, and I knew she wanted to reward me for making such a good run. Stoked by the opportunity, I blocked out the pressure and placed the ball carefully on the white spot. The referee shooed both teams out of the penalty box. As the crowd quieted, Tig's words flashed through my head. *Be unpredictable.*

What did that mean on a penalty kick? Should I kick it right at the goalie, hoping he would dive one way or the other? Try to fake him out with my run?

Charlie clapped his hands and hunkered down in the goal. "Hurry up, Leo," he said. "You know I'm going to stop this."

I smirked and backed away, trying to decide what to do. The referee blew the whistle and waved a hand for me to proceed.

Though my hesitation only lasted moments, it felt like a lifetime, with everyone in the stadium staring at me. I again debated shooting the ball down the middle, then decided to go right. It was my best shot, and I knew I could score. No goalie could stop a perfect penalty kick.

With a deep breath, I ran onto the ball, leaned to the left to throw Charlie off, and blasted the ball towards the top right corner. The shot felt great as it left my feet, and I knew it was on target.

And I was right. The ball went just where I had planned. A real screamer. The only problem was that Charlie dove to his left just as I kicked the ball, and saved it, punching the ball out of bounds as I stood there in disbelief.

I missed the penalty kick that would have tied the game. A penalty kick!

"Shrug it off, Leo!" Samantha said. "It's okay."

It wasn't okay. I might never forgive myself.

"Told you," Charlie said with a smirk, as I remained standing by the penalty spot, embarrassed and dejected. "You'll never score on me."

The missed penalty kick seemed to take the air out of my team. For the next few minutes, the Komodos pressed the attack hard, and we scrambled to keep up. Fabio finally slipped free of José in midfield, and wasted no time chipping the ball over the defense to Diego. The Mexican striker beat everyone to the ball by two yards, took one dribble, and sent a missile into the bottom left corner.

Koffi never had a chance.

I put my hands to my head, feeling as if the game was over, but as the Komodos began to celebrate, I heard a flag snap on the sidelines. I whipped around to see the lead referee point at the ground where the infraction had occurred.

Offside!

The Komodos argued the call to no avail, and a sigh of relief swept through our team. We had dodged a bullet that might have put the game out of reach.

When the play restarted, Garika kicked the ball upfield to Julian. We held possession for awhile, trying to get our swagger back, until I decided it was time to attack. I slipped a pass to Javier down the sideline. He dribbled it inside, passed it back to me, and I sent a one-touch, no-look pass right to Dayo.

Smack!

Dayo's right leg connected squarely with the ball, but it went right to Charlie. He slung it downfield to Fabio again, trying to start a fast break—only this time José read the play. He stepped in to steal the ball, and sent it straight back to me.

The counterattack was on. I turned and passed to Robbie, who was streaking in from the left side. A Komodo defender had no choice but to slide into him, drawing a foul five feet outside the penalty box.

This time, Samantha told Robbie to take the kick. As the Komodos made a wall ten yards in front of the ball, Charlie shouted instructions, positioning the wall where he wanted them, in front of the near post. Samantha let Brock move up to crowd the box.

The wall was too close for Robbie to try for the near post. No way he could bend it over the top or curve it around the side. And Charlie would be all over the far post. The best bet was a chip into the middle, where we could try to take advantage of the chaos.

After the whistle, I circled around to dart into the box as Robbie ran onto the ball. Everyone was pushing and shoving. José and Fabio were climbing on top of each other, trying to gain position. Brock created havoc as usual.

Surprisingly, Robbie kicked the ball with his left foot. His right foot was much stronger, and we all thought he would use it to chip the ball inside.

Even more surprising, the shot skirted the left side of the wall, an inch wide of the player on the end, and went straight into the near side of the goal.

Charlie had edged towards the opposite side of the goal and had no chance to save it. Defending the near post was the job of the wall. For a moment, both teams were stunned, unsure what had happened. Had Robbie kicked the ball too soon?

When the ref pointed at the center circle, signaling a goal, the Iguanas mobbed my roommate, who had a huge grin on his face.

"What happened?" I said as we ran back. "How'd you sneak it in?"

"I've been watching the Komodos play," Robbie said. "Charlie likes to place the wall super tight, so he has less space to cover. This time he went too far. The wall was a foot to the right. No one realized but me."

I slapped him on the back. "All that studying finally paid off, roomie!"

I was happy for him, and even happier his goal had tied the game. We had new life.

"Ten minutes!" Samantha called out. "Push, Iguanas!"

The stadium was rocking now, the atmosphere electric. With time running out, energized by the crowd, both teams played harder than ever, sprinting to every ball, diving, lunging, giving it everything they had. I felt as if I had wings on my shoes. I made pass after pass, trying to drive a wedge into the Komodo defense.

But Diego had another gear on his bicycle. Every time he touched the ball, it seemed he was able to get a shot on goal. He dribbled around defenders, ran through double teams, and rose above the crowd to blast the ball towards the goal with his powerful headers.

Somehow, someway, our defense held. Koffi made save after save. Alejandro sacrificed his body for a slide tackle that avoided a sure goal. Garika used his long legs to annoy Diego and force him into bad shots.

"Two minutes!" Samantha yelled.

After another Komodo charge, Brock kicked the ball out

of bounds so far it went into the stands, giving us a breather. "Hang in there, Leo," José said, seeing how hard I was breathing.

But I didn't want to *hang in there*. No way did I want this game to end in a penalty shootout, not with Charlie lurking in the goal. As exhausted as I was, I vowed to make one more run—if only we could get the ball back.

A Komodo midfielder threw the ball to Fabio deep in our half. He danced around José, looking for an opening to get the ball to Diego. I knew I was supposed to wait higher up the field, but I threw caution to the wind and ran back to help José. My arrival took Fabio by surprise. Someone tried to warn him, but he turned right into me, and I stripped the ball. Fabio came right back at me, even pulling on my shirt to regain possession, but my duels with Brock had toughened me up. I shielded Fabio off and passed the ball ten yards ahead of José, into a square of open space.

"Go!" I said.

With a defender on his heels, José ran onto the ball and carried it upfield. My legs felt as heavy as anchors, but I reached deep inside, somehow finding the energy to sprint alongside him. Instead of passing it back to me, José pushed it further ahead to Robbie, who surveyed his options and pushed it higher yet again, to Javier on the wing.

A Komodo defender dove at Javier, trying to slide tackle him. He evaded the attempt and cut the ball inside. I was still racing upfield, José right beside me. I gained a step on him and called for the ball. Javier saw me but sent it all the way across the field to Sven. Two Komodos closed him down at once. Sven passed back to Julian, which almost made me scream in frustration. *There's not enough time! We have to push forward!*

Julian was looking for a good place to pass the ball. Creativity was not his strong suit. I spotted some open space on the left side of the field, about ten yards outside the penalty box, and raced towards it. Simon was nearby, but he was playing deeper, near the edge of the box, since the space I was running towards was too far out to shoot. That was okay. I planned to put a move on him or pass the ball off.

"Here!" I called out to Julian, waving an arm. "I'm here!"

Julian looked as if he was about to make the safe pass to José, who was still lagging behind. At the last second, he swiveled his body and chipped the ball my way to avoid the defender between us. The pass was on target, but it was going to be a tough ball to control. I saw the referee raise the whistle to his lips, ready to call the game. He would let this final attempt play out, but only for a moment.

Think quickly, Leo. As the ball came in, I noticed Simon hanging back. He would close in as soon as I trapped the ball, and cut off the angle of my shot. Dayo was being closely marked in the center. Not a good option. The logical choice was trying to hit Sven for a header on the wing, but he was also marked.

Julian's pass was a high, looping chip shot. I was facing the right sideline to receive the ball, half-turned away from the Komodo goal. As the ball descended, I made a snap decision. *You want something unexpected, Tig? How about this?*

For a split second, time seemed to slow to a standstill. I saw players scrambling around me, and, at the edge of my vision, Charlie pacing back and forth in the goal, doing his best to read the play. As the ball continued to fall, I clenched my stomach muscles, lifted my leg, and prepared to swivel my hips for maximum power. Trying to volley a ball off that high of a pass was extremely difficult. Maybe even foolish. But I was desperate, and had a good angle for my right foot, so that's what I did. I watched the ball all the way in as Tig and Samantha had taught me, and just before it hit the ground, I struck it square on my laces.

The ball took off like a guided missile. Somehow, I managed to kick it cleanly, surprising even myself. The goal was so far away, I hadn't even tried to aim for a corner. I was just trying to put the ball on target, hoping for a lucky bounce or to catch Charlie off guard.

Not expecting a crazed volley from thirty yards out, Charlie had crept too far forward. As the ball soared in, he stumbled backwards, trying to get back into position. But he was too late. The volley sailed above his outstretched arms. He managed to brush the ball with his fingertips, but he couldn't slow it down enough, and my long-range shot thumped into the back of the net.

Almost at once, the referee blew his whistle long and hard.

Iguanas 3, Komodos 2.

We had just won the World Cup.

You Can't Always Get What You Want, But Sometimes, You Get What You Need

After my goal, the stadium exploded with cheers. For a moment I just stood there, stunned that we had won. The Komodo defenders slumped to the ground, distraught by the last-second defeat. My teammates tackled me, shouting my name as they formed a pile on top of me. I laughed and climbed out, then whooped and ran around the field in celebration. They all chased me, and we fell into another heap near our bench. Samantha stood on her crutches right beside us, her smile wider than I had ever seen it. Tig ran down from the stands to join her, cheering along with the team. I saw her reach over to grab his hand, and I knew things would be all right between them.

When the chaos subsided, Director Hawk presented the Iguanas with the World Cup trophy, right there on the field. We hoisted it high as everyone clapped and the announcer roared our team name throughout the stadium. During the ceremony, the winning goal—*my* goal—replayed on the digital screen in the stands high above the field, causing the fans to go wild again. I had never felt so good in my life.

We returned to the Castle and celebrated late into the

night. Samantha and Tig ordered pizzas for our whole team in the break room, and we stayed there for hours, cutting up and playing FIFA and stuffing our faces with cheese and pepperoni.

The party ended long after midnight. It was only when I returned to my room, as exhausted as I had ever been, that I remembered that the next morning I would discover whether or not I had earned an invitation to the London Dragon Youth Academy.

When the alarm jolted me awake, sunlight slanting through the blinds, I realized it was the last day of summer camp. My plane home left the next day at seven in the morning, so I wouldn't have time to do anything except rush to the airport. Would I return home a member of the London Dragons, with a fat check in hand, or would I go back to being Leo K. Doyle, a normal kid from Middleton, Ohio?

Once all the players had assembled for breakfast, Director Hawk didn't waste any time. He took the podium with a clipboard in hand and cleared his throat. I squirmed in my seat, hopeful but unsure of my fate. Before the World Cup, I would not have expected the coaches to select me. But after my performance in the tournament, especially over the last three games, I thought I had earned my way in.

"Good morning," Director Hawk said. "I hear there's an important announcement to make today."

Everyone in the room cheered, releasing their nervous energy.

"It's been a long, tough summer," he continued. "We're

proud of each and every one of you for persevering. Even for those who will not be asked to return, the very fact that you've made it this far speaks highly of your character, not to mention your talent. It should give you the confidence to endure life's challenges, both on and off the field." He placed the clipboard on the podium and folded his hands atop it. "To make it this far means you're an incredible footballer. Some of the very best in your age group in the world. But not everyone can be a London Dragon. I know that's tough to hear, but life is about managing disappointment as well as success. I hope none of you go home disheartened, but instead empowered to work harder and improve your game. Perhaps we'll see you back here one day." He flipped a page on the clipboard and looked slowly around the room, raising my anticipation to a fever pitch. "Without further ado, I'd like to announce the eleven players we have selected to join the London Dragons Youth Academy."

Beside me, I saw Robbie's hands clench atop the table. Alejandro had his hands clasped behind his head, yawning as if this was any other morning. How could he be so calm? Under the table, my left leg was bouncing up and down on its heel like a pogo stick.

"From the Gilas, we've chosen Sergi Hernandez, Sebastian Kowalski, Conor McDougal, and Miguel Arias."

The selection did not surprise me, except for Miguel. He was a center forward, and they *have* to select Diego, so where did that leave me? Would they choose me as a number ten?

When everyone started to clap, Director Hawk asked the room to hold its applause until the end. "Representing the Monitors," he said, when the players quieted down, "are Hans Keller and Mateo Holmberg."

Only two Monitors? That meant that Mahmoud, their crafty Egyptian forward, was left out. That surprised me. Mahmoud was *really* good. But it also gave me hope. I realized Director Hawk was announcing the teams in the order they had finished the World Cup, which meant we would be last.

"Diego Garcia, Fabio Calvino, and Charlie Lawson from the Komodos."

Diego, Charlie, Fabio. No way any of those three would be left out. I counted up the positions in my head. So far, two midfielders had been selected, one goalie, three defenders, and three forwards—two in the center and one winger.

"The last two picks, but certainly not least, are from our World Cup champions, the Iguanas. José Duarte and Dayo Achebe, congratulations. You're the final two selections. Now, can all eleven players please stand, so everybody can give our new Dragons a huge round of applause?"

A few seats down from me, José and Dayo rose to their feet, beaming as if it was their birthday, Christmas, and the last day of school rolled into one. Dayo looked a little dazed, as if he had not expected to hear his name called. As the clapping began, I joined in, thrilled for my friends, but my throat felt too dry to speak, and all of a sudden I had lost my appetite.

When the applause died down and we took our seats, I noticed Robbie staring at the floor, his hands folded in his lap. Alejandro leaned over to whisper in my ear. "You were robbed."

I was too disappointed to respond.

The Director spoke for a while longer, something about photos and taking vans to the airport, but I tuned him out. When he sat down and let us finish breakfast, I stood and walked over to Dayo and José, then embraced them both. My dad had always taught me to be gracious in defeat, and besides, these were my friends. I truly was excited for them, regardless of my own sense of failure.

Dayo shook his head and looked away, as if embarrassed. "I can't believe they didn't take you, Leo. What are they thinking?"

"It's fine," I said, forcing a smile. "Maybe I'll be back."

José pulled me in close and held my head in his hands, pressing our faces close. "Listen to me, Leo. You deserve to be at the Academy. I'm going to tell them that when I arrive."

"Thanks José. It's okay. I'm fine."

"I'm going to see you in the Premier League one day, my friend," he said. "I *know* it."

I had not even started to pack, but I spent the rest of the day ignoring the sorry state of my room and saying goodbye to my friends. My disappointment in not making the Academy hung over me like a dark cloud. Realizing I had to leave my friends made it even worse. We lingered in the break room during the afternoon and into the evening, exchanging contact information and promising to stay in touch. Alejandro, Garika, Dayo, José, Javier, Sven, Koffi, even Robbie: the Iguanas had been my family for the summer, and I didn't want to say goodbye.

Alejandro and I were taking the same van to the airport in the morning, so at least the two of us would have time to chat on the way. I had no idea how far away Costa Rica was, or how much it would cost to fly there, but I hoped I got to visit one day.

Robbie had left for his flight earlier in the day, so when I returned to my room to pack, I was alone. Soon after I gathered my clothes on the bed, I heard a knock at the door. I opened it to find Tig and Samantha standing in the hallway.

"Not trying to sneak out on us, are you Boss?" Tig said.

I invited them in and returned to putting my shirts in the suitcase. My mom, when she was alive, would have rolled them up nicely. I just stuffed everything inside as quickly as I could.

"We're on different planes this time," Tig said, "but I'm riding in your van to the airport."

"Okay."

"Can I get a goodbye hug?" Samantha asked, holding out her arms.

I obliged the request, then reached for a pair of socks.

"Listen, Leo," she said. "We came to say goodbye, but also to tell you a few things. I want you to know that I voted for you to join the Academy. So did some of the other coaches. The decision not to keep you was the closest one of all."

I kept on packing, not sure if that made me feel better or worse. When no one spoke for a moment, I blurted out, "Why didn't they take me? Dayo didn't even score in the World Cup. I'm glad he got in, I really am, but . . . ."

She hesitated. "While every club has a different philosophy, most coaches select players at your age for their athleticism as much as for their talent. Often more so. It's the *potential* they're trying to judge. But in your case, I'll be honest and say I think they made the wrong decision. You have something the other players don't, Leo. Something even rarer than world class speed or strength."

"She's right, Boss. Every last word. You've got the goods. I know it."

"Thanks," I said. "I guess not enough of the coaches thought so."

"Hey," she said, squeezing my shoulder. "They underestimated you from the beginning, Leo. Go home and prove them wrong. Keep training and working hard, and I know you'll have a bright future."

I slept most of the flight home. Whenever I was awake, I watched movies and pestered the stewardess for extra snacks. I was trying my best not to feel as if my life was ruined. My friends had said all these nice things about me, how I had a bright future and all, but that's like your parents telling you that you're great at something. *Of course* they're going to. If the coaches really thought I was talented, why didn't they invite me to join the Academy?

I smelled a rat.

When I saw my dad, waiting for me as soon as I stepped into the Detroit airport, my mood lifted. I realized how glad I was to be home. He picked me up and squeezed me so hard I thought I might break in half.

"Easy, Dad!"

He laughed and set me down. "Welcome home, kiddo. I missed you so much."

"Where's Ginny?"

"She's at home with Aunt Janice. I didn't want to put her through the drive. Here, let me get your bags. So how was it? Did you make the team?"

I hadn't even told him the news yet. "No."

"That's too bad," he said, with about as much emotion as if I had just lost a game in the YMCA league. He ruffled my hair. "I bet it was an amazing experience. I'm sorry we didn't get to talk more while you were away, but I want to hear all about it on the drive home."

On the long journey back to Middleton, Dad made me suffer through a John Denver CD as I told him about my new friends and everything that had happened at camp, especially the World Cup.

"Wait—you scored the winning goal?" he said, a proud smile creeping onto his face as he changed lanes. "In front of all those people?"

"Yep."

"That's my boy. I told you that you'd be great."

His praise caused a lump to form in the back of my throat as I thought about how the money I had lost could have helped our family. "It doesn't matter," I said. "I didn't make the team."

"It doesn't matter? You scored the winning goal in the final game against some of the best youth players in the world and *it doesn't matter*?"

"But I didn't . . . we didn't get the money, Dad. I know you needed it for the house. I really wanted to help out."

He looked away from the road to give me a sharp glance. "Are you talking about the money Mr. Niles discussed? Way back before you left?"

"Yeah. The fifty thousand we get for making the Academy."

"Son," he said, shaking his head, "that wasn't cash he was

talking about. It was scholarship money for school, room, and board. There was never any cash."

All of a sudden, I felt very foolish. "Oh."

"Leo, did you—" he cut off as his voice started to crack, and he waited a few moments to speak. "Thanks for thinking of your family, Son. But we're doing just fine. I don't want you to *ever* worry about money, or losing the house." His voice hardened. "Do you hear me?"

"Yes, Sir."

"I will always take care of you and Ginny. Always. And something else. I don't care about some fancy academy, or whether you're playing for the London Dragons, or the Middleton Badgers, or the Cincinnati Fart Blossoms."

"It's the Middleton Beavers, Dad. That's my team."

"Whatever. I just love to watch you play. And so did your mom. It was her greatest pleasure in life. London *Dragons*," he said with a snort, then turned his awful music up louder and concentrated on the road.

As we turned onto our street in Middleton, and I saw our little house and the maple tree out front I had spent my childhood climbing, a rush of warmth flowed through me. I realized how good it felt to be home, and how ready I was to see my friends and my bedroom and my pet lizard again.

"I wonder if Carlos is around," I said.

My dad parked the car. "Good question. Why don't you take your bag to your room and then go see?"

I threw my backpack over my shoulder and opened the door to the house, surprised by how much I wanted to see my sister. Only for a moment, though. Then she could go away. As soon as I stepped into the living room, the lights came on, and a bunch of people jumped out from behind the furniture.

"Surprise!" Aunt Janice yelled, just as I thought our house was being robbed.

I looked around, stunned by all the familiar faces: Ginny, Carlos, Dennis, and a dozen of my friends. There was a huge "Welcome home, Leo!" sign above the fireplace, balloons on the ceiling, and a table set up along the wall with burgers, soft drinks, chips, and a chocolate cake.

"We thought you might be hungry after the flight," my dad said, coming to stand beside me.

"So?" Carlos said, running up to chest bump me. "Did you make the team or not?"

I told them the bad news, causing Aunt Janice to hug me and Carlos to shake his head in annoyance.

"What am I supposed to do with my life now?" he said. "You were my ticket to the big time. I was going to join you at the Academy next year."

I couldn't help but laugh. "Sorry. You'll have to be the first one in."

"Tell them about the tournament," my dad said. "How you scored the winning goal."

"Wait—for real?" Dennis said. "You scored a goal *there*?"

With my friends gathered around me, chowing down on burgers and chips, I told the story again, or at least the highlights. They all *oohed* and *aahed*, and Ginny recorded the whole thing on Aunt Janice's phone, providing commentary along the way.

I went to use the restroom. After I finished, I realized I

hadn't said hello to Messi yet. Feeling guilty, I went to my room and lifted him out of his cage. He walked back and forth in my palm, then arched his back and stared up at me, fixing his beady eyes on mine. Somehow I knew that he, too, was asking me about the trip.

"I did my best," I said, as we locked gazes.

His little pink tongue flicked out.

"I almost made it, but not quite."

Now his beard flared, signaling he was upset.

"What?" I said.

He turned his back on me and faced the wall.

"Uh, Leo?" my dad called out.

I set Messi down in his cage, annoyed by his behavior. What did he want from me? "Yeah?"

"There you are," my dad said as he came into the room. "Someone's on the phone for you. I think you'll want to talk to him."

"Who is it?"

A grin started to creep onto his face, but he worked his jaw back and forth to make it disappear. "Just come."

Curious as to the identity of the mystery caller and my dad's weird behavior, I followed him into the living room, where the party was in full swing.

"Turn the music off!" my dad ordered. "Everybody listen up!" When the room quieted, he said, "Janice? Do you still have him on?"

Aunt Janice walked into the room from the kitchen, holding my dad's cell phone. She handed it to him. He must have had the phone on speaker, because he held the phone out as he spoke.

"Here's Leo," my dad said, and handed the phone to me. No one else seemed to know what was going on, either. It was probably my grandpa on the line, calling to say welcome home.

I took the phone and realized it was on video, because I saw a man about my dad's age on the screen, wearing a blue Polo shirt with a silver logo on the left breast that looked familiar. Dad had a Verizon phone, so this must be a Skype call. But I didn't recognize this man. Who in the world was he? And why did he want to talk to *me*? What was going on?

I glanced at my dad, but he signaled for me to take the call. With a shrug, I kept the phone on speaker, and everyone quieted so I could hear. "Hello?" I said.

"Hello, Leo," the man said in a serious voice with a British accent. His eyes reminded me of the surface of my dad's old pool table in the basement, green and worn and comforting. "My name is Giles Pearson. I realize you have no idea who I am, but I saw you play a few days ago, at Dragon Stadium. I'm the Director of Scouting for the Lewisham Knights Youth Academy."

Carlos gasped from behind me. The Lewisham Knights were another Premier League team from London, and bitter rivals with the Dragons. I looked closer at Giles's shirt, and realized it was the sword-and-shield logo of the Knights.

Everyone crowded in around me. Carlos and Dennis got so close they appeared onscreen, which caused Giles to smile. "Hi everyone. Leo, knowing each academy can only take a limited number of players, and that different teams look for different skillsets, it's not unusual for Premier League teams to send representatives to events such as the one you played in. You probably had no idea half the scouts in the EPL were in attendance, did you?"

"No," I managed to croak.

"I was extremely impressed by your performance. Quite frankly, I'm stunned the Dragons did not extend you an invitation, but, well, as they say, there's no accounting for taste. The Lewisham Knights feel quite differently about your professional prospects. In fact, after seeing you play, our selection committee was unanimous in our vote to extend you an offer to join our own academy this fall. Not a camp or a tryout, but as a full member of the Lewisham Knights youth squad."

For a moment, his words failed to sink in, and I stood there holding the phone in a daze. Carlos pinched me and whispered, loud enough for everyone to hear, "Leo! Say yes!"

I glanced up to see my dad's eyes twinkling as he watched me, his arms crossed against his chest. How much of this call, I wondered, had he known about beforehand?

Giles said, "We'll send your dad an official offer letter with all the details by tomorrow morning. I understand you'll need some time to think it over—"

"Nope," I said. Part of me would be a Dragon for life, since they had found me and given me a chance, but if they didn't want me, and another team did, I planned to embrace my fate. "I'd love to be a Knight."

The director smiled, Ginny squealed, Carlos staggered back with a hand on his chest, Aunt Janice whooped and threw her hands in the air, and everyone started to clap and cheer. My dad came over to squeeze my arm, then took the phone and disappeared into the kitchen to finish the conversation with Giles. I didn't care about the details. All I knew was that I was going back to London in the fall, to join the youth academy of a Premier League team. It didn't even matter which one.

I felt as if I was dreaming.

"Finally, Leo," Carlos said with a deep sigh, as if the weight of the world had just been lifted off of his shoulders instead of mine. "You got something right."

To stay up to date on Leo's future adventures and other stories by T.Z. Layton, it's best to join his newsletter at: www.subscribepage.com/tzlaytonbooks

ACKNOWLEDGMENTS

First and foremost, I would like to thank a few special advance readers—Temai, Ollie, Miller, and Owen—whose love of the first draft and encouraging words gave me confidence in the story. Without you, I might have left the book in a drawer. Thanks also to Tinashe for his passion for life, the beautiful game, and the pursuit of excellence in all things, all of which helped shape Leo's journey. A multitude of other people helped bring this project to fruition, my core team that has been with me for years. I can never thank you enough. A huge shout out to the BCFC players, coaches, and parents for all those wonderful years. Finally, thank you to Triangle United, AYSO, and all the volunteers and organizations everywhere who support the kids.

T.Z. Layton is bestselling author Layton Green's pen name for books aimed at younger readers. The author's novels have been nominated for many awards, translated into multiple languages, and optioned for film. The author is also a soccer dad, youth coach, referee, former collegiate player, and lifelong fan of the beautiful game.

Word of mouth is crucial to the success of any author. If you enjoyed Leo's adventures, please consider leaving an honest review on Goodreads, Amazon, Barnes & Noble, or another book site, even if it's only a line or two. (Note: if you're under 13, please ask a parent to help you.)

You can visit T.Z. on Facebook, Goodreads, or at tzlaytonbooks.com for additional information on the author, his works, and more.

Made in the USA
Las Vegas, NV
20 November 2023

81106427R10184